APR   2005

Life Studies

STORIES

SUSAN VREELAND

Viking

VIKING
Published by the Penguin Group
Penguin Group (USA) Inc., 375 Hudson Street,
New York, New York 10014, U.S.A.
Penguin Group (Canada), 10 Alcorn Avenue, Toronto,
Ontario, Canada M4V 3B2 (a division of Pearson Penguin Canada Inc.)
Penguin Books Ltd., 80 Strand, London WC2R 0RL, England
Penguin Ireland, 25 St. Stephen's Green, Dublin 2, Ireland
(a division of Penguin Books Ltd)
Penguin Books Australia Ltd, 250 Camberwell Road, Camberwell, Victoria 3124, Australia
(a division of Pearson Australia Group Pty Ltd)
Penguin Books India Pvt Ltd, 11 Community Centre, Panchsheel Park,
New Delhi - 110 017, India
Penguin Group (NZ), Cnr Airborne and Rosedale Roads, Albany, Auckland, New Zealand
(a division of Pearson New Zealand Ltd)
Penguin Books (South Africa) (Pty) Ltd, 24 Sturdee Avenue,
Rosebank, Johannesburg 2196, South Africa

Penguin Books Ltd, Registered Offices:
80 Strand, London WC2R 0RL, England

First published in 2005 by Viking Penguin,
a member of Penguin Group (USA) Inc.

1   3   5   7   9   10   8   6   4   2

Page 293 constitutes an extension of this copyright page.

PUBLISHER'S NOTE
These selections are works of fiction. Names, characters, places, and incidents either are the product
of the author's imagination or are used fictitiously, and any resemblance to actual persons,
living or dead, business establishments, events, or locales is entirely coincidental.

LIBRARY OF CONGRESS CATALOGING IN PUBLICATION DATA
Vreeland, Susan.
Life studies : stories / Susan Vreeland.
p.   cm.
ISBN 0-670-03177-1
I. Title.
PS3572.R34 L54 2005
813'.54—dc22   2004049487

This book is printed on acid-free paper. ∞

Printed in the United States of America
Set in Vendetta with Isadora

To my great-grandfather,

Herbert Henry Smithers,

*who unveiled to me the magic
of a paintbrush*

Contents

The real question is: To whom does the meaning of the art of the past properly belong? To those who can apply it to their own lives, or to a cultural hierarchy of relic specialists?

—John Berger, *Ways of Seeing,* 1977

Then

Mimi with a Watering Can

Paris, 1876

Jérôme did not want to go to his sister's garden party. He did not want to mix cordially with her motley Montmartre neighbors, did not want to sit on a crumbling stone wall among buzzing insects in her half-wild yard drinking that sharp *piccolo* from the last scraggly Montmartre vineyard, making trivial conversation with some tinsmith or shoemaker or painter Claire might have invited.

"But this is the second time she's asked," Élise said, sipping her coffee in the sunny breakfast room with their four-year-old dancing a paper doll around her bowl of porridge. "She'll think you despise her."

He loved his sister, but he would much prefer to stay in his dressing gown all morning reading Baudelaire and Verlaine, his method, though of dubious effect, of resisting self-pity, and to spend the afternoon walking one of Baron Haussmann's new grand boulevards with Élise and Mimi, which might make him feel expansive. Maybe stopping for lunch at Chez Edgard might help him throw off this malaise of dullness. Then they'd stroll home through the Tuileries, or cross the river to Luxembourg Gardens, and not have to talk to anyone else.

All week at the bank he had to be with people, affecting cordiality to clients and to *Monsieur le directeur*, when there was no juice of cordiality on his tongue. He saw only gray walls, gray desktop, gray ledger books, gray suits, gray hair. He had stood face to face with the director the day before, not even listening to him, only noticing the sickening grayness of the man's skin. He'd wanted to scream, to curse the monotony right in front of the man, to leap out the door and never come back.

A disappointment in life had taken hold of him lately, originating nowhere, everywhere, a resentment with no logical reason because he had all a man could want—except the thing he couldn't identify. This morning the dull power of that irony had shocked him. As he lay in bed, just at the moment of waking, the instant when he became conscious that it was Saturday, which should have made him happy, he couldn't open his eyes. They were stuck shut. With a shudder of panic, he'd made a conscious effort to lift his lids, but the dryness underneath had sealed them shut, and all he succeeded in doing was raising his eyebrows. He lay disoriented for a long time before he tried again. One eye opened part way, with a soft pop, but he'd had to push up the lid of the other with the pad of his ring finger. An absurd experience. Ridiculous to attach any significance to it. Still, he wanted to erase the fear of its happening again by doing something absorbing, by thinking of something exquisite—by reading poetry.

He finished his coffee and noticed Lise's hopeful, liquid blue eyes. "All right, we'll go," he said, not sure that he could be very sociable.

Mimi jumped down from her chair, and stretched her arms out to her sides, raising one arm while lowering the other. "Can we see the windmills, Papa?"

"*Naturellement.*" He touched Mimi's head and felt her blond childhood curls slip between his fingers like silk threads.

Upstairs, in their bedroom easy chair, he had time to read one poem before Élise came in to sit at her vanity and dress her hair and prepare her *toilette*. In a moment she would talk, and the poetic thought would fly away.

C'est l'Ennui!, he read, *l'oeil chargé d'un pleur involontaire.* An involuntary tear. And for what? Because Baudelaire couldn't recognize present beauty? Because life is too good? Because in a moment the silk of his wife's dressing gown might slide down to reveal the shape and smoothness of the globe of her breast and he might smell her sweet musk scent? It made no sense.

"Life *is* good," his father had affirmed the last time he'd seen him, chuckling before he added, "but better spent if not devoted to making a living." This from a man who worked all his life at a desk, uncomplaining, until a month before he died. His father's declaration ought to have alerted him to something important, but instead, this discontent had taken root.

What was he, some immature, spoiled Romantic overcome with pity that life was smaller and meaner and duller than he would have made it if he'd been the Creator? His gloominess disgusted him, that it clung to him like a stale odor, that it lay like a thief in some deep part of him he couldn't reach, that he couldn't shake it. If only his father had lived just two months more, he could have asked him if he'd ever felt this way.

Élise came into the bedroom in a swirl of her dressing gown, talking. "I should not have been able to bear it if you had insisted on staying in today." Her dimple appeared in her left cheek when she scrutinized herself in the glass. "The view from Claire and Paquin's garden will be gorgeous."

She lit the small spirit lamp on her dressing table to heat her curling irons. "Maybe you can leave your moodiness at home and manage a little gaiety."

Her words stung. It was only two months ago that his father died. That wasn't quite fair. Surely she wouldn't have said that if she knew about his eyes not opening. He wanted to tell her. Today. He wanted her to see it as a thing quite apart from his own doing, as some unwanted heavy-heartedness come upon him, bearing down, filled with portent. She would comfort him, he was certain of that.

She caught his eye in her wall mirror and smiled in a coquettish way. "Do you know what day it is?" she asked, dampening her curling papers in rose water.

"Saturday."

Her hands fell to her lap. She turned toward him and waited, her smile devastating him.

"June thirtieth," he added.

Palm up, she bent her slender index finger toward her.

"Eighteen seventy-six."

A look came over her face, not of exasperation, which would have been understandable, but of mystery, a faraway look, her eyes lit by a secret, if only he knew what it was.

"Six years ago today . . . at Bougival . . ." Her voice trailed off as though blown on a cloud, teasing him.

He heard Mimi fussing with her nursemaid in the hallway. "No, I won't," her high voice protested, and there came through the half-open doorway the sound of a dainty tantrum of a stamped foot. "I want to wear my new blue one with the lace. And my blue shoes."

"It's much too fine for a day in Montmartre," the nursemaid said just as Mimi burst into the room and flung herself on Élise's lap.

He had lost the moment of telling her.

"Why can't I, Maman?"

Élise looked at the maid. "Let her," she said, and then turned to Jérôme. "It's a special day."

Hands on hips, Mimi brushed past the maid out the door.

"Six years ago today," Élise said, "was the first time I saw you. The boating party at La Grenouillère. Remember? You were smoking that silly, long porcelain pipe like a Dutchman and were wearing a striped jersey and a straw hat. Monsieur Seurin mistook you to be an expert oarsman and let you take one of the skiffs and we went down-river and got out to walk among the poplar trees and wild poppies and cornflowers, and then you picked a daisy and put it in my hair and said, 'Adornment for the adorable,' and you dared to put your hands on my waist, and we slid into each other's eyes and both of us knew we wouldn't be strangers any more."

Mild shame that he hadn't guessed swept over him and quickly faded. She had already forgiven him, or rather, she had not thought to take offense, enjoying the memory so much. How could he invade her reverie with the mundane absurdity that his eyes had been stuck shut?

"As thin as a pencil," he said.

"My waist?"

"That skiff. If I'd made one wrong move, everything would have been ruined. With the boat and with you. I had all I could do to get you back safely."

"Because of the skiff?"

He chuckled. "Because of me. Because you were so beautiful."

The heath separating Montmartre from Paris seemed narrower than the last time they'd visited Claire. New houses with their unsooted red chimney pots were creeping down from the Butte and the city stretched to meet them.

"Jérôme, see how the heath is absolutely covered with mustard blossoms? Mimi, look. It's like yellow lace."

Mimi stretched out her arms to gather in the whole heath.

At the base of the Mont, the open-air horse cab lurched sideways on the cobbles of rue des Martyrs, past the shabby used-goods stores with paintings, lamps, and rickety tables and chairs displayed right out in the street. They climbed the Butte on rue Lepic past the plaster quarries and small, perched houses. Like so many rabbit hutches, Jérôme thought, smelling the air. He held Mimi so she could stand up in the carriage and watch for the black windmills along the way. In front of a narrow rooming house, two old women were combing lice from children's heads clamped between their knees.

"What are they doing, Papa?"

"Playing a game."

"What kind of a game?"

He shrugged.

"What game?"

She drummed on his thigh for an answer, but he had no playful spirit to make something up like he used to. Élise glanced at him as though waiting for him to come up with something. He saw that she realized he couldn't.

The people living their tawdry lives on the way up the Butte had little to speak of, but they were always singing in the streets or laughing around the hurdy-gurdy. He couldn't understand it. What did they know that he didn't? Even among the rag-and-bone men and the flower girls and laundresses with chapped red arms, there was a robustness, an insouciance that quite overcame him. It was absurd, really, to envy them. He spotted four Parisians dressed in affected rustic costumes—peasant shirts and muslin dresses, pretending to be denizens of Montmartre. Their fine shoes and precise haircuts and coiffures gave them away. What were they seeking in those getups?

"Look, Papa. The big windmill is turning." Mimi slapped his wrist, unable to contain herself, as if the whole world, not just a windmill, were turning and turning for her sake.

The narrow black sails of Le Moulin de la Galette near the top of the Mont and its smaller neighbor turned only to attract attention now. Their use as grinding mills was long past. The Moul' had become an open-air dance hall. With the buildings and fence repainted in green, the acacia trees and trellises and tables, the globed gas lamps strung tree to tree, it was an unpretentious gathering spot for the working people of Montmartre. Already a few musicians were tuning their instruments and one violinist was playing a melody.

"It's 'Amanda,' the song he's playing. Isn't it lovely?" Élise said.

He chuckled wryly. In the song, Amanda tosses away her maidenhood in a dance hall. A mix of sadness and guilt came over him. He hadn't made love to Élise lately.

A block beyond, at the crest of the hill, he noticed an unsightly new telegraph pole on the plain round tower of the old Church of Saint Pierre. An indignity, he thought sadly, not to let something remain as it had been for seven hundred years. From there, he could see the huge foundation for Sacré-Coeur, a basilica planned to be as magnificent as the cathedrals of the Middle Ages. Though it meant little to him, he didn't particularly like that it would be so monumental. Maybe none of it made any difference. Another seven hundred years would go by in a blink and none of it would matter.

They turned left onto rue Cortot and its worn, uncared-for homes, Claire and Paquin's among them. Two centuries earlier his sister's house had been a grand residence of a gentleman vintner. Now it was chopped up into small flats, and the garden in the back was shared by all of the tenants.

The door was ajar, so they stepped inside the dim maroon parlor.

"Claire? Paquin?" Élise called.

Laughter floated up from the garden. They went through the stone kitchen and Jérôme hesitated on the back porch. How would he get through the afternoon? Mimi hopped down and ran past the people at the table to chase a cat under the arbor, and Élise joined the women picnicking on the grass.

"Jérôme!" Claire cried. "I was beginning to think you weren't coming. I was afraid you'd chosen some dead book in a stuffy room over this." She waved her arm toward the garden and the view.

To the right, cream-colored gravel paths wound through banks of flowers planted in front of a tangle of vines and lilacs and wild roses climbing the arbor. To the left, poppies bobbed their heads between the vegetable rows, and sunflowers grew along a shed. Beyond that was the henhouse. Nasturtiums and mustard were taking over the apple and pear orchard which sloped downhill so that over the tops of trees he could see as far as Saint-Denis. The countryside was dotted with smoky factories, but here, high in his sister's overgrown garden, he felt surprisingly light-headed.

"I thought it might be too breezy up here. For Mimi and Élise, I mean."

Claire took Jérôme by the elbow and pulled him toward the rustic table spread with too small a cloth. "Our mother had to push him out-of-doors every spring like an old dog," she said to the guests eating in a blue haze of pipe smoke.

Her saying that made him feel foolish in front of these people he didn't even know.

Claire patted his cheek. "I'm only teasing, brother. Don't look so glum."

She introduced him to the vintner, his toothless, smiling wife, a quadroon who made saddles and smelled of leather and sweat, a young Italian frame maker missing a finger, and a high-booted Cuban painter whose odd-colored trousers were tucked into his boots like a soldier. *Merde*-of-goose green, those trousers. What did he have to say to such people?

"Auguste Renoir is coming too. The painter. You've heard of him? He lives just upstairs."

Jérôme looked with detachment at the shapes of the women's hats—an inverted pan, a mountain of flowers, the feathery body of a headless chicken—and watched Mimi pick a dandelion and wave it to release the seeds.

"Jérôme, are you listening to me?" Claire shook his arm. "Why, here he comes now."

The man was in his thirties, like himself, thin, dressed plainly, with reasonable brown pants, a round felt hat, and with a fringe of beard at his jaw, like his own only not so carefully trimmed. The painter had an air of absent-minded study as he looked across the garden, taking in the women, the lilacs, and Mimi following a bird along a path.

Coming out of the orchard, Paquin set down a basket of pears and swept Mimi up in his arms, lifting her high in the air until she squealed. Jérôme watched his thick fingers with split nails grasping her waist. Paquin kissed her, set her down, and picked up the basket. "A pair of pears, or a game of chess, anyone?"

"Better not today," Renoir said. "With you, one always leads to another."

"Afraid of losing again, eh?" the vintner said and began setting up the chessboard opposite the Italian.

"I've got something more important to do." He grinned and raised his eyebrows. "My painting. The Moul' will be filled in an hour." Renoir took out a tobacco pouch to roll a cigarette. "I can only stay until Georges comes to help me carry it down the hill. He's going to pose in a dance position with a seamstress I know. I don't want to be late."

Working on Saturday, and he sounded elated about it.

"Seamstress? The Butte is full of seamstresses." Paquin grinned. "Aren't you going to tell us who?"

"From the rue Saint-Georges. Aline." He smiled again, shyly, Jérôme thought.

"*Une amoureuse?*" Paquin puffed on his pipe, pretending disinterest.

"Not yet." Renoir looked down at his foot tamping down a patch of grass, the smile diminished but still detectable. He scratched a match on the table edge.

Paquin rolled his eyes at Jérôme as if to say, "Get on with it, man." He went to fetch them each a tumbler of *piccolo*.

Mimi sat in a low swing under the chestnut tree. "Make me go, Maman."

Élise got up from the picnic blanket and pulled Mimi back in the swing seat and let her go, still chatting with the women across the grass. Only snatches of their conversation drifted to him in waves— "an old prune who won't allow herself to smile" . . . "mutton with cumin" . . . "crêpe-de-Chine, I'm certain." How they flew from one topic to another baffled him. He watched Lise, tall and graceful, holding up her hand, laughing, saying, "It's true. I saw it with my own eyes. I'd rather be flogged in public than to wear such a dress." Her carefree air captivated him. Six years. He couldn't believe it.

Renoir sat down with the Cuban painter, the framer, and Paquin, and soon was railing against the new façade of the Ministry of Defense decorated with sculpted heads. Claire sighed and went inside, as though she'd heard it all before.

"They look like gorgons made of molded rubber," Renoir said. "A waste of good quarry marble. What's wrong with the style of the old kings' heads of Pont Neuf? Each one is noble and unique. And after two hundred and fifty years, each one still bears the irregularities of expression of its creator. Now, that's immortality, and that's art. But there's no taste in these monster heads."

Claire brought out a platter of couscous with sweet onions and muscat grapes, and a plate of Brie. "Taste! Here's something if you want taste. Just the way you like it, Auguste. Not too runny but ripe enough."

"There's no more taste these days because no one sees his own work to the finish," Paquin said. "That's the trouble nowadays. Everything's broken up."

"What do you mean?" Jérôme asked, sitting down and making an effort to join in.

"For thirteen years I've made the legs of chairs. Another man makes the backs. Another assembles them, but I never make a whole chair. Where's the enjoyment in that?"

"At least it's making *something*," Jérôme said. "You see it." He gestured to an imaginary chair. "There stands the chair. There are the legs supporting it. They serve a purpose. Someone likes it, buys it, sits in it, passes it on to his children."

By contrast, what did he do? Subtract numbers. Try to guess the *bourse*. Draw up lending documents. Smile and say no, or smile and say yes, it made little difference to him.

"After a while, a man who can't enjoy his work loses something—taste or aesthetics or wholeness. That's what produces ugliness." Paquin balled up his fist and leaned toward Renoir. "What if you just painted one figure, passed the canvas to another man to do the still life on the table, another man to do the background?"

Renoir waved his hand. "That's the way they worked for five hundred years on ceiling frescoes and cathedrals."

"But a man's more important now." Paquin brought his fist down onto the table. "And you know it, Auguste."

"Yes, yes," he said, sounding tired of the argument. "Producing only part of something is the evil of the century."

"Because it's separating the craftsmen from the designers," Paquin said.

"That's what I didn't like about painting porcelain in a workshop. Plate after plate, the same design." Renoir screwed up his face.

Jérôme recognized the man's angst in his flash of memory, and it silenced him. No, Renoir couldn't have loved to work on Saturday in such a factory. As for himself, he was working in a loan factory, just as his father had done.

"I don't see it that way," the Italian said. "There's nothing wrong with the workshop system if the design is well conceived by the master and executed by the planers, carvers, and joiners. Faster production, more frames, more money."

"Fine," Paquin smirked. "So long as you are the master. All the others will learn is to copy."

"So? If they have any talent of original conception, they'll rise to be the masters," the Italian said.

"But everyone ought to be allowed to create something whole." Paquin swung his arm toward the back door. "My father designed and made a whole chair, carved every bit of it, and it's sitting by the fireplace and there's nothing more important in that house."

Jérôme sucked in air through his teeth. What did he have from his father? Nothing.

Mimi tapped his arm. "There's nothing to do."

And what would he be able to leave Mimi?

He offered her a piece of bread with cheese but she shook her head. "Close your eyes and open your mouth," he said.

When she did, he put a strawberry between her lips. She squealed and ate it, then opened her mouth for another. Three strawberries later, he stood up and gave her his index finger to hold. "Show me what you found in the vegetable garden." He made her guess the plants—carrots, onions, leeks, cauliflowers.

"Cauliflowers! Those aren't flowers! I like real flowers better." She skipped through the dappled shade of the chestnut tree toward the flower beds in the sunlight. The air around her seemed to vibrate.

Élise was standing on the swing now, statuesque, presiding. Strands of her light brown hair had blown loose from her chignon and trailed down her throat. The other women looked lovely too, with their skirts spread out around their picnic on the grass. The sun coming through the leafy branches made pale yellow patches on their dresses. My God, if he'd stayed inside today, if his eyes were still stuck shut . . . He didn't want to think about it. Was a man to resign life or die bitter because he only had two days of every seven to call his own?

He found a place to sit in the sunlight, and listened to the women across the grass, amused. Apparently two conversations were going on at once. "You refused him? That's monstrous of you," one of them said. At the same time, Élise and Claire were trying to determine precisely where in the neighborhood Berlioz had lived when they were growing up. He chuckled. As if the exact house mattered a great deal.

Mimi ran across the yard, arms outstretched, chasing a butterfly. It landed on a lilac bush.

"Stand still, Mimi, then creep up slowly so you won't frighten it."

She froze until he gestured for her to go ahead, then tiptoed forward, her dimpled hands out to catch it.

"It's velvet, just like my dress," she said.

One step too close and it flew away. She followed it, her eyes lit with wonder. "How can it fly, Papa?"

"By moving those big wings and catching the air."

She flitted away in imitation, elbows tight to her sides, forearms up, hands gently flapping like wings. He wished his father could have seen her right then.

He remembered how his father had liked to reach down and find him, *petit* Jérôme, skipping beside him when he was Mimi's age. Just a few months ago, his father had reached down and found her instead, and looked up bewildered. Jérôme knew with a start, the same instant that his father knew—the terrible swiftness of it all, as fast as a wingbeat, the cruelty of its brevity.

The *piccolo* made him drowsy. He closed his eyes, surrendering himself to the heavy scent of lilac, letting the sunlight warm his lids. Was it dangerous to close them? Even briefly? From the vicinity of the table he heard the yearning in Paquin's voice. Even the legs of chairs were something. He tried to think of all the shapes a chair leg could take.

"Maman! Papa! Come quick!"

He bolted out of the chair and ran toward her voice, thinking something had happened to her. Everyone laughed. She was standing safe as could be, pointing to thin air.

"Look," she cried.

"A spider's web," Élise said. "Look, Jérôme. How beautiful."

It was strung from a tree branch to two places on a lilac bush. The sunlight turned the silk iridescent. How that tiny creature could launch himself into the void, spinning a filament of thin trust, and catch hold of something, anything, and build his three-pointed kingdom from such a slender thread.

"It's miraculous," Élise marveled and explained it to Mimi, pointing to a fly tangled at the web's edge near the lilac bush, buzzing in panic.

"Trapped," Jérôme said.

Élise looked at him and smiled wanly, as though pained, as though understanding something, not about Mimi. About him. It was comforting. He appreciated it and drew a chair next to his for her. Maybe he could tell her about his eyes now. When she sat, he lifted her hand onto his palm.

"I'm glad you managed that skiff six years ago," she said softly.

He smiled and was about to speak when Mimi said again, "There's nothing to do," in a tone close to a whine but not quite.

"How would you like to help Claire water the plants?" Élise asked and went to fetch her a small tin watering can.

Mimi's chest puffed out like a little sergeant when she took it. She tipped the watering can to sprinkle the iris, scooting back her feet so as not to wet her blue boots. She doused the sweet peas twined on strings, the clumps of daisies. He saw her against pinks and green and yellow gold, lavender and deep purple, but no gray. She sprinkled the cascade of wild roses spilling over the sweet alyssum in joy. Water drops moistened the young rosebuds, tight, mauve, as full of promise as Lise's nipples that first miraculous time he'd seen them.

Mimi came to the pansies bordering the path, and pointed. "Papa. They look like butterflies. They're taking a nap."

She scowled when the water ran out, then ran back to the house to refill her small container. Puckering her mouth with the importance of her task, she carried on.

There was nothing unusual about that watering can—tin turned bluish green, with a sprinkler head on the spout—yet he felt a tenderness toward it out of all proportion to its value. How Mimi's fingers, like little white minnows, grasped its handle. How she wielded it with an authority beyond her years. It made no difference that the trickle of water drops falling on leaves and petals was a mere decoration and would never nourish the plant deep down in the earth where the roots searched for sustenance. She had a job, a purpose.

If only he were a poet. Or if Baudelaire could see her, and see inside him to his love for her, he wouldn't have written about *l'ennui*. He watched her dance through her enchanted world, arms out to catch the fleeting impossible, her world where sprinklings on petals mattered, and his heart followed her.

Renoir plucked him by the sleeve. "A blue hummingbird bent on visiting every flower, with blue eyes to match. Continually astonished at things, that's the way to live, don't you think?"

He couldn't answer.

"She's exquisite," Renoir said.

"I know."

"She'll stay the way she is today no more than the flowers will."

"A thought I try not to think."

"Does she ever stand still?"

He chuckled. "When she wants something her way."

Renoir puffed on his cigarette. "What would you think if I asked to paint her?"

He saw her then with a frame around her, adorable and full of life, with that silly watering can as ineffective as a thimble of water against a field in drought. A painting would make her immortal, not only the girl immortal, but this day when his three-pointed kingdom was of one accord, in one place. It would be a way to beat back the brevity.

"I'd think you have a fine eye."

"I only work on my Moulin painting on Fridays, Saturdays, and Sundays when the place is filled and the atmosphere is right. During the week, I have other ones going. I can't pay much for her to model, but it'll put butter on the spinach."

"Pay me nothing. If you can get her to stand still, you've earned the pleasure." He looked at Mimi. "But I warn you, that might be as hard as making time stand still."

"That's what a painter does." He put out his cigarette in a saucer. "Will she come if you call? So I can make friends with her?"

"Mimi, come here, *ma minette.*"

She looked at him with incredulity. "I have to water the flowers," she said in a voice taut with exasperation and responsibility. "I'm not finished."

An acute joy overcame him. He wanted Mimi, and Mimi's daughter, and even her daughter, to look at him just that funny, exasperated way. Fifty years of such pleasure. Not a day less.

Renoir chuckled. "Women, even little women, instinctively value the right things. You're a fortunate man to live with two of them."

He thought he detected a wistfulness in Renoir's tone. "I know."

Renoir approached Mimi and crouched down. "How did you know the flowers were thirsty?"

"They told me."

"Will you come back another day to water them again?"

Mimi looked at Jérôme for permission, and then nodded.

Renoir spotted his friend Georges coming into the garden, wearing a bowler hat cocked forward. He returned to Jérôme. "Ask your wife to bring her next week. At her convenience, of course, but the sooner the better," he said, and went with his friend into the barn. In a few moments they came out carrying an enormous canvas, so large it caught in the breeze like a sail and they had to wrestle with it to hold on to it.

In the foreground of the painting some figures seated at a table appeared to be nearly completed, but the dancing area and the background were still empty canvas. Even so, Jérôme could already see the love the painter had for the crowded Montmartre gaiety. To launch forth on a blank canvas of that size, to trust enough to go forward, brushstroke after brushstroke across the canvas, filling in with color and life, working, yes, but out of the pure, intoxicating compulsion to create a vision he held inside—it was astonishing.

He felt a faint beating inside him, like hummingbird's wings against his chest. He sat up straighter and slapped the arm of the chair. It's not too late, he thought. He could learn. Not painting, but something that would be his. That's what he needed. Nothing grand, just something that would have taste and expression and love. Paquin could teach him woodworking and he could make a dollhouse for Mimi, or a birdhouse for their terrace. Or he could write a poem for Lise about the little skiff of their family floating past La Grenouillère.

Possibilities rose inside him as the small orchestra from Le Moulin de la Galette burst into a lilting melody. Élise beckoned to Mimi, and with hands joined, mother and daughter swung in a circle to the music. He felt a joy that exceeded art, love for two breathing

women, one once within the other before they unfolded into two be-
ings, for whom and by whom he would, someday, find himself
whole. He could not look at them enough.

Fifty years. If he did nothing more in those years than open his
eyes in the morning and go to the bank and be cordial and read
Baudelaire, no, maybe not Baudelaire, and see that face of Mimi grow
up to have some of Lise in it and some of himself, and not miss a
wink, that was the essential thing, not to blink, and if he could make
some small thing now and then, for them, for himself, if he did just
that, then . . .

He couldn't bring himself to finish his thought. Finishing it
might make it dry up and fly away. Instead, he let the music, Lise's
whirling grace, and Mimi's laughter wash over him. He thought of
Renoir and wished him well with his seamstress. He hoped he would
take a few minutes from painting to dance with her.

Riding home past the massive foundation of Sacré-Coeur, he imagined how it would tower over the little Church of Saint Pierre. He
worried that it would change the village on the Butte. Sometimes the
futile mattered a great deal.

"Did you and Claire decide where Berlioz lived?"

"Yes. Right at the corner of our old street, rue Saint-Vincent. Just
think of it!" The brightness in her voice sharing this trivia amused
him.

He thought of taking Mimi home and coming back with Lise to
the Moul'.

"We haven't danced in a long time." He pulled out a daisy from
his sleeve and threaded it through Élise's hair above her ear.

Winter of Abandon

Vétheuil, 1879

We looked for little movements, a finger, an eyelid, the pulse in her throat. "Camille," he said again, to rouse her, as he had all morning, intoning her name in a loving chant. There was a wheezing breath, a long, frightening stillness, and then another. Claude looked with bewilderment across the bed from his wife to me, as though I could do something. Four days since Father Lévêque had given her last rites, but Claude still hoped. I couldn't tell him that last week she'd whispered to me, "You've been an angel, Alice. It'll be over soon. Then you can rest."

I spooned water into her mouth, and wiped the dribble from her chin so it wouldn't tickle her. God, take Rottembourg and all its rooms of paintings, but leave us Camille. For his sake.

Claude's head nodded and his chin fell to his chest. As he breathed, light glinted in his beard, chestnut-colored. Poor Claude. He'd stayed by her all night instead of waking me at two to switch as we'd done for months. In those hushed times together alone with everyone else asleep, we breathed our anguish deep into each other's lungs, and poured our tangle of feelings into each other's eyes. "In the night, without light, I feel as though I'm the one dying," he'd said this morning. And last night I wasn't there to comfort him. Sleep at such a price.

I stood up. His arm shot out to stay me.

"I'm only going to get you a coffee." He didn't let go of my wrist even though he didn't take his eyes off his wife. "It will just take me a few minutes." Slowly his grip relaxed.

When I came back with the tray, he was whispering to himself. "Blue-gray under her eyes. Losing the blue. Light magenta fading from her cheeks. Yellowing."

My stomach knotted. What if she heard? They say hearing is the last to go. His eyes were fixed on her.

"Antwerp blue. Graying."

It was the moment. I took her hand, he the other, kissing it, holding it to his cheek. Perhaps she could still recognize the soft, spongy feel of his beard. We waited until we were sure. I touched her throat and the pulse was still. He left the room abruptly and came back with easel and paints and a canvas.

"Claude, no!"

"The colors. Everything's changing. Passing in an instant." He set the easel at the foot of her bed.

"The children, Claude. How could you—?"

"Move, please."

"Aren't you anything more than an eye?"

I did not love him then.

"This is the point I've reached. It's all I understand."

I closed Camille's door behind me and sank onto the sofa in the parlor. Silence lay thick as the dust dulling the table next to me. My God, what do I do now? Tomorrow? Next month? What do I really want?

Märthe came to sit next to me.

"She's gone," I said. "You're my eldest daughter. You'll have to be strong, for the others."

The final reality flooded her eyes—Märthe who never shed a tear for anything.

"You *have* been strong, and helpful." I put my arm around her, almost a young woman already. "Last week Camille said to me, 'My boys. Jean is afraid of his father's rages. Little Michel needs a mother's love. You'll see to it, won't you, Alice?'"

"Then we'll still be living with them?" Märthe asked.

I lifted my shoulders, and pushed the future away. What did I need to do now, this very minute? I should tell the children. No. Claude should tell his two children. I should tell mine, that is, the three who were here. Thank God my sister took the middle ones for a while. My littlest one, Pierre, wouldn't understand. Should I tell Germaine and Blanche together? No. A six-year-old needed different words than a thirteen-year-old. What a troupe we were—two needy families at their lowest times, a painter's and a patron's, sharing a rented house.

Claude should be telling his boys right now. Painting! Unbelievable.

I went outside to look for his eldest, Jean. A chill raised the hair on my arms. Autumn had crept over the countryside without my noticing. The hay in the fields was already being stacked. Only last week the poplars were green and lush, and now they were golden spears, and the hillside aflame in gold and orange. Trees were dearer to me now, because of him. Water, too. Across the lane and beyond the garden, aqua vapor lifted off the Seine, the river he loved. Colors spoke. He was teaching me to see, and in spite of Camille fading away for the past year, the world had burst into intoxicating life. Sometimes I felt guilty for such joy.

We'd need a fire tonight, but there was no wood chopped. That was Ernest's job, the absent husband scrambling for money in Paris, trying to recover our losses. My loss. His ineptness. His inattention.

But my inheritance. I lifted the axe over my shoulder, brought it down with all my fury, burying it in a round of oak. I staggered backward, surprised, yanked it free, and whacked recklessly, splitting the round, splintering the wedges.

"May I go back in now?" Jean startled me, kicking at dry leaves behind me. My Blanche stood behind him, nearly a head taller, inseparable from him.

I sat wearily on the bench. "Not yet. Your father is with her saying his goodbye."

"Is my mother dead?" A cold, demanding voice.

I took him in my arms. "Think of her as still the same. She's just away." He struggled free and ran up the steps into the house. Blanche and I ran after him. He stood frozen before Camille's closed bedroom door, his back so small, his neck too delicate for the weight of his head. How would he ever grow into a thick-chested, broad-shouldered man like his father?

"Don't go in."

He spun around and flung himself out the door. Blanche followed him at a trot.

I found Germaine and the two-year-olds, my Pierre and Camille's Michel, rolling down the grassy incline at the edge of the orchard. I held both boys' hands and we walked down to the river where Jean and Blanche were skipping stones, making bright splashes alive for only an instant before they sank through murky jade and forest green water. Sitting on the grass, I drew Michel onto my lap. I took his fingers out of his mouth, and wrapped my hand around his fist.

"Look at the river, *mon chéri*. See the colors dance? Your mama's gone now, to another place. As beautiful as this. A river just like this is carrying her to another land."

"With boats?"

The small ferry to Lavancourt was making a crossing.

"Pretty ones in all colors. Like a rainbow." I rocked his little body, too young to cry. He would someday. "Always remember she loves you."

Jean dropped a rock on a worm and watched it writhe.

"Will we go back and live at the château now, Maman?" Germaine asked.

"No. It doesn't belong to us any more."

I drew her to my side, my chin on her head. Her hair smelled dirty. Maybe this afternoon I could get to it, or Märthe could.

"Why not?"

"My little question box. Is that what it means to be six years old? A hundred questions a day? You know why."

Le Château de Rottembourg at Montgeron, the most beautiful place in the world. My father's, then mine—never Ernest's. Thirty rooms. A music salon in mauve velvet with a concert grand. A ballroom. The wisteria garden. The park and pond. Outlying studios for visiting artists. The private rail line from Paris. All lost.

"Why not?" Germaine pulled my sleeve. "Why isn't it ours?"

Fifty paintings. Twelve of them Claude's, but Auguste Renoir's, Édouard Manet's, and Alfred Sisley's too. Ernest had bought with a passion. He loved to surround himself with talent, the one thing we had in common, both of us suitors to beauty. How could I fault him for that? He would go down in history as a collector of aesthetic acumen, brilliant in his choice of what the world would love someday, brilliant in spending my money. Paintings, furniture, even our clothing—all auctioned. The indignity. Ernest had been beside himself with shame. Twelve of Claude's most important paintings went for ridiculously low prices, which hurt his reputation. The auction gavel had split my heart like an axe.

"Why isn't it?" Germaine shook my arm. "I'm asking you."

"The department store went broke," Blanche snapped. "How many times do you have to be told?"

"Blanche! No, it didn't go broke, completely." I couldn't say more. Ernest had never explained it to me.

"We're poor now." Accusation threaded Blanche's voice.

"No, we're not. Not poor like a peasant. We just don't have servants or a house of our own." I patted Germaine on her belly. "Things change, *mignonne*. Just like the seasons."

Around noon Claude came out of Camille's room, breathing heavily, his face drawn, his pupils wild from having stepped into the maw of death.

"Is it finished?" I asked.

He turned toward my voice, but his gaze wasn't focused. Absently, he wrapped his arms around me, which sent a tremor to my toes. One big hand held my head against his beating chest, his thumb moving back and forth on my cheek as if it were the most natural thing to do. My eyes burned. He smelled like oil paint and something else, less pleasant, sour. Her.

"Yes. It's finished." His husky voice vibrated through his chest into my ear.

Märthe walked in from the girls' room and I pushed away. "Make a lunch, Märthe, and take it down to the river so the children won't wander home until I come to get them."

"Take a blanket. The little ones can have their naps in the studio boat," Claude said, "but settle them in one at a time and stay with them."

Märthe turned abruptly and went into the kitchen.

"I'll make arrangements at the church," I said. "Father Lévêque

knows me more than he knows you." I gave him a little smile, real-
izing I'd just teased him. "You stay with the children. They know."

A grateful sigh came from his mouth. "You're a marvel, Alice."
His lips brushed the hair at my temple, making me pause a moment.

I put on a shawl and went up the lane to the village, little more
than one street, the odd-shaped houses and a few little shops strung
along the river and dominated by the church tower. I passed the
boucherie where the butcher had run me out of his shop once because
I owed him money for a month, until my sisters' allotment came.
On the rise to the church, my legs quivered from exhaustion. Bells
chimed the half hour. Camille loved those bells.

"Thirteenth century bells," she'd mused. "They tolled for Joan of
Arc, and for the slain of the Hundred Years War. The sweep of human
history rings in those noble bells," she'd said. "Someday they'll toll
for me."

I found Father Lévêque sitting at a desk in the rectory surrounded on both sides by crucifixes, and with a painting of the Holy
Family behind him. A round man with a double chin, and a face that
always struck me as kind, he recognized me when I entered.

"Madame Monet died this morning."

"I'm sorry, madame. You can take comfort in knowing that she is
resting in the mercy of the Lord."

I felt the sting of tears forming. "I've come to arrange for her burial and service."

"You? Not Monsieur Monet?"

"I . . . It was a way I could help."

"I meant to ask you when I saw you at the Monets' house, do you
live in this parish now, madame . . . ?"

"Hoschedé. Not permanently. I'm a family friend. I've been staying with the Monets, my husband and I, to help."

"So I understand, but I do not see your husband at mass."

"No, he has business in Paris."

"Ah. And soon you will be going home?"

My stomach cramped. I looked over his shoulder. The Holy Family seemed a portrait of rebuke.

"Monsieur Monet has very little money for a burial. It will have to be the simplest. But not crude, Father. She was well loved."

"The Brothers of Charity will take care of that. It is left for you to take care of yourself, madame, in all ways earthly and heavenly." He clasped his hands on his desk.

"Yes, Father. I understand. And the service?"

"It can be on Saturday at noon. Tell Monsieur Monet that the church will accept whatever he is able to give."

"Thank you." I turned to go.

"I remind you that the church is always open for prayer for our souls as well as for the souls of the dead. Our Lord is merciful, but also firm in His sacred judgments. Confessions are heard from noon to two daily."

"Yes. Thank you." I backed out of the room.

The empty church was cool and dark but not unpleasant. I lit a candle for Camille, and one for Claude, and watched the two flames glow golden, side by side, their two aureoles mingling. I chose the same pew we had sat in the last time she and I came together to mass, near a side chapel where we had knelt side by side, both of us praying for her life.

Last things. Her last meal was only broth. Nearly two years of pain. Months of retching. Apologizing when I had to clean it up. She didn't deserve any of it. God, how hard a thing You've asked of me today, to believe in Your mercy.

Camille's last words to me were whispered, slowly, deliberately, when Claude was out of the room: "If you have not been before this, you will soon be lovers." Even then, in extremity, her words were gentle. She knew, and had said nothing until then. Claude and I had barely touched for more than a year, but there'd been an earlier intimacy, and ever since, there had grown an intimacy of the soul, deeper than of the body, and that we could not hide. A spasm of guilt shook me. My head sank to the pew in front of me.

I would return to grace, if I could. I would make an effort. I would not look into Claude's eyes to read his passion. He was selfish, ill-tempered, always needing praise.

But he made the world luminous. He was vastly talented. He was opening me to earthly glories, the heavenly ones having grown oppressive. He gave more love to my children than Ernest did. And he still needed me.

Surely some woman, a baker or ferryman's wife in the last five centuries, knelt where I was kneeling, tormented by loving the wrong man, or loving the right man at the wrong time. What did *she* do to quell her love? To forestall the sin that lay behind Father Lévêque's pointed inquiry? To go on living with equanimity and in the grace of God? Or did she plead for pardon and still succumb to earthly rather than heavenly love?

For more than a year we'd lived in taut proximity with only a brief touch, a look, a knowing, never taunting or teasing one another with lingering hands, for we knew the anguish that would cause the other. It was a love that came from another part of us, separate from our bodies, which had to suffice. Did that restraint mean anything to God?

I sat for a while in a stupor, not knowing what I could pray for with honesty, thinking instead of all the things that needed doing at home. I slipped past the confessionals, and on my way out I touched a new candle wick to Claude's flame, for me, and set it next to his. Mary, have mercy on us all.

In the *boucherie* I smacked my few coins on the counter before I asked for a quarter kilo of meat for *ragoût*. I watched the butcher's hands wrapping the meat, smeared with blood.

Outside the shop I asked myself—would I still love Claude if he were a butcher and not a painter? If he had not painted me so tenderly?

It had been three years ago that Ernest had commissioned Claude to paint four large panels to decorate the dining room at Rottembourg with scenes from the estate. Ernest would be represented in a hunt in autumn, and I in the setting of the pond.

That's where it started, with a look across the still pool as I was pretending to fish with a willow branch, resting my hand against a tree trunk. "Lovely," he'd murmured. "You're a wood nymph," and I'd felt so.

When he closed his paintbox, he gave me a brief sweet kiss, on my mouth, a thank-you for posing. It was only because he was exuberant about the painting, I'd told myself. A forgivable indiscretion.

"Both of the things I love, wood nymphs and water," he'd said, his eyes glinting playfully, "and I've never thought to paint them together. You're my muse, Alice!"

And I'd felt that too, rumbling distant and deep, the power of his fantasy tugging me.

No. It was laughable. Definitely not if he were a butcher.

At home I filled a bowl with warm, soapy water and went in to wash Camille. The painting was turned to face the wall. I didn't touch it. Sitting next to the bed, I tested the water and stroked the cloth across her forehead, cheeks, under her chin, her neck, then her arms and hands. I think she knew I would do this now, just as I had for months. She always murmured with pleasure at the warmth of the cloth and the gentleness of my attentions. How powerful a thing love is, that one loves past death, past regret, past all logic, and feels purified by that loving.

I lay my head next to hers and whispered, "Would you mind if I stayed on here, just until I'm sure Claude will be all right, and for the children's sake?" I tried to feel her answer, to hear it truly despite what I wanted, but I could not.

I closed her door and wandered from room to room, my footsteps creaking the wood floors in the silence. Soon, the tolling of the village bell resounded dark and deep, cracking my heart. I sat down and wrote to Ernest.

> Camille died this morning. I am distraught, even though we expected it, but expectation only causes the imagination to create grim pictures. It doesn't give peace. I am trying to hold things together. For weeks I've hardly left her bedside, watching for her slightest need. I've had all the housework except what Märthe can do on weekends. I even chopped wood today. My hands are blistered. I've been exhausted since the housekeeper left. She's not to blame. Four months without pay? A woman's got to find a way to live. Thank God she taught Märthe and me some things about cooking or we'd all starve.
>
> Please come for the funeral on Saturday. It will look bad for me to live here now without Camille if you don't come more often. You must bring us some money. Surely you're receiving something from these last auctions. What my sisters sent this month is nearly gone. Claude has had to help support us. If you and I are husband and wife at all, then you'll tell me how things stand, money and all. I deserve to know.
>
> Yours,
> Alice

The scratching of my pen in the silent house was a painful sound.

I wrote more letters to tell Camille and Claude's friends, Auguste

Renoir, Alfred Sisley, Berthe and Eugène Manet, Suzanne and Édouard Manet, and to tell my sisters. I felt drained by the time the Brothers of Charity came to take her. It was good that I was in the house alone. I rolled up the blanket and sheets, sprinkled her rose talcum powder on the mattress and rubbed it in, and aired out the sickroom, what was to have been my room after she was well enough to climb the stairs and sleep with Claude again.

Finding no more ministrations that I could do, I went outside. Claude had gathered everyone in the orchard to pick the last apples. His youngest, Michel, was riding on his shoulders to reach the branches.

"Are you all right?" Claude asked. He was holding himself in, for the children's sake.

I nodded. "There's something each of you can do to help." I handed Märthe the letters. "Please post these in the village. Blanche, you can pick some basil and thyme. Germaine, you remember what scallions look like? Pull up four or five. Jean, you know how to set the rabbit trap, but be careful. Later, your father can teach you to chop wood. Twelve is not too young." When all of them left except the two toddlers, I said to Claude, "It's better if everyone has something to do."

"Do you mind how countrified we've become?" he asked.

"*We've* become? We?"

I thought of the multitude of servants at Rottembourg, where I never needed to do anything difficult or humbling or heroic. Ache traveled up my arms. I showed him the blisters on my palms. His mouth dropped and the apples he held in his loose smock tumbled into the bushel basket.

"I don't know if I should stay now," I said.

"Where would you go?"

"Paris."

"And do what?"

"Just what I did after I left Rottembourg. Find a few piano students. Do dressmaking for the women that used to come to parties there."

"Ridiculous. I won't hear of it."

The *ragoût* was thin, the conversation just as sparse. After the children were in bed, Claude showed me the painting in the sickroom. A great wave of blue bedclothes almost smothered her. The brushstrokes swirled over Camille's disembodied head and under her chin, like blue-white clouds lifting her, swallowing her up in the universe. Her face was pale violet and blue-gray—sweet and insubstantial.

"She's there yet dissolving, on the point of not being there at all," I said.

He'd poured out his anguish and love on that canvas, yet he'd calculated his colors carefully, which made it a chilling achievement. He'd frozen the moment of change when pain was loosening its grip and her forehead and the skin around her eyes were finally relaxing. She was holding dahlias, but we'd had no flowers for weeks. It had grieved him that she couldn't lie in a room filled with flowers.

"You've given her permanence."

"I think of it as continuity."

We looked for a while in silence, rooted in front of the painting.

"I will always love her," he whispered.

"I know."

He turned to me. "Will you sleep here tonight?"

I felt a small, sudden contraction in my chest. Sleep here, alone instead of in the crowded bedroom with the girls?

"Not yet."

Ernest sent a paltry forty francs, but was conspicuously absent at the funeral. Either something in Paris meant more than how his family was managing or . . . There was no *or*.

Auguste and the Manets came to the service, but they had to take

the coach to the rail station in Mantes right after the burial to catch
the last train back to Paris. Édouard and Suzanne kissed each child
and we said goodbye. I thought of how they had played croquet with
the children at Rottembourg, and had always brought them some
sweet thing.

Walking home from the village, Claude carried Michel in the
crook of his arm. His other hand rested on Jean's shoulder. He nodded toward a farmer's field. "Look how the sunlight bends around
that haystack and blurs the edges."

I didn't know what to make of it, that he'd notice, even now.

"It's too far, Maman," Pierre whined, dawdling behind me in the
lane. I picked him up and kissed him.

Blanche fell into step with me. "Are you going to be their mother
now too?" she whispered.

"Shh. I don't know."

Claude spent the next days along the Seine, in the hills above
Vétheuil, or taking the farmers' ferry across the river to Lavancourt.
Searching for painting motifs, he said, but he didn't take a sketch-
book. I worried. He'd told me once that in despair over being unable
to support Camille when Jean was a baby, before they were married,
he'd thrown himself into the Seine, and then crawled out, ashamed.

"Why doesn't he stay home if he's not painting?" Jean asked.

"He needs to be alone. In nature."

I didn't know if we were losing him to nature, or if nature would
make him whole. I wondered if it was shame, because of me, that
kept him away. I waited and watched, hoping he'd come back excited
about a weeping willow branch dipping into the river, or a magpie
perched on a rustic fence.

"Nature makes a person humble," he said one evening. "All that
life pushing through the earth one season. Dying back another. Re-

peating endlessly. You can't fight it. All you can do is stand in awe and let it work its mystery in you."

"Take Jean with you. Tell him that. He's longing for you, Claude."

The next morning they went off together, he tousling his son's hair, Jean skipping every few steps to keep up, holding his father's hand. Blanche stood at the window watching them go, and then turned to me with a suffering look. The weekend after, I asked him to take Blanche too.

"Jean isn't as sad when he's with her. She makes him forget for an hour if they're absorbed in something."

He smiled wryly. "That's the general effect of Hoschedé women."

The weather turned cold early. Wind bent the bare poplars, rain blew sideways, and puddles froze. After Claude slipped and fell in his *sabots*, he bartered a painting for the postman's treaded boots so he could still tramp the riverbank, its icy edge wider and thicker each day.

Snows started early in November and still I stayed on, not knowing from day to day what I'd do. Being indoors more, the girls and I were cramped in one room. "Ridiculous," Claude said and moved my things onto the bed in the room where Camille had died.

Her presence seeped from every corner. Her tortoise-shell hand mirror was still lying on her dresser. If I picked it up, it would leave its imprint in the dust on the cherry wood. Touching the doorknobs where her fingers had been, I opened the armoire and found our one elegant dress, the only one saved from the auction. Before she'd become too ill, she and I longed to go to Paris together, to see the friends we'd known, or to go to the opera, but we never could go together because we shared the dress in order to keep up appearances.

That night, Claude stepped into the doorway, his thickset body filling it, as if making a point not to cross an invisible line.

"What shall I do with her things?" I asked.

"Use them. It would please her."

He came into the room, two steps, a pause, then a few more, lifted her straw hat with the black streamers from the bedpost where she'd left it in summer, and positioned it on my head. His eyes were soft, the way he looked at nature.

"Don't see her in me, Claude. I'm someone different."

"I know." A touch of peevishness edged his tone.

I took off the hat. "May I give it to Märthe?"

"Whatever you'd like. Give her Camille's slippers too. I noticed she has none."

"I don't want to do anything hurtful."

"You won't. Use everything of hers. What we both do is going to be remembered, though, by more people than just our children."

"That's your desire for fame speaking. You care painfully what people think."

"It's also my concern for you. I just want you to be aware of that."

"I am."

Taking that for a sign, he kissed me, softly at first, then pressing. The knotted, bittersweet tension of more than a year of untouchable closeness unraveled. I felt my knees buckle. His hand moved down my spine, holding me against him. I quivered involuntarily and he smiled in a knowing way. Where was my will? A moment longer, to savor it for the days ahead. I pressed my hands against his chest, and he stepped back, out the door, and went upstairs.

Emptiness flooded me.

I opened a drawer. Camille's rose-colored nightgown that I'd washed dozens of times lay just as I had folded it. I couldn't touch it now.

Beyond the pity given a woman whose fortunes have fallen, there was this new badge: the mistress of a painter. A reckless hedonist, that's what they'd call me, or worse, if I stayed on here. I piled my clothes on the window bench and slid into her bed, my skin hot, the sheets cold, crawling into her skin, one step closer to his bedroom, which frightened me with longing.

In the morning I wrote to Ernest.

> This is the sixth letter I've sent without a response. Do your duty by our children and by me. Either send for me to come to you with the children, or come here yourself. I'm risking all by continuing to live here. No one has come to see how we are, not even Suzanne and Édouard. That should tell you something. I will not be cast as a bohemian.
>
> We have no more credit in the village. Claude still owes the doctor a thousand francs, yet he hasn't touched a brush to canvas since the day she died. I don't know when he'll paint again. That's what worries me the most. You've got to see what that means, Ernest. We are in peril.
>
> This is the last pleading letter I will write. I am at the edge. Come and save me.
>
> > Alice

Bohemian. I already was one—unless he would come.

Claude wrote to him too, and to Édouard, offering paintings, asking for money, even to Auguste, knowing he could ill afford to lend a bean. The bald importunity of his letters embarrassed me. Claude still wasn't painting. For someone who normally finished a painting in four days, this was dire. How long would that go on? Every week he took an older painting or two to Paris dealers. Landscapes aren't popular just now, they told him. Half the time he came back with nothing. Once he saw Ernest, who convinced him he could sell them, so Claude left a couple with him too. When he went to collect, he couldn't find Ernest at his city flat or at any of the usual cafés.

One morning Claude stood smoking a cigarette before the large painting of Camille and Jean as a toddler walking in a hillside of red poppies in Argenteuil. She was wearing the straw hat with black ribbons. He stubbed out the cigarette and lifted the painting off the wall.

"No, Claude. Not that. Take one without her."

"Bigger ones will fetch a larger price."

"Then take two small ones. Take the boats at Argenteuil. Not her."

He blew a puff of air out his mouth and shook his head. "It's a confounded profession, selling what you love, and then convincing yourself it makes you happy when someone buys it."

Snow billowed in as he went out the doorway clutching the painting against his body. "I'm taking it to Durand-Ruel, not to Ernest."

He came back the next day with two hundred francs, canvas, stretchers, paint, a bag of potatoes, and a newspaper, saying that the Seine had frozen in Paris and snow shoveled from the streets was being dumped in huge mounds on top of the ice. "Let's hope it lets go slowly, or there'll be a monstrous debacle. The papers are full of grim predictions."

"Did you see Ernest?"

"Yes, at the Guerbois with Édouard. He was surprised when I walked in. He looked awful. He made me wait while he wrote this."

Claude handed me an envelope from his breast pocket. I tore it open.

My beloved wife,

What may I call you now? Don't curse me. I've struggled. I've nearly lost my mind. I've wanted to kill myself out of shame but I lacked the courage. I've lost the Paris apartment. I should have told you everything earlier, as it was happening. The partners are exacting the last franc from me, and will not even let me into my old office. But I've invested what was left in a new magazine. I'm sure it will be a success. I've named it *L'Art et la Mode.* Tell me to take heart or tell me to disappear.

Ernest Hoschedé

The city is frozen solid. If you wish, I will come at Christmas.

I handed it to Claude. "His last name. As if *I'd* forgotten."

Was he preparing to make the grand gesture at Christmas, arriving on the wings of a success so large it would shame me for doubting him? Or would he creep home morose and dangerous and stir up the children? Or was I being abandoned, clean and simple? I wasn't sure I cared. Yet I wrote the next day, come.

Bitter cold set in. The parish school closed early for the holidays. The garden and countryside that had shouted their glories only a few months before, now presented the bleakest picture I'd ever seen. The river froze here too, so Vétheuil was cut off. Only draft horses pulling sledges could travel. One day I hoped for Ernest's coming at Christmas. The next day I hoped he wouldn't be able to get through.

"You don't want Papa to come, do you?" Märthe said as she peeled an onion while I washed the turnips.

"How could you say that? Pierre and Germaine would be inconsolable if he didn't come."

"But you don't want him to."

"I want him to fulfill his responsibility."

Shame that my feelings were so transparent made me silent. As a gesture of contrition, I tried to think of the Ernest I once knew, to make me want his coming. Dashing, exquisitely dressed, confident,

Ernest lived every day with zest, constantly devising new entertainments. He was so pleased with himself when he bought his first painting, regaling dinner guests with how he'd discovered Alfred Sisley, that when I choked on a fish bone and couldn't stop coughing, he kept talking, happily telling his story.

Happiness wasn't love. I chopped a turnip in two. The halves fell away from each other and rocked a moment. At least not a love deep enough, since he kept from me the events that changed our lives. Not like Camille loving Claude enough to outwait his parents' disapproval, subsist on turnip broth, pack up and escape from creditors in the night in order to share the life of her beloved. Love wasn't just some delicacy served on a silver spoon in the glow of a gala evening. It had to be richer, demanding more resilience and honesty and self-forgetfulness and risk.

"Mother, stop! Look what you've done."

I'd chopped the turnips too finely. They would be mush.

Late that evening while I was taking down my hair, Claude came into my room and closed the door. He sat on the bed behind me. In the wall mirror I could see the ardor in his eyes. Gently he took the brush from my hand and pulled it through my hair, long, slow strokes, his other hand gathering up loose strands at my temples.

"Like spun bronze," he murmured.

His fingers trailed from my temple to cheek to throat, and his head sank slowly, the softness of his beard tickling my ear, the kiss resting on my shoulder.

"The children are all asleep," he said. "What's to stop us?"

A quick intake of breath. A flush of warmth. A hammering in my heart. To feel his thick hands firm on my body, to relax in his arms . . .

"I'm still his wife," I said, my throat scorched dry with longing. "He has a responsibility. If we become lovers—"

"We already are, save for the new beginning."

"If we begin again, it lets him be negligent. It would mean I was leaving him. That would let him abandon me."

He squeezed my shoulders. "Open your eyes, Alice. Where is he?" He stood and flung his arm toward the parlor. "Do you see him here? When was the last time you saw him? Six months ago?"

"He might come for Christmas."

"Or the Second Coming."

"I have to wait and see."

The morning before Christmas, Claude took down Ernest's shotgun from the high cupboard in the utility room, and stuffed a cartridge box in his overcoat pocket.

"Claude! Don't!" I flung myself at his chest.

He eased me away from him. "What's the matter?"

"The shotgun."

He chuckled. "I've seen bird tracks in the snow. They might be game birds."

I flushed with embarrassment and relief.

He put on his jersey, jacket, overcoat, muffler, and knit cap. "You and the children ought to have something decent for Christmas dinner." He pulled on his gloves. "A man has a responsibility," he said pointedly. And then softer, "If I want you to take her place, upstairs, then I have to take Ernest's place."

He picked up the shotgun.

"Do you even know how to use it?"

"Ernest showed me when I painted *The Hunt.*"

Jean came running into the room from the kitchen. "May I

come?" he asked, positioning himself between us and looking up at his father. "Please."

Claude squatted in front of him and put his big hands on Jean's waist. "Another time, son. When it's not so cold."

Jean whirled around and bumped into me. I put my arms around him and he allowed me to hold him a few moments before he pulled away.

From the narrow kitchen window, I watched Claude trudging away through deep snow, and tried to remember his painting of the hunt. It was one of the dining room panels. Claude had come back to finish it that last winter at Rottembourg, three years ago. That first winter of abandon.

A winter so mild that Claude and I took walks outdoors, Claude so robust in his country tweed and muslin shirt covering the dark, coarse growth on his chest. So different from Ernest, who wore only the finest cambric and virgin flannel and stayed inside all winter. We said how foolish Ernest was to remain in Paris, and we went to the pond where Claude had painted me the summer before. All the exuberance of that painting day bubbled up again, and opened me, and he entered.

He stayed four more precious days, ostensibly to paint Germaine as a gift for me, but it was the nights and what we felt that held him there—the nights, a sin to swoon over a hundred times in memory. He left to spend Christmas with Camille and Jean, and when Ernest came home for Christmas dinner, I stared across the dining table between Märthe and Blanche to Claude's painting of the pond and its wood nymph. The following August, Ernest admitted bankruptcy in a letter to me sent from Paris, and I gave birth to Pierre in a rail coach as the children and I were leaving Rottembourg forever.

A knock at the door brought me to my feet. Ernest! My throat tightened.

"Papa!" Germaine shouted.

It was the postman for Vétheuil and Lavancourt, with packages and a letter.

"How did they get through?" I asked.

"By sledge to Lavancourt. I carried them across on foot. I didn't trust the ice with more weight. It's warming up," he said with an exaggerated shiver, grinning.

All my breath leaked out of me. Then it *was* possible.

We gave the postman coffee, and he warmed himself by the fire.

"I'll bet you're sorry you bartered away those boots," I said.

He looked around at the paintings, as though that were the real reason he had come. "No, madame. Someday all of France will know the name Claude Monet." He chuckled. "In the meantime, I have his river in my parlor."

A wild wave of happiness swept over me.

"Merci," everyone chorused as he left. *"Joyeux Noël!"*

"Are they from Papa?" Germaine asked. "The packages, are they from Papa?"

"No. They're from the Manets." The letter was from my sister.

Dear Alice,

 I don't know how, in all good conscience, you expect me to send more money for you to continue living in such a disreputable way with that painter. People are talking. Besides, it's absurd for you to live wondering where your next meal is coming from. Listen to reason, Alice. As soon as the thaw permits, you must come to Biarritz with your children. Then we'll make a plan. Do not make me ashamed. In any event, the twenty francs is for the children for Christmas.

             Ever your sister, Cécile

I crumpled the letter in one hand. Märthe watched with a concerned scowl. "Is it from Father?"

"No." I went into the bedroom and dropped it into the bureau drawer. I couldn't pretend I didn't have a choice now.

Claude came home numb, his fingers stiff around the shotgun, ice crusting his beard and eyebrows. His cheeks above his muffler were rosy and exuberant as he held up two pheasants and two small plovers. He laid them on the kitchen table, swept up the nearest toddler—it happened to be Pierre—and lifted him high over his head until he squealed and giggled, and Claude set him on his shoulder. Michel flung himself at Claude's legs and he bent down to lift him onto his other shoulder. "My two baby boys. Just like puppies, both of you. Someday you'll be too big for me to do this."

"It's a good thing you have two broad shoulders," I said.

"Birds," Michel said, and pointed.

"They're pretty, aren't they?" I said. "I never knew feathers could be so beautiful." The plovers were plain tan but the pheasants had red masks, white patches behind their beaks, and intricate markings of brown and iridescent purple. I stroked the sheen on top of a green head.

"Don't pluck them yet."

"Pluck them! How in the world does one pluck a bird?" Camille would have known. What was inside that had to be gotten out? "You just assume I could do anything."

He opened his eyes wide. "Can't you?"

Warming himself by the stove, he worked his fingers gingerly until they were supple enough to move freely.

"You're at least going to help me with them, aren't you?" I asked.

His face stretched slowly into a smile. "No. I have my own work to do."

He left and came back with his easel and a small canvas.

"You're going to paint again!" I clasped my hands under my chin. "The birds?"

He positioned them on a white cloth. "These will feed us twice. Once when we eat them tonight, and again when the painting sells. I know it will. People who go to the Salon buy still lifes by the crate. I'll do more. It's not what I want to paint, but that has to wait."

He started right in, painting at white heat, painting to become alive again. He was working. For this day at least, he was free from the grip of grief.

Germaine came into the kitchen and pressed herself against my legs. "Papa's not coming, is he?"

"Whose little voice is this that sounds like it's coming out of a well?" I bent down and covered her neck in kisses.

"Is he? I'm asking you."

"No, I don't think so, ma chérie. But we'll have a nice Christmas anyway."

"Will there be almond cakes?"

"No. But we'll have these fine birds. See?"

"A maman, a papa, and two babies."

"Yes. A family. Will you do something for me? Will you find Märthe and tell her she can help me now?"

Germaine left, scuffing her feet through the kitchen.

After painting awhile, Claude said, "You can start on the pheasant on the right. I'm through with that one."

I grimaced and carried it to the counter. Märthe came in and laughed.

"Don't be so quick to think it's funny, Märthe. You're going to do the next one," I said. "Bring a bucket."

I gathered some soft down below the neck and tugged in a downward direction. Nothing happened. Märthe giggled. I held the breast with my other hand and yanked harder, and the feathers gave but the skin tore. Somehow, I denuded the bird, cut a slit, and held my breath as I pulled out the slick soft shapes. My stomach revolted at the smell. My hands became gooey with blood. I brushed my hair out of my eyes and feathers stuck to my face and hair, which made Märthe laugh even harder.

Claude lifted them off and handed her the next bird. "Pluck up your courage, girl."

Her smile vanished. "I can't."

"You do what life gives you to do," I said and whacked off my bird's head so its golden eyes wouldn't look at me, and dropped it in the bucket. There it was, life pared down to essentials—food and work and love, and beauty too.

In the painting, the birds lay alone against the white cloth, as if it were snow. His feathered brushstrokes were so tender, the bird family so forlorn.

Claude scoffed at it. "It isn't much."

"It's a new beginning."

Our spirits turned inward after dinner, with Camille so hauntingly here and not here. Thank God for the Manets' gifts, for the brief pleasure of opening them—a wooden toy for each of the little boys, a doll for Germaine, gloves for the older girls, a cap and muffler for Jean.

Claude held Camille's Michel and my Pierre on his lap, one on each leg, letting them worm their fingers into his full beard to find each other's hands. Both of them his. Both of them equally loved. If I left to live with Cécile, that would deny him his own son.

If any traveler were to peer through the frosty window, we would look like any large, happy family living decent lives. And if I could peer in at Rottembourg tonight, I'd see its new occupants, a happy, ignorant family, having their Christmas Eve dinner served in the glow of the chandeliers, poorer than I because no one there had tramped through ice and snow in below-zero temperatures all morning to provide the meal.

I opened the door a crack and looked out into the night—clear and silent and still. Cold burned my nostrils. Light from the doorway spilled onto the snow, turning it into pale gold satin. Stars sparkled like a thousand shards of crystal, a chandelier as broad as heaven.

"Claude, Jean, Blanche, come see this. Everyone. Put on everything. Coats. Hats. Mittens. Mufflers."

I pulled blankets off beds and made everyone line up on the porch wrapped up together. If they kept slapping themselves and hugging each other and stamping to keep warm, maybe they would feel some joy in our little world. We sang out to the stars, *"Il est né le divin Enfant. Jouez hautbois, résonnez musettes."* Claude bounced Michel and Pierre in his arms to the rhythm, and then gave them over to me. He stayed outside longer than everyone else and sang out bravely in his baritone, *"Ah, Quel grand mystère,"* and I knew he was singing to Camille.

As I cradled Michel and Pierre on the sofa, wrapped in a blanket, I knew, finally, what to pray for—that Camille had died without noticing the resemblance of my Pierre's eyes to Claude's—not just to wish it wistfully, but to try to know as a certainty that since God is merciful, He would grant it.

After the children were in bed, Claude and I stood watching sparks fly out from the fireplace onto the hearth.

"If sledges got through to bring the post, Ernest could have gotten through too," I said, my voice more bitter than I intended.

Compassion puckered the skin under his eyes. I felt ashamed for my self-pity when he had the greater grief.

"Does his letter alarm you?" he asked.

"That he would kill himself? No, not if he was showing his face at the Guerbois. He's probably there tonight, unless some family invited him to share their hearth and holiday."

Claude wrapped a single blanket around us both as we faced the fire, his body next to mine, so solid and *there*.

"Some men don't need to have a hearth and family," he said.

"No. Apparently not."

His held breath let go in a hush of, "I do."

I chuckled. "You've had rather more than a family." Joint by joint my body shaped itself to his.

He responded with a look that was both amused and thoughtful. "Have you noticed that Jean and Blanche are always together now?"

Joy surged up in me. "They've been inseparable for months. Ever since the diving match off the studio boat last summer. I was wondering when *you'd* notice."

"I've seen it all along. I didn't want to say anything to disturb it."

Leaving would take away Jean's closest friend right when he needed one. Our lives had become so intertwined, I didn't know how we would ever unweave them.

Claude's expression changed from amusement to seriousness. He squeezed his bottom lip between his teeth, and turned me toward him. "I have to have continuity to work. You have to have a place to live."

"I have one."

"Then you'll stay?" His eyebrows lifted and his cheeks rose over the top of his beard.

"Cécile's. A letter came today. She's demanding that I bring the children and stay with her as soon as it thaws and we can travel."

He burst out of the blanket and paced. "What right does she have to tell you what to do?"

"The right to protect the family name."

"Protect! It's already a ruined family, Alice. That husband of yours—"

"Don't say it. I know."

"Continuity, family, love—they're all right before our eyes. Can't you see them?"

"Yes. You've taught me to see."

He stopped pacing. "Then you'll stay?"

"The world is frozen. Right now I can't move, even if I wanted to."

"And after the thaw?"

I lifted my shoulders. "After the thaw comes spring."

A slow, tentative smile spread over his face. He reached for my hand, and took one step backward. I came forward. He reached for my other hand and stepped backward again, leading me toward the stairway, gentling me to walk step for step with him, not letting his eyes off me, as though I were a vision that would vanish, feeling with his foot behind him for the first step up, then the next, up, up and into an early spring.

Cradle Song

Paris, 1879

Today is the day of the christening and I am allowed to go. I'm jittery right now because I'm putting baby Julie in her long white lace christening gown and Madame Berthe would be terribly upset with me if I let her spit up on it. Such a baby's dress!

I feel Julie's diapers. Wet again. I lay her down to change her. There is no limit to the number of diapers Madame lets me use. When I think of my few poor cloths at home for my Félix, probably ragged now, and rough from hog tallow soap, my heart aches. I wish I could send Maman some of these soft ones.

Julie clutches at my ear with her tiny fingers while I'm working. Oh, the feeling I get when she does that. I bury my face in her belly and tickle her and kiss her from the top of her wispy head to the soles of her feet. I think of Félix, and long to kiss his dimple. I sing a little to Julie. Madame doesn't mind it if I don't sing loudly like I used to do in the woods at home, but softly.

I put on the leather shoes Madame Berthe gave me to wear to the christening. They're very dainty but so tight. I like my wooden *sabots* better only she doesn't want me to wear them in the house. The noise on the floors aggravates her when she's painting, she says.

This is their first baby, just like Félix is Pascal's and mine, so it's a special day. I want to do everything right. I go down the grand staircase with the baby. Madame looks beautiful in a pale blue dress. She has piled her dark hair on top of her head. She is tall and graceful and her fingers are long. Monsieur Eugène Manet looks at her with goose eyes and whispers some funny soft thing. Poor man. He gets terrible headaches.

When Madame and I get into the carriage to go to the christening, she leans over and says to me, "I'm sorry Julie isn't a boy. To pass on the Manet name. I think she looks like a boy."

"I don't," I say. "She has the sweetest little-girl point to her upper lip."

"No, she doesn't. That head, flat as a paving stone. Don't you think it's ugly?" she asks.

I don't want her to fall into one of her gloomy moods so I say, "No. Julie is the most perfect baby that could be."

It wrenches me inside to say that, but I tell myself that I meant a perfect girl baby.

The church for the christening is as grand as a palace built for baby Jesus. I gaze at a stone carving of him in Mary's arms. I don't listen to the priest. I am cold and my feet hurt. I have all I can do to keep Julie quiet and look up and up to the colored windows shining like jewels.

In the carriage coming home Madame nibbles the baby's toes, gently of course. She hands Julie to me and I do the same thing.

"Don't do that, Sylvie," she says as hard as stone.

"I'm sorry, Madame. I won't ever."

Madame changes her mind about the baby being ugly, though. After the christening, her sister, who also has a baby, and Monsieur Manet's brothers, Gustave and Édouard, and Édouard's wife, Suzanne, come to the house. The brothers all look alike, with high foreheads and thick, dark beards, only Eugène's upper lip pokes out from his mustache in a point.

"Julie is like a kitten, always happy," Madame says. "My daughter is a Manet to the tips of her fingers. Even this early, she's just like her uncles. She has nothing of me."

Oh! It's terrible for her to say that and not say Julie is like her father. Which uncle she means I don't know, but Monsieur Eugène just stands there looking at Édouard's shiny shoes, and Suzanne Manet pulls in her double chin and glances sideways at her husband. Madame Berthe's sister covers up the moment by talking about Julie's christening dress, but they've already talked about it.

Something is not right in this house. I don't know what it is.

Monsieur's brother, Édouard Manet, is a famous painter. On Tuesday nights, Madame and Monsieur go to *soirées* at Édouard's house to talk about painting with other artists and to listen to Madame Suzanne play the piano. Sometimes they meet here instead and they listen to Madame just as though she were a man. She's as good as any of them, Monsieur Eugène told me. She is always teasing Monsieur Édouard to get him to paint outdoors. Once they had an argument over using black and white in paintings. He said, "My blacks are not pure black any more than your whites are pure white." It wasn't a hard argument. They laughed and touched cheeks when he left. I don't understand. Black is black and white is white.

I don't understand Madame Berthe's paintings either. They don't look finished. She leaves empty spaces. She must think they're finished because she's forever setting them aside and starting a new one. She must love painting more than anything.

I love Félix and Pascal more than anything.

On the next sunny day, I take Julie out in the baby carriage on the streets nearby. A little way from our house twelve streets come together at a big arch. I used to be afraid that coming home I'd pick the wrong street and get lost, but not any more. The arch faces the grandest boulevard in the world. Under rows of trees there are toy and gingerbread stalls and merry-go-rounds for children. If I hadn't promised Pascal that I'd save all the money I earn, I would buy something for Félix there. In the toy stall, I look at the stocking dolls. He probably has nothing to hold but an old rag. There are some fine red ones. I think red is Julie's favorite color because she always reaches for red things. I wonder what color Félix likes most.

It's a beautiful baby carriage, Madame has, dark blue with a ruffle around the hood, and easy wheels. I feel like such a lady pushing it, but of course everyone I pass knows by my white pleated Burgundian bonnet and *sabots* that the baby carriage and little Julie aren't mine, just as sure as if I were wearing a sign on my back saying: *nourrice.*

I know I should never pretend I am what I am not, but sometimes, on Tuesday nights, I do pretend. When they're out, I take the baby from the nursery and sit in the pink silk chair in the parlor or the striped sofa and pretend that this is my house with those flowered carpets, and that Pascal will come home any minute, all clean and dressed in as fine a coat as Monsieur wears, and smelling as nice too. Or I walk the baby through all the rooms if she needs quieting, looking at all the vases and running my hand along the polished banisters and the posts of Madame and Monsieur's bed, as grand as any for a queen. Once Madame left the doors of her armoire open and I could see her dresses. Oh, such beautiful cloth. I made sure my hand was clean, and I touched them. They were cool and smooth.

Tonight is Tuesday and they are away again. I sit at Madame's dressing table with Julie in my lap, so it's not like I'm not working. Rouges and powders and perfumes and face creams are lined up in rows. She has tweezers too. I dare to lift them off the embroidered doily and pluck an eyebrow hair that is too long and curls. I have to rub it out, it stings so. Madame has a box with satin ribbons, a painted fan, a hair brooch, and a tray of earrings. I hold one up to my ear and it slips out of my hand. A frightened sound escapes me. It didn't land on the table or in my lap. I have to set Julie on the bed and get down on the floor to look for it. Julie starts to fuss, and I think that she might wet the bed. I check her. She's still dry. I crawl around until I find it. Julie is crying. How was the earring sitting on the tray? Just next to the other or . . . ? Julie screams. I drop the earring on the tray, pick her up, sweep my hand across the bed to smooth it, and hurry back into the nursery.

By the time I hear them come up the stairs, Julie is lying quietly in her cradle, and I am rocking it with my foot and singing,

> *"Sleep, sleep, baby, sleep.*
> *Now then, baby, don't you peep.*
> *Sleep, sleep, baby, sleep."*

Madame comes into the nursery all red in the face. Her eyes dart around and she is wringing her hands.

"Is everything all right?" I ask, too loud. I must not have put the earring back exactly, or pushed in the dressing table chair.

"Yes. Why wouldn't it be?"

"No reason. I just thought—"

"Don't think, Sylvie."

She sees that Julie is quiet but she doesn't leave. It's as if she has to settle herself before she goes into the bedroom with Monsieur. She pushes open the window curtains. Only a few stars glimmer.

"They're like blessings, aren't they?" I say. "These are the same stars that Pascal sees, if he is looking up tonight." Then I am embarrassed.

She leans on the windowsill and lets out a long, deep breath that she must have been holding all evening.

*"Sleep, sleep, baby, sleep.
It's time you were asleep,"*

I sing softly to the three of them even though Pascal can't hear.

It's the middle of summer now, the time of the dying of babies in the country. I get worried. Maman might be working in the fields and forget the feedings. Maybe she can't come home during the day. I hold on to the hope that my sister, Natalie, has hired out to a farmer so Maman doesn't have to.

Because the days are warm, I take Julie in the baby carriage to a lovely wood called Bois de Boulogne. It has sycamore trees and several little waterfalls spilling through rocks into two small lakes. There's a dark grove of fir trees, and if I sit there and close my eyes and take a big breath of the trees, I can feel as though I am home in the Morvan and that the baby suckling at my breast is Félix.

Other *nourrices* go walking in the Bois with their madames' babies too, and sometimes we talk of the Morvan and our poor dear mountain villages. It's because no vegetables grow in our stony gardens that so many of us are *nourrices,* we say. We talk of the Bureau des Nourrices too, and the *meneuses* there who got us our places and took our own babies back to our homes in the Morvan. I hear horrible stories. "One in five city babies put out to nurse in the country dies," an older *nourrice* says. I learn that sometimes a city family puts their baby out to nurse and doesn't know it's only a dry nurse using animal milk in those clumsy new English bottles Maman uses for Félix. If the city baby dies, they sometimes just replace it with a foundling the *meneuse* brings from Paris and never tell the family.

I tell Madame this and she is horrified.

"The Société Protectrice de l'Enfance tries to stop such things," I say. "They want to start a nursing colony and have fairs where *nourrices* present their babies to be judged for prizes."

"Ugh! Like cows," she says.

"Sometimes the parents don't pay and just abandon the baby."

"How could a person ever do such a thing?"

"I don't know, Madame."

I don't tell her that my own Pascal was such a baby brought to the Morvan and left there twenty-three years ago. That makes me think of him more. I find out from the other *nourrices* how to go to the Bureau des Nourrices to send a letter if you don't know how to write. Pascal would forgive me, I think. I am only spending a franc of what I promised him I would save.

I practice what I'm going to say as I walk, and I ask the writing clerk at the bureau to send it to Father Baudouin in Saulieu for him to read it to them. The clerk is ill-tempered, and it would cost another franc to write more, so this is all I say:

Dear Maman and Natalie,

I hope Félix is as plump as this baby, Julie, is. She weighs more every week so I know I'm feeding her well. Natalie, don't let Maman work at any farm. Don't even let her glean the oats. She'll be too tired to tend to Félix. My bed is upstairs in the nursery so I can feed the baby in the rocking chair the minute she wakes up at night and not let her disturb them. I mean Madame and Monsieur Manet. They are very kind. They let me eat in the dining room with them, on white plates with violets. When Pascal comes home, tell him there is easier work in Paris than in the mines, if he'll only come and have a look. Maybe a fine house needs a caretaker. But he is stubborn, and afraid of cities. If you can, ask Father Baudouin to write to me at 9 Avenue d'Eylau to tell me where he is working, if you know. Don't worry about me. Give a thousand kisses to Félix, especially on his dimple, to make him know I love him. Make sure the bottles are clean, like the *meneuse* said. Please talk to him about me.

Love,
Sylvie

I long for Pascal every night and wish I could write to him. Even if I knew which mine he's working at on his *campagne* away from our village, he wouldn't have anyone there to read the letter to him. I worry. There are accidents in mines. And even though he is a good man, every mining hamlet has a house of temptation.

Sometimes Madame goes with me to the Bois to paint. Monsieur Eugène carries her easel and canvas and paintbox. He kisses her on the forehead sweetly, and they clasp hands a moment before he leaves. He comes back to carry her things home late in the afternoon. Once she brings two hired models with us, Marie and Aimée, who are about my age. They are very pretty, with straw hats perched on their curls. One of them has a blue ruffled parasol which must have cost dearly. They are working women too. I want to ask how much Madame gives them, but I do not have a chance.

They sit in a little boat tied to a dock where she sets up her easel. The scene looks lovely from where I sit on the grass, but when I come up close to the painting, the geese in the water turn out to be only white smudges with dabs of orange for beaks.

One day there is to be a meeting of painters here which makes Madame talkative. They are to decide something about an exhibit. Madame is a leader, I think. She bustles around preparing the parlor, humming. The pot of violets that is usually on the windowsill for light she sets on a side table. Then she moves it to a round table next to the sofa.

"We have wild violets in the woods at home," I say.

"Oh, that would be lovely to see."

"You must like violets a lot."

"Why do you say that?"

"Because of your plates, and the painting you made of them."

"I never painted them." She shakes a pillow hard to fluff it up and sets a footstool in front of the sofa. It think it must be for Édouard, who has a slight limp.

After everything is ready in the parlor, I go into the dining room to look at the painting I meant. I remembered rightly. It does have a bunch of violets, and a fan, and a note. It's a curious combination of things. Monsieur Eugène finds me looking at it.

"Did you paint this?" I ask, because sometimes of a Sunday afternoon he tries his hand too.

"No," he says.

"Then your brother?"

His nostrils flare. He turns and walks into the parlor.

He is the shyest man I've ever known, even in his own house.

I look more closely at the painting. I know the alphabet enough to guess the name Berthe at the top of the note, and the name Manet at the bottom. Maybe it wasn't shyness. Maybe I irritated him.

Édouard and Suzanne Manet are the first to arrive. Édouard is full of words and so is Madame Berthe, and her eyes sparkle when she looks at him. They talk and talk about this artist and that, and about sellers of paintings. Sometimes Suzanne and Monsieur Eugène join in, but mostly they are quiet. I think for a moment that the two couples are wrongly matched, and then I am ashamed for letting my imagination go.

When the other painters arrive, the noise in the room makes the baby cry so I take her out to the Bois and am nursing in the fir grove when a woman wearing a Burgundian *bonnet de nourrice* stops to speak to me. Everything about her is small. Her shoulders roll forward and her hair isn't tucked neatly into her bonnet. Maybe a baby just pulled on it.

"You have a healthy baby there. You must be young in your milk," she says.

"No. Ten months from my first milk," I say. "I came at two and a half months."

"I'd give three francs to rent that baby for a couple of hours."

"What for?" I look at the front of her dress and she is dripping, fresh. Her mouth moves in a little jerk when she sees that I noticed, and her eyes fill. She has a haggard look.

"You lost one, didn't you?"

She nods.

"Your own?"

"No one will hire me if they know that. The agency won't offer me. I have to have a healthy baby to show, just like you had to."

That makes me remember how miserable I felt kissing Félix on his dimple for the last time and handing him to the *meneuse* at the bureau to take back to Maman.

"Where are you from?" I ask.

"Saulieu."

"I'm from the next valley south. A farm near the river ford."

"Four francs. Please. It's the only way I'll get a place."

"A city place or a nursling to be put out at home?"

"Either. I can't be fussy."

Four francs would mean four letters. Or maybe I could send home some softer diapers or that stocking doll.

"You can't follow me in, though. They'll know if they see you. You'll have to wait a block away. And I can't hand back the baby until we're around the corner."

"I can't watch? To make sure nothing happens?"

"No."

"How do you know all this?"

"I've done it before."

What if she dropped Julie? What if Madame found out?

"No. I can't."

"Five. Do this for three others after me and you'll earn enough for a rail ticket home."

"There are that many?"

"Five and a half francs."

"No. I'm sorry." I turn the baby carriage the way I came and hurry back. I couldn't possibly put Julie in the arms of a *nourrice* whose own baby died. I don't want anything to do with a *nourrice* whose baby died.

The next time Madame and I are in the Bois, she wants to paint me nursing Julie. I am surprised. We go to a cool, wooded place off a path and she has me sit on the grass under a chestnut tree and bare my bosom to Julie. She sets up her folding easel and paintbox.

It is my job now to be still and to keep Julie still and quiet. I think about the women Madame hired for the painting at the boat dock. "Does this mean I am working double?" I ask.

She only smiles. She's happy today, and kisses Julie on the top of her head. "Yes, Sylvie, this is going to be a work scene. You are working so that I can work."

She lays down her straw hat on the grass next to me and arranges the ribbons. "There. Now they'll know there was another woman and wonder why she isn't in the painting. Then they'll know it was the mother who painted this, since you have on your *bonnet de nourrice*. Two working mothers." She chuckles she's so pleased with herself. "I doubt if this situation has ever been painted before."

At noon we stop to eat our picnic. I shake my shoulders and am glad I can move around now. She eats and plays with the baby and I laugh at the funny sounds she makes when she nuzzles her.

I feel bold, having worked alongside her. "Do you know what Pascal and I are going to do with the money I earn?"

"I can't imagine."

It's true. She can't.

"We're going to start building a house. That's what young people in the Morvan do. Send out the wife on three *campagnes de nourrissage*, one to start the house, one to finish it, one to furnish it. Morvandeaux think it's cowardice if the wife doesn't do at least one *campagne*."

"Cowardice. Why?"

"I don't like to say."

She stops eating and looks at me. For once I think she might be interested in me. "Tell me."

"I— Sometimes nurses get the syphilis from their nurslings. But not in fine families, Madame. Not in yours. I didn't mean anything."

I wait without breathing. She reaches toward me and I think she's going to pat my arm, but she only picks up a piece of cheese.

She works all afternoon, and I do too, but I keep quiet, as I'm supposed to.

"Finished!" she says and closes her paintbox.

It doesn't look finished at all. The brushstrokes aren't connected. They make it look like she'd stopped too soon. My face is hardly a face, only a mound of bread dough. It could be anybody. It's a nothing. I'm a nothing!

"A letter!" Madame says one day at the end of summer. We sit down for luncheon with the baby nestled in a new rolling wicker crib. "There's a letter for you, Sylvie."

"Oh!" I squeal. "From Maman! Or Pascal!" She hands it to me across the table.

I hold it a moment and give it back to her. "Will you read it, please?"

She looks surprised, and then opens it.

"It's from a Father Baudouin." Madame's hand goes up to her lips and she gives Monsieur a serious look. The paper trembles. He puts his hand on her wrist holding it. She reads it.

> "I am writing at the request of your mother, Adèle Tournais, who has asked me to tell you that your Félix has been sickly for some weeks. Finally he succumbed and is buried here in the churchyard of Saulieu. Since your husband has not returned from the mine yet, there is no money for a headstone. The babe is resting in Jacob's bosom now. Try to know that in all things, our Heavenly Father knows what is best for His children.
>
> Madame Adèle wishes me to tell you that you might do well to bring a middling woman's nursling home when your time is up, unless you can obtain another place in Paris.
>
> With deep sorrow for your misfortune,
> Father Nicolas Baudouin, 28 July 1880"

I feel dizzy.

I will not cry. Two tears fall onto the plate. Water drips from my nostrils and I grab my napkin. There is nothing to say. I back away from the table. The last thing I see is Monsieur's forehead lines wriggling into furrows. I run to the nursery and sink to my knees before the cradle.

I think I knew all along.

For a few days I cannot look at Madame or Monsieur. I take my meals in the kitchen and stay in the nursery all day. On the fourth morning Madame gives me a new dress. It is not one of hers that she doesn't want any more. It is from the new Galeries Lafayette, she says. Something called a department store. It's a lovely pale gray with a pink, see-through tie at the throat.

"I have never had such a dress," I say.

"Wear it today," Madame says. "We'll go to the Bois. I want to paint you."

"Again?"

"This time in profile. It will be good for you to be outside."

We don't go to the fir grove. Instead, we take the Allée de Longchamp. "The fashion promenade used to take place here every Passion Week, before the war," Madame says cheerfully.

I can't imagine such a thing.

She chooses a bench, and sets up her easel. She wants Julie to be sitting up on my lap. Julie is making sweet gurgling sounds. I can't murmur back to her because I'm supposed to be silent. I steal a sideways look at Madame every so often and I see her working with half frowns coming and going on her face. How can she frown even once? She has everything.

I think of home, quiet as a cave now without Félix, Maman and Natalie hardly talking. I'm sure Maman feels terrible. I want to put my head in her lap and cry. Maybe I can go back to the Bureau des Nourrices to send her a letter. I try to think of what to say.

Maman, do not cry. I . . .

My heart . . .

I must be brave but . . .

Ohh.

It's good that he died, Maman. Now he won't have to stand by and watch someone he loves die and not be able to do anything about it.

That's what I'd write. I blink back angry tears. I don't want Madame to see. She is too far above me to understand. Her mind is too filled with her painting to know how I feel. A new dress is not a child.

Words burst out of my mouth. "Your painting must be very important to you."

"Why, yes, Sylvie. You know it is."

"As important as a baby?"

She dabs more paint on the canvas as though she doesn't hear me. How could her smearing of paint on a cloth be as important as a child? She doesn't even finish a single painting.

"As important as a baby?" I ask again.

"Yes, as important as Julie."

"I meant Félix."

She looks confused. "Why Félix?"

"Because if I were home instead of working for you, Félix would not be dead now."

"Sylvie, please. I'm sorry, you know I am, but I can't have you talking while I paint."

My mind goes numb to shut out those words. I feel a heaviness in my lap. It isn't Madame's baby there. It's only a dead weight.

Nothing. Nothing else in life can ever be this hard. I realize that there is no reason now to go back to the Morvan after I'm through at the Manets, but no fine Parisian family like them will want a *nourrice* seventeen months gone from her first milk with no baby to show. I'll have to accept a middling woman's puking urchin, and take the risk.

Nourrices stroll by, and governesses with older children. One girl turns a hoop with a stick. She is quite good at it. She probably has dozens of toys at home. I see the *nourrice* from Saulieu. She is pushing a baby carriage and has lost that haggard look. She sees me too, but I cannot get up to tell her that I'm glad she found a baby to rent, and a place. I wonder if she sees in my face the one thing that over-shadows everything now.

On Tuesday night when Monsieur and Madame are gone, Julie is fussing so I walk the whole house with her and stop in the parlor in front of the small painting of Madame. "See, Julie?" I bounce her in front of it as I often do. "There's your maman." She quiets down.

In the painting Madame's eyes are large and dark and full of feeling. She is looking out with an open look. At whom? The person painting her? She is wearing a black bow around her neck, and her black dress has a low, lacy neckline. Men would like it. She is beautiful. She's almost lying on a sofa in an inviting way, but her face is calm. The painting has been cut off just below her waist so I can't be sure where her feet would have been. Until now I never noticed the writing at the top corner. I study it and go to the painting of the violets with the note and the fan, and then come back again. The letters are the same shapes.

Édouard, not Eugène, painted both of them.

A shock ripples through me.

She lay like this for him. That isn't one of the sofas in the house. She went somewhere else and lay like that. I shiver at the thought. How horrible for Monsieur Eugène to have that painting in his house. How can I look at him, knowing why she's gay and talkative when his brother comes to the house, knowing why she moved the violets from place to place? I go into the dining room to look at the painting of the violets and the note and I am furious that I cannot read it. But I know enough to hate her tonight for wanting more than all she already has. To be that greedy in life disgusts me.

I set Julie on the flowered carpet to crawl a bit, and I try to decide how loving starts. Does it come by surprise, without a person helping it along? Is it impossible to stop, like a river after a storm? If I could know that she was fighting against loving the wrong brother, I might be able to forgive her.

I want to see her pain of wanting too much, wanting what can never be. If there's any place in the house that might show me, it would be her studio. I carry Julie in there and light the gas lamp. Paintings are hanging all the way to the ceiling, mostly of women and children in gardens or rooms. I look at the ones drying on easels, her oval board with smears of paint, and her table full of paints and brushes and pots of smelly liquids. Nothing gives me a clue to her feelings.

I mustn't get my dress dirty. Then she'd know I was here. I lay Julie on my shawl on the floor. Some strange urge enters me and I put on Madame's smock. The last painting of me holding Julie is on an easel, still wet. I like this painting more than the first one. The gray dress is pretty, and the bow tied at my throat is filmy, like what a sea creature might be. The side of my face is clearer this time. It shows me looking down at Julie with love, and that is the truth of what I feel.

Two dark beads of Julie's eyes look back at me in the painting, but the little point I love on her upper lip isn't there. How could it be that Madame never noticed? I'll always remember the shallow dimple on Félix's chin. Isn't that pucker in the center of her baby's upper lip important to her?

Julie has crawled away from my shawl. I bring her back and sit her up. The point has not disappeared as her face has grown. I think of Monsieur Eugène's lip poking out from under his mustache. Édouard doesn't have that. Pretending, that's what Madame was doing by not painting it. Pretending that Julie is Édouard's baby and not Eugène's. The awfulness of pretending enters me like a knife. It hurts me that she doesn't love every bit of this baby who will live and have everything.

Julie's lips and cheeks in the painting are the same color as the bow. I look at Madame's board of paint smears. The pink is still there. I want so much to do it that my hands are clenched. I shake them and walk in a circle to get it out of me, but I come back to the painting. If I wait too long it will be too late. My heart is pounding. I rifle through her brushes and find one with only a wisp of hairs. My hand shakes. I hold it with the other. I barely make a touch, pointed downward, so slight no one will notice but me.

And her. Some bad, hurting place in me wants her to cry out when she notices. Wants her to stop pretending that the point isn't there on Julie's lip.

I don't know what to dip the brush in to clean it, so I dip it in all the jars and wipe it off with a paint rag that already has that color on it. I'm frightened now by what I've done. It could cost me my place. I put back her smock, pick up Julie in my shawl, blow out the light, and hurry back to the nursery.

I am not sorry I did it. Maybe that dot of color will save her. And Eugène. But I am ashamed of other things—the joy I took in pretending I was the lady of the house and Julie was mine. Now, more than that, I am ashamed of the first faint feeling of ease since my Félix died.

In the nursery I put Julie down for the night and open the curtains. A crescent moon is tumbling down the sky, and I sing softly out to the universe,

> *"Rock me, tumble me, sing me to sleep.*
> *Hushabye, lullaby, my babe to keep."*

Madame bursts into the nursery. Her hands are shaking. She glances at Julie and flings herself at the window ledge. Her breast is heaving, and she sobs quietly at the moon. Her fist pounds the windowsill softly. I feel helpless to know what to say, seeing her pain so plain.

I give her my handkerchief, and whisper, "I know what it's like not to have the thing you want most."

She straightens her back. "How dare you . . ." She is stunned a moment, then cries harder, pressing my handkerchief against her mouth to muffle the sound. She tries to quiet herself.

"We'll both carry our longings privately into the next world," she says, giving me a stern look when she says "privately."

We face each other, our eyes blurred but seeing each other clearly. All I can do is croon, "Hushabye, lullaby, sing us to sleep."

Olympia's Look

Paris, 1883

Suzanne pushed Édouard's heavy fan-backed armchair in front of the empty fireplace, facing the chair away from it so she would not imagine she saw the thing lying on the grate. Sitting there and putting her feet on his cushioned footstool would be a victory unrecognizable to anyone else, out of all proportion to the act, but she was determined to do it. Now the chair faced her piano and the painting of Olympia above the sofa. She smoothed the lace antimacassar, took in air with a shallow, abrupt breath, turned, and was about to sit when the sound of the door knocker startled her.

Where was Hélène? She didn't like to answer the door when she wasn't expecting someone, not with all the paintings.

"Who is it?" she asked at the keyhole.

"Your nephew, Albert."

She undid the lock. "Oh, wonderful! I didn't expect you until tomorrow." She kissed him, a brush of the lips on both cheeks in the French way she'd adopted. "Come in. Sit, please."

He gave Édouard's burgundy chair a curious look, it being out of its normal place, and then sat in it. "Is Léon here?"

"No. He was exhausted, tending his papa for so long. I sent him to the country for a fortnight." She sat on the blue sofa opposite him.

"You shouldn't be alone, Aunt Suzanne."

"Hélène is here. I'm all right. I have plenty to do. I have his clothes to go through, for one thing. I've started a pile for you. You could use a top hat. Léon already has one."

"That's generous of you."

"How he loved his top hats."

"I'll be proud to wear it. You know that."

"And I'll be proud to see you in it."

She clapped her hand over her mouth.

"What's the matter?"

"It's . . . it's just that for an instant, you sitting in his chair, I thought I was looking at Édouard. Young. The same full beard, your hairline receding the same way—all his brothers have it, and now you." She managed a smile. "You're a Manet through and through."

He gave her a sympathetic look. "Is there anything I can do for you?"

She took a big breath and sat up straighter. "Yes, an enormous thing, which is why I asked you to come. You're a better painter than you think, Albert. Édouard said so."

"He did?" His eyebrows lifted.

"Most certainly he did."

"That's good to hear, but I still have a lot to learn."

"Learning never ends. The moment you think you've learned it all, you're doomed. Take a look at *Olympia* there. What does it show about his figure technique?"

He grinned. "Are you quizzing me for a purpose?"

"Of course."

"There isn't much gradual shading to create shape."

She tried to determine if he was just repeating Édouard's words without understanding. "What else?"

"The contour shadows are so narrow they're practically outlines."

She smacked her fist into her other hand. "Yes, that's it! Do you think you could reproduce this painting?"

"I suppose, if I had the original to study while I painted. The genius was in his conception, not in its imitation."

"And the rest?" She gestured to other paintings. "Could you do those too? Same sizes?"

He glanced around the room. "Yes, but why?"

"I can't keep them. There'll come a time when I'll have to sell them to live."

"Suzanne, no!"

She held up her hand to silence him. "It was what he wanted. One fell swoop. An auction would be easier to take than the constant search for buyers, with prospects always traipsing through the house."

"I'm so sorry. I wish you could keep them."

"Not a word more. I've already spoken to Théodore Duret. He will arrange it."

She stood up and looked at all the vibrant faces, flowered bonnets and top hats, fans, gloves, swirls of silk, vases of peonies and lilacs, Victorine Meurent clothed and unclothed, Berthe Morisot in a speckled white dress with a black velvet band cinching in her waist, a wistful look on her face.

"A house with empty walls would be a house without him. I couldn't bear that. So, if you can make replacements, it would mean the world to me."

"Copies?" His eyes opened wide. "Was this his idea?"

"No. My own. Your mother agrees. She has every faith that you can do it, and so do I."

"I only want to do what eases you."

"Good, then. You're a dear boy." He looked at her with good-humored exasperation, and pointed to his receding hairline. She chuckled. "I mean, young man."

He walked over to the sofa. "Should I start with the *Olympia*?"

Her breath caught in her throat. "No, not yet." Victorine Meurent looked out at her from the canvas with that brazen look, in silent defiance of being copied.

"Shouldn't I take the most important ones first?"

"Yes, but . . . I need it here awhile yet. Take another."

"Which?"

She surveyed the drawing room, and went into the dining room. She'd known that Albert couldn't do them all before the auction, but she had not expected the choosing to be so difficult. She looked at *Déjeuner sur l'Herbe,* his first nude, and felt a surprising smile creep up her cheeks.

"When I called this one *Victorine's Notorious Debut,* Édouard was furious with me until I said, 'Better to be notorious than ignored.' That surprised him so much, coming from me, that he laughed. After that I kept my own names for his paintings private."

"Will you tell me?"

She pulled in her bottom lip and rolled her eyes in a teasing way.

"How can it hurt now?" Albert asked.

"Promise you won't tell Léon?"

He put on a mock grave expression and held up his hand. "I promise."

"Well, then, this one, *The Street Singer,* I called *Victorine at Work.* And this one which Édouard called *The Railway* . . ." She giggled. "*Victorine Abandoned at Gare St-Lazare.* There's something very satisfactory about that."

"What about this one? I've always liked it."

"Édouard called it *Before the Mirror.* To me, it's *Henriette's Vanity.*"

Albert went back into the drawing room. "What about *Portrait of Méry Laurent as Autumn?*"

She felt a conspiratorial glee in this telling. "Now, you mustn't breathe a word." Albert shook his head. "I call it *Courtesan to Half of Paris.*"

"Suzanne! I never knew you were so—"

"Wicked? A woman in my position has to have some private revenge, no matter how trivial. Regardless, I love those quick, sharp little brushstrokes." She flicked her hand at the wrist as if painting. "See how they flash and dance? At the moment he painted them, he must have been carried away with happiness."

Portrait of Isabelle hung above the fireplace. "I like that one the least. You don't have to paint it."

"But it's beautiful." Albert looked at her, expecting a title.

Her mind flew backward.

It was just by chance that she had seen Édouard slip Hélène an envelope. The way Hélène slid it into her ruffled apron pocket and went about her dusting, pointing her long nose downward, told her she knew just what to do with it. She'd probably done it dozens of times.

She had followed Hélène into the dining room and closed the double doors behind her.

"Give it to me," she'd said, the firmness in her voice surprising her.

"Monsieur said I must deliver it to the post."

"So all loyalty is to him, is it?"

She'd looked at Hélène steadily, trying to make her expression as commanding as Victorine's was in *Olympia*. She held out her hand, palm up. Hélène glanced toward the kitchen door as if to escape.

She thrust her hand inches from Hélène's ribs. "I am your employer as well as he," she said quietly, steeling herself to wait, to hold that position, that look, as a model would.

Hélène crumpled, smacked the letter onto her hand and left the room.

Now, standing before the painting, she could still recite the words three months later.

Jolie Isabelle,

This is a hurried greeting. I should like to get a loving one from you every morning, when the post comes. You certainly don't spoil me. Either you are very busy—or very cruel. Today I am imagining you at the seaside, a pretty sight. I would kiss you under God's own sun, had I the courage.

E. Manet

"What do you call this one of Isabelle?" Albert asked.

She shook her head and wouldn't say. To her, it was simply *Betrayal.*

"He relished all of these women as though they were succulent fruit," she said.

But how often did he go beyond the act of painting to other intimacies? She quailed every time she suspected it, never with dear friends like Berthe, but with the women who were models first.

"Despite his attentions to his models, from those first breathless days as his piano teacher, when I felt the whole world sing, and in the twenty years after, when I hardly had time to dry the vase before he'd bring me another bouquet of tulips or a pretty new handkerchief or hat, or when his touch made me feel beautiful, we loved with a love beyond all dreaming." Her throat tightened and her voice became a squeak. "Remember that about him, will you? Put that in his paintings, the bounty of his love. That was the wonder of the man."

"I'll try." Albert's eyes shone dark with doubt.

"Don't remember his illness, Albert," she cried.

The look of the thing in the fireplace flashed in her mind again. A whimper escaped her. Albert enfolded her in his arms, his hand stroking her back and his soft sounds soothing her.

Would it have been any different if she'd confronted Édouard? If she hadn't been the placid, tolerant Dutch wife wanting peace at any cost, turning a blind eye every time he burst into the apartment flushed and elated, passing it off as the joy he took in painting? Now if she were French, she might not have been so troubled.

"You've done paintings of women from a model, haven't you?" she asked, her mouth against his chest.

"Yes, of course."

She drew back to look at him. "And you found them beautiful?"

"Yes."

"And alluring?"

"Yes."

"French or Dutch?"

"Both."

"Just be careful, Albert. If you choose a Dutch wife, remember. The Dutch may seem tolerant, but they're not particularly forgiving."

He looked embarrassed for a moment. "I'll keep that in mind." He drew her toward Édouard's pastel of her reclining on the startling blue sofa. "What about starting with one of you?"

"O-ho! You know as well as I do, his best work was not lavished on me. That shapeless egg of a face daubed with rouge. That equally shapeless hat, like a fallen soufflé. Those tiny black beads for eyes."

She grimaced, hating how her double chin showed. Her belly ballooned out of her jacket as though she were pregnant, and her stiff fingers were splayed ungracefully. He'd posed her with her feet up on the sofa, indelicately, with shoes on, angled away from each other in fatigue like an old man.

"Ugh! I don't care if I ever see this one again. There's one of me I prefer at the studio. He posed me in profile in a big hat that covered most of my face. It's the only painting of me that's flattering."

Albert turned in a circle. "So now we're back to *Olympia*. What did you call her?"

"*Olympia*. Eighteen years that painting has been here, and I never dared to rename it, even in secret."

Unabashedly naked she was, her taut little body startling and beautiful, dressed only in a thin black velvet ribbon around her neck and dainty satin slippers. Olympia, a courtesan lounging on a divan and receiving a bouquet of flowers while coolly assessing her gentleman client.

"She's too imperious to countenance any other name. Besides, I like what Édouard named her. It's similar to Olympe, an alias used by some courtesans in the city. It's Victorine Meurent, you know."

The directness of her look, straight out of the canvas, ostensibly at her male client, was silently confrontational. The French had a way about them, an assurance she envied. Her deferential Dutchness kept the peace, but that was all, while Olympia had mocked her with that barefaced impudence every day of her married life.

She went back into the dining room to consider *Lunch in the Studio*. In it, Léon appeared as a bright, fashionable young man in a straw hat leaning against the table, and Hélène was pert and precise in her starched maid's dress, holding a pitcher of water. "Take this. I couldn't bear not to have Léon with me in the years ahead."

"A good choice. I'll start tomorrow."

She kissed him goodbye at the door, and his beard against her mouth gave her a shock. It felt like Édouard's.

She wrapped her shawl around her, sat on the sofa, and looked at the chair. Not the worst, but one of the worst memories was Dr. Tillaux whispering to her, right in that chair, one phrase at a time, "The paralysis will creep up from his foot. It's caused by syphilis. At this stage incurable." That was only a few months ago, after three years of pain. She'd cried that night, her anger and grief and love spilling out in the bathtub with the faucet on so Édouard wouldn't hear.

The next morning she had begun her private program of self-development. She would be alone. She'd have to get over anger, timidity, and grief all at the same time. She'd have to speak her mind. She couldn't retreat into her music. How inconsequential her first efforts were. *Hélène, this soup is cold,* and, *Édouard, I'd prefer the window closed.* At least it was a start.

The day she seized the letter had been a big step.

Isabelle Lemonnier. At the time she couldn't believe it. Isabelle was only twenty. A frivolous child. She'd only begun to sit for him because she fancied him a leader of the avant-garde and therefore fashionable. Was it a mere flirtation from a dying man envious of freshness and youth, or something more? It wasn't just the note itself that hurt her, but the furtive way in which Édouard had handed it to Hélène and her understanding that it was to be kept secret.

She had put it in her copy of Giorgio Vasari's *Lives of the Painters, Sculptors and Architects,* a bookmark sticking out on Fra Filippo's page, and laid the book on various tables in the drawing room. If he sees it, she had thought, we'll talk about it. If he doesn't, we won't.

Now here it still was, clearly visible out the top of the book where she'd left it in plain sight every day. Maybe he noticed and didn't want to bring it up. She opened the note and looked at the small watercolor on the bottom edge, two open halves of a Philippine nut, so sweetly, humbly executed. She wasn't sure, but thought that it was a French symbol of love. There wasn't anyone she could ask except Berthe, but Berthe was still so broken up she didn't want to disturb her.

She took up reading Vasari again to occupy her mind, although if she admitted the truth, it was really to discover just how frequently artists made their models into lovers. The most despicable so far was Fra Filippo Lippi, he a holy brother once and his lover a nun. Maybe he abducted her while she sat for a Madonna and Child or a St. Theresa in Ecstasy. She read the page again:

Fra Filippo is said to have been so amorous that when he saw a woman who pleased him he would have given all his possessions to have her, and if he could not, he quieted the flame of his love by painting her.

Maybe Vasari could have written the same about Édouard. What existed between artist and model that made it so likely that they would become lovers? That, Vasari didn't say. She read on.

He incurred heavy expenses in love intrigues which he indulged in until his death, even refusing a papal dispensation to marry the nun, Lucrezia, in order to legitimatize their son, because he wished to give full rein to his appetite.

She felt a little flare of sympathy for the nun, and hoped she didn't have to pass off a son as a brother, like Édouard had made her do with Léon. Eleven years she'd had to, until Édouard's disapproving father died and she and Édouard were finally married.

She laid her head back and thought of their artist friends. Young Aline was Auguste's neighbor, then his model, then his secret lover, before she ever became Madame Renoir. And poor Camille Monet had been wasting away with consumption not knowing that Claude was the father of Alice Hoschedé's last baby. Or perhaps she did know. That would have been worse. Auguste Rodin had lived with Rose for as long as she could remember—they had a child, in fact—yet Camille Claudel, his model and student, was his lover. Everyone knew it.

She'd seen all of them only two weeks earlier, at the funeral. Five hundred mourners packed the Church of St-Louis d'Antin. All the people of consequence were there—their artist's circle, and Émile Zola and Georges Clemenceau. Paul Cézanne had even come up from Aix. Édouard would have been pleased, and satisfied. Everyone from Montmartre came, but she knew the truth of it: They came to see, or to be seen. Where had they been when he needed a shred of support in the early years?

The moment the service was over, while everyone was still sitting, Edgar Degas said loudly, "He was greater than we thought." Everything around her had blurred. Sitting behind her, Berthe patted her shoulder, and she reached up and held Berthe's hand, which gripped hers with sudden fervor.

Léon picked a lilac for her from the casket, then offered her his arm to walk up the aisle, like a wedding only in reverse. She couldn't control her thoughts as she followed the coffin toward the double doors. She noticed a familiar hat with ivory ruffles and a pink and black satin crown. It was Jeanne de Marsy with that black bow under her chin, the actress whom Édouard had painted as *Spring* in that hat. She remembered how he had asked one morning at breakfast who her favorite milliner was, and when she said Madame Virot, he went off to her shop to buy that hat for Jeanne—not for her at all. Was Jeanne wearing it now as a tribute to him, or did she just want people to know it was she who had sat for the painting? Jeanne's friend Méry Laurent, Stéphane Mallarmé's lover who posed for *Autumn,* sat next to her, Méry's red hair so startling against her brown dress, maybe the same one as in the painting.

It was a bit unnerving—the paintings come to life, the painter dead. All the models he'd used over the years were looking back at her. Eva, Claire, Marguerite, even Ellen who posed with a plum in brandy at the Café Nouvelle-Athènes. Their dresses made them stand out against the grays and black of the men's clothing. Henriette Hauser, that grand *cocotte,* wore a fluff of yellow-orange chiffon at her throat. That was brazen, considering she was kept by the Prince of Orange and everyone called her Citron. That pretty mulatto, Jeanne Duval, had been Charles Baudelaire's mistress, and next to her, Madame de Loubens. Édouard had painted her in a bed, which had always made her suspicious. After all, that was *her* place, Suzanne Manet, the wife.

Through the haze of incense like the cigarette smoke in her painting, she saw Suzon, the barmaid from the Folies-Bergère. She still had those long thick yellow bangs, not at all attractive. And that famous eccentric, Nina de Callias, was wafting away the smoke with one of her enormous painted Japanese fans. Finally she found Isabelle Lemonnier looking subdued but elegant in a pert black hat with net veil, as if she were the widow.

Any one of them could have been the one to have caused his death.

Everyone there had seen the public man, gay in his silk cravat and silver stick pin, his fine shoes and buff-colored trousers, always knife-creased and immaculate, a pansy in his buttonhole, and always, while in the cafés of Montmartre or promenading on the Champs, a top hat. She'd seen him vulnerable—pacing before the opening of every exhibit, staring at a critic's words in *Le Figaro* the morning after until his eyes seemed to burn out the words and leave soot-edged holes where the printing had been. She preferred that authentic man to the witty counterfeit she imagined holding court at the Café Guerbois or the Nouvelle-Athènes, the ebullient *enchanteur* thriving on confrontation.

She paused at the door of the church which opened onto rue Caumartin. As soon as she stepped outside, a different life would start. She'd have to live on her own, state her own mind, do things that satisfied her, not anyone else. She stood near the waiting carriages, determined to respond with grace to the people queued up to offer condolences, but she felt smothered by the strain of repetitions. Their dirge of voices merged into nothing more than variations on a minor-key melody.

Isabelle approached her, trembling. *"Je suis désolée,"* she squeaked, and sniffed into a lace handkerchief.

The display irritated her. "There's something you should see." She fastened her eyes on Isabelle's unlined porcelain face as she slid the letter out from her black sleeve, put there just in case she'd have the delectable opportunity to let Isabelle know that she hadn't put anything over on her. She unfolded it and showed her, holding it firmly, just out of Isabelle's reach, and it did not quake.

Isabelle read it quickly, her throat reddening. "May I have it?"

"A *memento mori* from a famous man? A paper trinket you can sell to an antiquarian someday when his paintings are finally praised?" She snapped it in the air and slid it back up her sleeve. "You care less about him than you do that carriage horse."

Enjoying the fineness of the moment, she had turned her back on Isabelle to greet the next person in the queue.

She should get back to the clothes-sorting, but she didn't have the will. The house seemed sepulchral. She gazed at the keys she hadn't played for a month. Léon and Albert had moved his bed out here so the stream of visitors would have places to sit and it would be near the piano. Right to the end Édouard put on his charm for Méry and Berthe when they came, even for Isabelle's maid who brought flowers every week. He often asked her to play Schumann's "The Merry Peasant" for them, saying, "*M'alouette*, you play like God's own daughter in Heaven."

But when Claude came, a different man showed. Once Claude inadvertently laid his hat on the end of the bed and Édouard shouted, "My foot, man! What are you doing? Trying to kill me?"

Claude snatched it up and looked at her helplessly.

"Here, sit next to him." She gave him her chair by the bed and moved to the piano. She had hardly begun playing when Édouard shouted, "*Pour l'amour de Dieu*, Suzanne, don't you know when a man wants silence?"

She'd fled to the bedroom and wept.

Now, idly, standing at the piano, she played the first two bars of the Schumann, only the right hand.

"Madame Suzanne!" Hélène burst into the drawing room, gesturing over her shoulder to the dining room. "The painting's gone! Of Léon and me."

"Don't worry. Albert took it just now. He'll bring it back eventually."

"Oh. Well, then, here's the post."

Suzanne leafed through the letters. More condolences. One caught her eye, from 7, boulevard de la Seine, Asnières. They knew no one out in Asnières. She opened it and read:

> Madame,
>
> I beg you to excuse me if in what follows I revive your grief over the extraordinary and greatly mourned Monsieur Manet.
>
> You know that I posed for many of his paintings, notably for *Olympia,* his masterpiece. M. Manet took much interest in me and often said that if he sold his paintings he would reserve some reward for me. At the time I refused, saying that when I could no longer pose I would remind him of his promise.
>
> That time has come sooner than I had thought. Misfortune has befallen me. I can no longer model. I have to take care of my sick mother all alone, and I have broken my finger and will not be able to do work of any kind for several months. It is this desperate situation, Madame, which prompts me to remind you of M. Manet's kind promise. If, in my misfortune, you will be so kind as to interest yourself in my destiny and can do something for me, please accept my deepest gratitude.
>
> Respectfully yours,
> Victorine Meurent

Mademoiselle Olympia certainly hadn't wasted any time in writing her.

She did not doubt that Édouard had promised her. It would be like him. He probably promised something to all of them. A dutiful wife, an acquiescent wife would carry out her husband's wishes even if they were contrary to her own.

She looked up at *Olympia*. The frank intimacy of that painting, and Victorine's look of cool confrontation, had been the private trial of her last twenty years, had made her hungry for intimacy in all things—from handing him his scissors for his meticulous beard-trimming, to nursing him with bedpans and warm milk, and later, holding him during his nightmares, him thrashing in the bed and calling out, "My leg, my leg!" She had wanted to be skin to skin through it all.

Waking in a sweat once, he had murmured, "Alexandre . . . the boy . . . his face purple . . . his rope so thin."

She'd bent over him, held him, tried to contain his shaking. "It was only a nightmare," she said to soothe him.

"Stiff already."

"It wasn't your fault," she said just as she had so long ago when Édouard had found the street boy he'd hired to clean his palette and brushes hanging from a cord and a nail in his studio.

"Boy with Cherries," Édouard murmured, the name of the painting he had done of the boy smiling under a red cap.

"It was in his nature. His mother said so."

"I was sharp to him," he said.

"So was the whole world. It wasn't you."

She'd stroked his cheek above his beard which had grown ragged in his last weeks, put a new, cool cloth on his forehead, and knew then she'd have her own nightmares. It was the price of intimacy.

"A wreck. I'm through. Victorine . . ." he said through pain-clenched teeth.

For a moment she thought he'd confused her with Victorine.

"Tell her she started it."

It. What? His reputation in the avant-garde? His paintings that scoffed at hypocritical bourgeois morality? The new art for art's sake, throwing out classical narrative so that a nude could be simply a nude and not a goddess? No. This wasn't just a senseless torment of his delirium. It meant something else.

Now, with Victorine's pitiful letter in her hand, *Olympia* still held for her a haughty look. What she would give for one ounce of that self-assurance. She studied the painting up close. For the first time she noticed something about the eyes only three-quarters open, the shading of her lower eyelashes, the set of her jaw beneath her full cheeks that lent a sad vulnerability to her nakedness. Maybe the imperiousness he painted did not represent what Victorine was, but what she wished to be.

She hired a hackney to take her to 7, boulevard de la Seine in Asnières. The poplar trees along the riverbank looked dusty in the yellowish haze. She held her handkerchief to her nose as they passed the outlet to the Paris sewer system. The hackney stopped at a three-story apartment building.

"Please wait," she told the driver. "I won't be long."

Not knowing whether the encounter would turn out to be an errand of mercy, a curiosity visit, or a trial of her courage, she pressed her handbag containing an envelope of francs against her ribs, and climbed the creaking stairs to Victorine's flat.

Victorine answered the door with a pair of scissors in her hand, her damp chestnut hair disorderly, cut in different lengths. Her skin really did have a yellow hue, just as he'd painted it, but there were dark bowls beneath her eyes and a puffiness to her cheeks, not of vigor but of inflammation. Her limp dressing gown the color of a bruise hung off one shoulder. It was trivial, she supposed, to give it any importance, but it gave her a turn that the poor woman had to cut her own hair.

She expected not to like her, yet seeing Victorine's own drawings and paintings hanging frameless on the walls, she was touched by her honest attempts at being a Salon painter. She had forgotten that. Victorine didn't try to straighten the soiled chenille spread on the sunken divan, or whisk away the empty wine bottles and cigarette butts.

Suzanne was startled to find a beautiful black cat—sleek and sensuous, all that Édouard loved in women, all that she wasn't.

"Surely this isn't the same cat as in the *Olympia*?"

"Two cat generations later," Victorine said.

The cat jumped into Suzanne's lap and settled itself in a winsome way that quite unnerved her.

They spoke vacant pleasantries first, inquiries about each other's welfare, followed by a pause and a cough from a room behind. The stale odor of shut-ins permeated the air.

She would have to leap the abyss of propriety to speak of what she really came for.

"How have you commanded his affection for these twenty years?" Suzanne asked.

"Affection. You say that as if it's a dirty word."

"No. Not dirty. Misplaced. Toward the end he said, 'Tell Victorine she started it.' Do you know what he meant by that?"

Victorine gave the slightest flicker of a smile. "No."

Suzanne pushed forward her ribs and chest. It was now or never. Say it. Coolly, as if prompted by mere idle curiosity. "Did he love you?"

Victorine hesitated, apparently calculating her answer. "I gave him something different, and he was grateful."

"What did you give him that I didn't?"

Victorine leveled at her that same look that had beguiled

Édouard, the look that so enraged the public, a look that seemed like a natural one for Victorine, a look not only tinged with insolence, but indifference.

"I collaborated with him."

"Collaborated! Who stood behind him at the scandal of *Déjeuner* when they called him a renegade and barbarian? Where were you when he was pelted with a hail of insults while the *Olympia* was at the Salon?"

"I'd done what he needed. That was all I owed him."

"Owed him? Then collaboration was a business transaction between you."

"Of sorts."

"A *mere* commercial venture. A deal. 'You give me what I need and I give you what you need.' Nothing freely offered. Nothing bountifully given from an overflowing well of feeling. Everything measured. Meted out."

She realized she must be looking at Victorine in Victorine's own way, imperiously, but as "the wife." She saw it reflected in the speck of fear in Victorine's eye, and felt a mounting thrill of exhilaration as she sat there petting the cat, long, slow strokes down the black sheen on its back, knowing that there was an aura of respect and deference due the grieving wife, knowing that she commanded it even more because Victorine needed what she could give her, knowing what she would say next.

"You didn't have him at the end, Victorine. Isabelle Lemonnier *thought* she did. In the small world of Paris, you must know of her, a silly girl engaged in clandestine fantasies with a dying man. Poignant or pathetic, I don't know which. The last thing he wrote was to her— but it was to me that he turned for things higher than need, things that neither of us measured."

She thought of how she had brought lilacs from the mantel to his bed, and he had held her hand for hours on his last afternoon while they reminded each other of their fondest times. He may have loved his models for what they allowed *him* to do, but he didn't love them for what they were independent of him. They were an adjunct to his own self-esteem. She, his wife, with her inelegant way of speaking French, her thick-in-the-middle Dutch body, she who had none of the French chic or *joie de vivre,* he loved for herself. He loved the soul of her, she thought defiantly.

Looking at Victorine now, at the shallowness of her expression, it went through her like a surgeon's cold blade, that she was probably looking this very minute at the very woman who had carried the syphilis. *Tell Victorine she started it.* Her mind veered. Her self-control vanished. What was she doing here with succor money in her pocketbook? If Victorine's look meant that she thought she shared his love, if she had, in fact, shared his bed, then she ought to share the horror too. Wasn't that what Édouard had meant when he said to tell Victorine she'd started it?

"Whatever they say in the papers, Victorine, he died of syphilis." She spat the last word. "More than three years of pain, first in his foot, then his whole leg. See him, Victorine. The dashing, witty, charmer, Édouard Manet, feigning insouciance, doubled up and hobbling like an old cripple."

She braced herself, her palm on the dirty chenille. "Paralysis and bedpans and hallucinations and a putrefying smell. Gangrene crawling up his leg, turning it black and blue, eating his flesh, and leaving a trail of pus. They amputated." She pushed the word out at her. Victorine winced and drew in her chin. "Surgeons clicking their knives right in our drawing room, claiming that the pain of being moved to a hospital would kill him.

"The day before, he was making plans to go to Rueil again this summer. A disguise it was. I had to say that we would, and remind him of the hollyhocks and peonies we would see. Peonies were his favorite. He painted only flowers in the end. Any figure was too much for him. *But still he painted.*"

She was losing ground now. What did Victorine care about his favorite flower? She shouldn't have given her that.

"His bravery demanded that I match it, Victorine. Could you have done so?" She stroked the cat more roughly. "Just before the chloroform, I held his hand, his artist hand with the enlarged joint on his thumb that supported the palette—surely you noticed—and made him think of pleasant memories—how we had walked against the wind along the dike roads in Brabant to see the windmills, how we had gotten lost in Venice and didn't even care. A collaborator"— she uttered the word as if its taste on her tongue were vile—"is merely a fleeting accomplice in a painting, which is, after all, a fantasy. A wife, the deepest kind of friend, is a life partner. Through everything."

Tell her. Right now when she looks so small and pitiful, hugging herself.

"The morning of the cutting, Victorine, imagine, his toenails fell off at a touch."

Victorine's face went pale. "Don't—"

"My son held down one arm, my nephew the other. I held his head and kept a damp cloth over his eyes." Her heart was hammering against her breast. "There was a saw, Victorine."

"Stop!"

"Imagine the sound it made. And my kitchen bowls full of blood." She could hardly breathe fast enough, and felt herself trembling, losing control. "They hadn't thought ahead about what to do with the severed leg. In the confusion they heaved it into the empty fireplace, and forgot it there until I discovered the thing on the grate the next morning, crusted and hideous. Would you have had the presence of mind to push a chair in front of it so he wouldn't see it?

It was I who was there when the surgeon, shamefaced, came to fetch it the next day. *No one* else. I who took no comfort in thinking that his infidelities received their just reward."

She stopped, spent, and waited until her heartbeat slowed. She unfolded Édouard's letter to Isabelle and laid it on the low table between them, careful not to let it touch the greasy plate of food scraps left there. She watched with cold anticipation as Victorine resisted a moment, but eventually allowed her eyes to look down and read.

"We each had our moments," Victorine said.

Suzanne looked away in disgust. Victorine had never become a courtesan. Only a cheap prostitute.

"Moments are not years. The deepest intimacy occurs when a man is frightened and powerless. That, no one shared with him except me."

She shifted positions and the cat jumped off her lap, arched its back, raised its tail indelicately, and sauntered away. She brushed off her skirt. "There'll be an auction soon." She picked up Édouard's letter to Isabelle and stood to leave. "You ought to be pleased to know that *Olympia* is expected to be the prize piece."

A spark of desperation flashed in Victorine's eyes. "And my letter? His promise?"

"I'll see after the auction."

Olympia didn't sell. No bid for it was voiced above the floor the auctioneer announced. The silence of the auction room that moment while everyone squirmed and waited gave Suzanne a curious satisfaction, a justification for not giving Victorine one centime, but back home that evening, the painting hanging in her drawing room again, she wondered whether it would come to haunt her in a different way—how she made that poor woman imagine what she didn't need to know. From her own nightmares and day visions, she knew what it took to keep the remembrance of the amputation at bay. Calling it forth for Victorine had cost her, and for no purpose. If that look was the only look Victorine had for the world, the manner of Édouard's death wouldn't penetrate anyway. If it wasn't, that look represented only one moment in time, and was not so commanding as she had once thought. Perhaps Olympia's look was merely defensive.

As for herself, she'd found no elation in confrontation for confrontation's sake. Indiscriminate anger was as reprehensible as indiscriminate affection.

A chill made her shake her shoulders.

"The first coolness of fall," she told Hélène. "Don't you feel it?" She pushed Édouard's chair out of the way and knelt before the fireplace.

"Oh, Madame. I'll do that."

"No, Hélène. I want to do it myself. I used to like doing it at home in Brabant." She lifted small branches from the kindling scuttle. "Watch. I'm better at it than Édouard ever was."

Methodically she placed the small branches, crisscrossing them right on the grate. She lay quarter logs on top. She tore pages of *Le Figaro* into strips, crumpled them under the grate, and did not cringe when her knuckle brushed the iron. She lit the paper in four places and backed away.

With a small intake of breath, she found herself sitting in his chair, and felt a sweet, unexpected hint of relaxation from a life of bracing herself. Her Vasari lay on the side table with Édouard's letter to Isabelle sticking out to mark her place. It had been foolish of her to think Victorine would have been hurt by it. She lifted her legs onto Édouard's footstool and noticed with amusement that her feet did angle outward. She wiggled them. A fine fire it was, full of satisfying crackles, just like the ones they had in the happy times in Brabant. She chuckled softly, remembering the funny, surprised look on Édouard's face when the wind racing over the flat land had whisked away his top hat on their wedding day and he went running down the dike road after it.

She slipped Édouard's letter out of the book, looked inside the envelope to make sure it was still there, and tucked in the flap. It was only a sweet, silly note. On the envelope where he had written *Mlle. Isabelle Lemonnier,* she put a comma, added the word *Collaborator,* and set it aside for Hélène to post in the morning.

The Yellow Jacket

Arles, 1888

On Saturday morning after trimming his mustache for the first time, Armand Roulin sat on the wooden bench in the kitchen polishing his shoes in the hope that Jacqueline might notice and think him debonair. He wished he had his uniform already. Today he would really talk to her in the *pâtisserie*. He would buy a pastry and ask her to take a walk with him along the quay under the Plane trees. Or maybe, like last Saturday, he'd lose heart and only watch her through the shop window.

"I don't like the idea of Armand idling away the day with that artist fellow," his mother said, coming into the kitchen. "He might get ideas. It's bad enough you stay out all hours of the night with him. I don't want Armand—"

"Just a few hours," his father said, following her and buttoning his vest. "To paint him. Our son. A painting of our son before he leaves to become a man."

"You asked that drunken lout to paint him?"

"No. He wants to paint the whole family." He smiled. "You and the baby too. I tell you, this Dutchman will be famous someday."

"He's odd, and he's disturbed, the way his eyes bore into you."

"He's my friend, and a decent human being. Be a little charitable, Augustine. He's just hungry for companionship."

Armand had forgotten his name, but he'd seen him roaming

around town and in the fields—a man with a bristly red beard and hacked orange hair wearing a gigantic straw hat, rumpled pants the color of bricks, and a blue peasant shirt buttoned wrong and hanging out of his trousers. Once he watched him walk in jerky movements down the center of rue de la Cavalerie, and stop all of a sudden right in the road. He raised his hands to make a square frame of his fingers, and looked through them at a raggedy acacia in the place Lamartine, muttering "God, God, how beautiful," then shook his head like a horse shaking away flies. He didn't even move when a carter shouted at him to get out of the way. Behind his back children imitated him and laughed.

"I want you to talk to him, Armand," his father said. "A very interesting fellow. He lived in Paris. Before that, he studied to be a preacher, and there's still something of that in him. Get him to tell you about the coal miners he knew. You'll learn something."

"What do I want to know about coal miners?"

"About life and work and struggle. About being a man." His father laid a heavy hand on his shoulder and Armand pulled away. "The yellow house on place Lamartine at avenue de Montmajour. He's expecting you."

His father had been talking about the Dutchman almost every day since the stranger had come to Arles last winter. As the postman, his father delivered letters and packages to him, mostly from the fellow's brother in Paris, and the Dutchman gave his father letters for his brother, sometimes four a week. "I've never known anybody to write so many letters," his father had said more than once, shaking his head and chuckling.

For another month, until he left in twenty-nine days, Armand had to do what his father told him to, so he went, and instead of trying to talk to Jacqueline at the pastry shop, he just watched her through the shop window, which was easier in a way. The pouty expression of her lips and the toss of her dark curls practically made him sweat. He watched her rest her hand in an old man's open palm a moment longer than necessary as she gave him his change, and the man doddered out of the shop smiling as though an angel in heaven had blessed him.

Armand felt like marching right in and . . . and what? Buying a pastry like that toothless pensioner? No. He had to have something to tell her or ask her. That's what his good friend Gustave told him, and Gustave always gave him good advice, like going into the army. In the evenings when they had a smoke on the quay, they talked about the girls in Arles. Brigitte, the laundress, so pretty both of them admitted they'd offered to pick up their mother's laundry. Christine, who helped her father deliver milk because she had no brother to do it. And Monique, who smelled like cheese. No matter whom they mentioned, their talk always circled back to Jacqueline.

He'd go see her after he went to the painter's house, and maybe walk her home. And if the painting made him look manly and handsome, he might persuade the painter to show it to her. That would be something important to tell her.

The Dutchman's house reeked of fumes and looked as though the mistral had blown through. Every paint tube was uncapped. Colors shouted at him. Brushes stuck out from under the mattress. The red floor tiles were spattered. Blue paint oozed out of a tube onto a half-eaten potato. Some spiky, wilted sunflowers in a clay pitcher were dropping their seeds and petals onto the table, and half a dozen paintings of sunflowers hung crooked on the walls. What would a man want with six pictures of the same thing?

The artist saw him looking at them and pointed with the mouth-piece of his pipe to one painting of them. "The closed ones remind me of small birds' nests back home."

The man's hand moved haltingly toward a closed sunflower in the nearest painting. Armand held his breath and watched the big-knuckled hand stroke the round blossom tenderly, as though it were a woman. He turned away. It was too private a thing to watch.

"Why did you paint the same flowers so many times?"

The artist stood straighter and pushed out his chest. "For my friend," he said loudly, fists on his hips. "To decorate the house for my friend. He's coming soon."

Peering out from under his overhanging forehead, the artist gave Armand a long, penetrating look, not a hard look, but a look of deep interest, as though he were trying to see beneath his skin.

"Why do you want to paint me?" Armand asked.

"Paint a whole family is what I want. Complete. Your father has a sturdy Russian look. He's a common man who shouts like a revolutionary when he's drunk, but looks like a saint from the old time when he's not. And you . . ." The man thrust his head forward, studying him with such intensity that Armand squirmed. "We'll see about you."

He set to work stretching a canvas onto a wooden frame. "How do you like being a blacksmith's apprentice? Making things."

"I don't, much."

"Make things?"

"Like it. I don't like it. My father made me. He said I had to do something, so next month I'm going into the army." He still felt uncomfortable saying it, but it was better than pounding iron all day until his arm ached.

"The army, huh?" the Dutchman said out of the side of his mouth where he held a few tacks.

"Tunisia."

The man pounded the tacks into the frame. "Just don't go to the all-night cafés in the bazaars and you'll never learn the taste of absinthe. You can ruin yourself in night cafés." His eyebrows squirmed toward each other like worms and the man shook his shoulders. "After the heat of the day you can go mad and commit crimes there."

He didn't like the fierce way the man looked just now.

Armand had heard about the bazaars—narrow, dusty, crooked alleyways where you could get lost forever, where you could buy anything—a pistol or a fine, curved sabre, a silk cravat edged with gold thread, jewels by the kilo, anything. He'd heard tales of slick, dark flesh in smoky rooms. He'd heard tales, and they had shocked and excited him.

The artist brushed his hand across the canvas, then tapped it with his middle finger, testing its tautness. "You have a girl you'll have to leave?"

How did he know?

He'd never so much as touched her. Round, rosy Jacqueline with the dark blue eyes that sparked with points of light. He'd walked with her once on the boulevard des Lices, and all she'd talked about was Gustave. Gustave, in his leather pants and Spanish boots and cattleman's broad black hat. Gustave, who could carry a whole calf on his shoulders, and ride across the Camargue in one day. Gustave, who sang her songs, sad and yearning *gardian*'s ballads that stirred her feelings. Gustave, his boyhood friend who'd been like the older brother he didn't have, who had taught him how to ride, his name now brassy in his ears. Home after a summer in the Camargue, Gustave was winning her right in front of his eyes, and Armand had lost the courage to speak to her again. But when he came back from the army with presents for her from the bazaar and heroic tales to tell, things would be different.

"You have a girl you'll have to leave?" the painter asked again, tapping him on the shoulder to get his attention.

"No. Not exactly."

"Then there's someone you want to have?"

Armand nodded, looking down.

"Nothing to be ashamed of. All young men feel it." His voice softened. "The touch of a woman—God does not desire man to live alone. Tolstoy tells us that."

The Dutchman gazed out the window. "Look. *Les petites Arlesiennes.*" Two girls were sitting on the grass beneath the acacia trees, their skirts spread wide. "My God, how pretty. Maybe a little sad, though, like Giotto's young women."

Whatever that meant. It seemed to Armand that this man was the one who was sad, not the girls outside.

The painter jerked into action. "Now we'll do a painting that will make her yours forever. Sit here, on this special chair for my friend."

The fellow pulled forward an ordinary, scratched wooden chair with a rush seat. There was nothing special about it, even though a painting of it hung on the wall behind it. What kind of man would paint what was already in the room?

"It's for my good friend. He is coming soon, from Paris, to paint the south. Someday this will be called the Studio of the South. When you come back, place Lamartine will be filled with artists, like comrades in arms working together"—he made a fist and swung it in the air—"and paintings of those girls out there will be in Paris galleries." He flung his arm wide toward the street and his chest heaved. He patted the chair. "Here. Sit."

The man looked for something on his tray of tools. "The army. People get killed in the army. Are you afraid of dying?"

He asked it casually, as he lifted blue paint off the potato with a razor and smeared it onto a thin board, as if dying were nothing, and not wasting the blue paint were everything. Maybe the man had felt that fear himself once, and now it didn't matter to him. That was the kind of man you had to be in the army.

"Are you?" the artist prodded.

He knew he was supposed to answer no, but he couldn't say the word.

"Be confident, my boy. No matter what, no evil exists in this best of worlds. Everything is for the best." His voice sounded pinched.

"Do you really know that?"

"I know it's good to think that way." He squeezed dark purplish blue onto the board. "If the fight is still ahead of us, we must try to mature quietly."

He couldn't figure out what that meant.

The painter looked up to study him. "White cravat," he muttered. "But not white. Slate blue, gray, pink in the light." The words brought them back to earth again, to the task before them. He smeared more colors on the board, put his thumb through a hole in it so he could hold a fistful of brushes with the same hand, and then he began, taking long, fast strokes.

Across the room Armand saw a painting of his father in his blue postal uniform. The eyes looked right, but the beard was curlier than his father's. His wide face was painted yellow, green, pink, even red. His father didn't have those colors in his face. Flushed from liquor—that's how this man saw his father. The realization hurt him, which was surprising to him because he'd had thoughts of his father lately that weren't kind at all. He couldn't help it, and so he was going away. But the painting made him feel good too, his father there in his postal uniform looking straight back at him, square-shouldered and forthright, like a general.

He wondered how the artist would paint his face. With colors like that? What about his mustache? He was proud of the way he'd trimmed it. He'd gotten it sharp and even.

Once the fellow started painting, he didn't talk, and hardly took a breath. He just squinted. Armand felt as though there were pins in the painter's eyes pricking the pores in his newly shaven face, a sensation that crept into his scalp, making him feel alive and part of something important and private. He couldn't explain it, and he would never tell anyone. The way the man studied every part of him, he didn't know how to describe it—tender and urgent maybe. He'd never been looked at that way before, except maybe by his mother.

It was hard to sit still. The artist kept him there a long time and he became restless, thinking about what he would do later that afternoon. When the man finally stopped and said he'd finish tomorrow, it was dusk, and the pastry shop was closed.

The next day on his way to place Lamartine, Armand lingered beside the ancient arena, knowing that Jacqueline would be in the pastry shop on rue Voltaire just beyond it. He paused, and his palm touched the warm old stone of the arena where centuries of brave men faced the bulls. The last bullfight of the season was a week away. There would be music and dancing, and people would be wearing their traditional costumes. He pushed off from the stone wall, determined to buy a pastry and ask her to accompany him. If she said yes, he'd offer her his arm and they would join the promenade around the ring, and he would feel her skirt brush against his pant leg. And during the bullfight, he would take her hand in his so she wouldn't be frightened.

Opposite the pastry shop his firm step faltered. He lurched off the curb and stopped in the street. Gustave strutted out the shop door, cocky and smiling, and hailed him. Before they even reached the end of the block, Gustave cupped his hands, palms up, as though he were holding two bowls. "Big as melons, the weight of them in your hands," Gustave said, grinning.

Armand felt his fist clench.

"And in your mouth—" Gustave pinched his fingers together and kissed them.

Armand felt his arm flex, his fist spring forward into Gustave's jaw. Not a powerful blow, but enough so Gustave staggered backward against a building and slid to the ground. Gustave stared at him, wide-eyed, holding the side of his face.

Armand trembled and his knuckles burned. He fled quickly down rue de la Cavalerie to place Lamartine, and arrived at the yellow house out of breath.

The Dutchman pulled him inside. "My boy, what happened?"

"I just punched a good friend. I knocked him to the ground." Armand slumped onto the chair. "I've never hit anybody like that."

"He was a comrade?"

"I thought so."

The artist moaned. "Awful how impulse takes over a man, even with a friend. Like a flash of madness. Like the mistral." A tortured scowl passed over the man's forehead and he seemed to sink into gloom with Armand. The metallic buzz of cicadas outside reverberated in Armand's head.

"It can't be helped now. Maybe someday you'll see it was for the best."

Armand nodded, just to get the painter to stop staring at him.

The man brought him an apple, held it up, and turned it like it was a work of art. The painter looked at that apple as if it were someone he loved. It was only an apple! He cut it crossways so that each slice had a star shape in the middle, and laid them out carefully on a white plate, then moved them to a dark blue plate and handed it to him. He leaned forward to watch him eat, breathing heavily, his paint-smeared hands rubbing his thighs. Nothing else seemed important to him. "Apricots and nuts in Tunisia, but probably no apples," the man said, watching him until he finished, practically feeding him the apple as if he were a boy prince. Armand Roulin. Himself. The postman's son.

"That friend who's coming, he must be important to you."

"Yes. He's coming any day now. You must meet him before you leave."

He hardly knew him, yet the man was talking to him as a friend, and looking at him in that deep way again.

"Did you hit your friend for a good reason?"

Armand nodded. "Jacqueline."

The man hung his head. "Anger, heat, hope—passions are what makes a man alive, but maybe it's also good for a man to go away when things stir him up too much." He covered his face with his hands, and then let them fall. "Working at something new can help too. Like last night. I painted in the dark."

"How?"

The painter grinned and showed him a hat with stubs of candles wedged in the hatband and the front brim cut off. "Here, look." He brought out a night painting of the café terrace on place du Forum.

The terrace was blazing in yellow and orange from the lights inside the café, scorching the night in that spot. Stars like chunks of quartz hung in the dark blue sky. "The sky has eyes," Armand said.

The painter nodded in quick jerks of his head, hard enough to snap his neck. "In Tunisia, don't forget to look at the sky at night."

They worked all afternoon while Armand thought of Tunisia and what he might find there. Maybe the bazaars at night would blaze like this café inviting a lonely person in.

As soon as the painter finished, he motioned to Armand to have a look.

Armand felt his breath knocked out of him. The painting was him, all right, his face turned to the side, his eyelids half down, his brimmed hat shabby and drooping, but he looked so lost and sad, the way the painter was sad, and, he couldn't help but think, *weak.* He had to look away. He could never have Jacqueline see it.

"I want to paint another," the fellow said. "Tell your father to buy you that wheat-colored jacket in the shop on the boulevard des Lices.

He knows which one. The color of wheat fields or a dusky gold sun. A young man going into the army deserves a new jacket. *Pour la bravoure.*"

In a few days, his father came home from the postal station and laid his leather postal sack on the kitchen table.

"Reach inside, son." His father folded his arms across his chest and leaned back on his heels.

Armand stared at the jacket he pulled out, soft suede, a fine cut with sharp lapels, a man's jacket, as fine as his father's postal uniform. He couldn't believe it. He hadn't told his father what the painter said. He'd never in his life tell his father to buy him something, but here it was in his hands.

"Why?"

His father smiled in a gentle way. "Having a son in the army makes a man proud." He gestured urgently to the sack. "Again. Reach in again."

He pulled out a new black felt hat. What in the world had the painter said to his father?

"A beautiful jacket," the artist said the next day. "You'll have to wear it for your girl. What's her name?"

Armand's voice croaked, "Jacqueline," and fury boiled up in him that Gustave could boast about what he, Armand, thought about only when he was alone in his dark room, Gustave bragging as though touching Jacqueline were as common as touching an old shoe.

"Ah, Jacqueline," the artist murmured. "To be united with a woman in love is the highest thing in a man's life. That's what opens the prison."

Armand saw that he blinked wet, bloodshot eyes.

"*La belle* Jacqueline. You feel that everything is yet to be done, no?" The man's arms spread wide. "A strong, fine feeling. I feel it sometimes too. Here. Sit in my good chair. The chair for my friend. He'll be here any day now." He put a new canvas on his easel. "Tilt your hat like a man who's just been to see his girl." Armand shrank inside. "More. Like he's just *made love* to her."

The painter jerked back his chin. "Why, look at you! Love is no sin, Armand. Don't let those purgatory carvings on Cathedral de St-Trophime scare you. That demon vomiting a serpent—silliness. You know which ones I mean?"

Armand chuckled. "Everybody here knows them."

"That one stunned man slumped on the ground doing nothing while a lion tears at him from one side, a monster on the other—he's given up. No! Never give up." He paced in a circle, his fists clenched, and he bent at the waist toward Armand and shouted, "We must not be like him."

He thumped Armand's chest and Armand sat up straight, adjusted his hat, and felt himself smile, remembering Gustave's astonished look as he slumped to the ground, as stunned as the man in hell carved on St-Trophime.

"That's it! That's the look. *Formidable!*"

Armand tilted his hat even more.

The painter worked faster this time, swaying toward and away from his painting, a rhythm that would last for a while and then abruptly stop, as if a pain were attacking him and he had to wait until it passed. A deep scowl would come and vanish just as suddenly. Every so often he murmured excited syllables—not words, just sounds.

While Armand sat, he thought of Jacqueline, of what Gustave might do to her next if he'd already touched her breasts. Now that he'd hit him once, if Gustave spoke one more word about her, he couldn't trust what he might do.

He looked at the stars in the painting of the hot night, like her eyes burning through darkness, and knew there were more beyond the painting's edge, the number of them dizzying.

"Enough!" the artist said, stepped back, loaded his brush with green, laid on a few more strokes, and flopped into a chair with a loud sigh.

Armand looked at the painting and gasped. The jacket wasn't wheat-colored at all. It was yellow, pure, shocking yellow, like the light of the café. He was facing forward this time, and his own eyes looking straight back at him showed that he was thinking of Jacqueline, that he wouldn't have her, that Gustave would, but in the rake of his hat he saw the tremendous, unlimited possibilities before him. It was true. Everything *was* yet to be done. He straightened himself and stood squarely in front of the painting. A man who'd cock his hat like that and wear a jacket that yellow was a man afraid of nothing.

Of These Stones

Aix-en-Provence, 1896

Four boys lay in wait for the slovenly man to come out of the church. The tallest of them, Maurice, was nearly finished carving *Cézanne imbécile* on the trunk of a Plane tree in the churchyard when he came out, hunched under a load, muttering, "Awful organist. If he can't play better than that, he shouldn't play at all."

The boys giggled as the man shuffled past, casting apprehensive glances behind him, his slouch hat pulled low.

"Look. He brought all his painting trash to church," Maurice said.

"What an idiot," Benoît said. "What was he going to do? Paint God?"

The boys burst into derisive laughter. They waited until Maurice had finished his carving, and then followed the man whom they had heard their parents revile. He turned onto chemin des Lauves, the road out of Aix to the hillside from which they could see across the fields and wooded valley to Mont Sainte-Victoire. When they were beyond the town, the boys shouted after him.

"Imbécile."

"Bête."

"Sauvage."

The man turned to look over his shoulder and knocked his chin against the folded easel strapped to his back. He stumbled and lunged onward, nearly dropping his large leather satchel and blank canvas.

"Look at his rat's eyes," Maurice said.

"Don't trip over your mustache, old man," Benoît shouted.

The smallest boy, Anatole, remembered the fierceness with which his mother had said, "Not even the decency to see his poor mother's bones laid to rest, painting the very hour they laid her in the grave."

One of his grandmothers had added, "He's a fool to paint the same mountain every day. Can't he get it right?"

And his other grandmother spit out a coffee ground and said, "Seventeen years with that Hortense woman before he married her. You know she's not an Aixoise. He found her in a Paris gutter."

Nothing he could remember had ever made them talk so meanly.

The boys followed at a distance, challenging each other with what they would shout at him next.

"Humps for shoulders."

"Rags for clothes."

At the quarry, Maurice picked up a handful of yellowish stones and threw one at a *Défense d'Entrer* sign, and it clattered to the ground. "That should have been the old man's picture," he said. At once they all knew what they were going to do.

Pockets bulging, they crept onward among the fig and almond trees edging the dirt road. Anatole hung back, wishing he had not come, and, seizing on an idea, emptied his pockets of stones and filled them with figs, which were, he thought, softer than stones. They waited for the man to set up his easel and paint awhile, long enough for him to forget them. Then, from behind the bushes, they pelted him with stones. The painting toppled. Stones rained on the man's back and a fig hit behind his knee with a thunk. His knee buckled and he fell.

Anatole went cold. The man staggered toward them, shouting, "Ruffians! The devil take the lot of you."

The boys scattered. As he was running, Anatole felt a rock strike the back of his thigh. He whirled around. It was Marc, his older brother, appearing out of nowhere.

"See what it feels like?" Marc shouted. "Go to my chapel unless you want Mother to hear of this!"

Anatole ran into the woods by himself, glad to be rid of his friends, hoping Marc wouldn't follow. He lingered by a dark pool and hurled the remaining figs into it. Their puny splashes were disappointing. His brother was a monster, spying on him just to catch him at something. Marc didn't care what happened to the painter. He just saw another chance to pick on him.

Slowly, he circled closer to the hill where the Château Noir loomed above dark pines. To Anatole, its black roof and three windows in the shape of pointed arches made it look like a monastery. Heavy with guilt, knowing what awaited him at his brother's hands, afraid to imagine what worse thing might await him if he failed to appear, Anatole parted the tangled bushes and entered the gloomy hollow overarched with pines that his brother Marc called his chapel. In an instant, Marc swung down from a branch, his boots thumping against Anatole's back, sending him sprawling. Both boys swung at each other wildly. Marc pummeled him, aiming right where the bruises from their last encounter had not healed yet.

"Confess. Say it. *Forgive me, Father, for I have sinned.* Say it." Marc twisted Anatole's arm behind his back and sat on him. "Say it!"

"Forgive me."

"*Father.* Say it all." Marc shoved Anatole's face into the dirt.

"Forgive me, Father, for I have sinned," Anatole whispered, dirt scraping against his lips, entering his mouth, and choking him.

"The rest too. *I'm heartily sorry . . .*" Marc yanked his arm tighter. "Speak up to your priest."

Anatole couldn't remember the words.

Exploding with rage, he twisted free, kicked Marc as hard as he could in the crotch, inflicting the one injury tacitly off limits. Then he did the unthinkable. He bolted.

Because Anatole hadn't said the whole confession, Marc told their mother. And because Marc was favored in the family for his simpering, fawning way, and for kissing the grandmothers, and because he was an altar boy and had declared early that year that he was going to be a priest, he was believed. Anatole knew it would turn out that way.

"Even if the man is a fool and a libertine, it's still a sin to throw stones," his mother said. "Your catechism tells you that."

For three days she fed him only bread and water while he smelled the pork sizzling as she cooked, and she sent the painter a note saying that for the next month her youngest son had to do penance every Saturday by working at Jas de Bouffan, Cézanne's family estate.

Anatole felt tricked. It was his mother who had spoken meanly about the painter in the first place, calling him a peasant for his clothes even though he lived in a house bigger than their own. Anatole had only done what plenty of others probably thought of doing, what Marc had probably done when he was Anatole's age. Marc gloated, walking around the house with his hand over his heart, whispering, "Sinners go to hell," when he passed him.

The first Saturday, Anatole and his mother stood outside the iron gate in the high stone wall around Jas de Bouffan. He peered through the grating down a lane between two long rows of chestnut trees to a large yellow stone house with an orange tile roof.

"Stand up straight when you apologize to him."

"If he lives here, why does he wear such shabby clothes?"

"He's a disgrace, that's why. And immoral too. And to think, his father was a prosperous banker."

A gardener let them in and took them to the house where Madame Hortense Cézanne greeted them. Curious yet afraid to behold the face of a woman as disreputable as his grandmother had said she was, he looked only at the uneven hem of her dress.

"His name is Anatole. He's not afraid of hard work," his mother said, "so set him to digging a trench or rebuilding a garden wall. That'll teach him what stones are to be used for."

"The wall in front? I can't even reach the top."

His mother grabbed the back of his neck and squeezed. "Shh."

Madame chuckled. "No, there's one in back which is more your height, but it's very long," she said and dismissed Anatole's mother with a nod.

The garden wall was made of the same yellow quarry rock as they had thrown, only much larger rounds. Climbing back and forth over breaches in the wall, he had to lift the heavy rocks that had fallen on both sides, and balance them on top of each other. After a couple of cold hours, he'd rebuilt only a few raggedy feet. He looked down the length of the broken wall. How could he ever do it well enough? He remembered the man's anger at the organ player in the church, and groaned. His repaired part barely looked any better than a narrow pile of rocks.

Madame came out with a coffee in an orange bowl and set it on the unbroken part of the wall. He glanced at it, thinking it was for her, and rolled a large rock end over end to get it closer to the wall.

"You ought to drink it while it's hot," she said and sat on a slatted iron bench not far away. "Go on. Drink it."

She sounded so severe that he obeyed and took a sip. He'd never had a coffee before so rich with cream. *"Merci."*

"How old are you?"

"Ten, madame."

Unable to contain his curiosity any longer, he lifted his eyes to see the face of the scarlet woman, and felt his shoulders drop. No red lips. No painted cheeks. Her brown hair was parted straight and pulled back just like his grandmother's.

"I meant nine and a half."

"Your father's the butcher?" she asked.

"Yes, madame. Phineas Ouessant."

"*Monsieur Centime,* I call him. Not a centime's worth more. He'll shave a slice of veal so thin I can see his round face right through it. An exacting lot, your family. They've lived in Aix long?"

"My grandmother was born here."

"Brothers and sisters?"

"Two baby sisters and an older brother. He's going to be a priest."

"Hm. It's easy to think that when you're young." She regarded him steadily while he finished the coffee. "When it gets dark, you come inside to warm yourself before you go home."

He shook his head. "Won't Monsieur be there?"

"He's out painting now. Come in even if he's home. He's gruff, but he won't bite." She wrapped her shawl around her shoulders, walked back to the house, and went in through a blue door.

Anatole worked until the weak autumn sun slanted in pale rays through the reddening foliage of the chestnut trees, and the wall made a long cool shadow in which he shivered. His hands were scraped raw and he'd gotten a blood blister on one finger. He told it not to hurt, and kept working.

When the woman finally called his name, he came to the blue door, and peeked in to see if her husband was there.

"He's not home yet. Come in."

He stepped into the kitchen, and saw shelves of pitchers, vases, bottles, teapots, crocks, tankards—more than he'd ever seen before. He counted thirteen pitchers. "Why do you have so many pitchers?"

"He paints them." She tipped her head for Anatole to follow her. In the dining room, the walls were filled with paintings of apples and peaches and oranges lying among the same vases and bottles he'd just seen. Green and blue bottles, a brown jug, a red pitcher. He couldn't understand why the people in the town thought his paintings were bad, except that the tables were tipped and crooked. He felt dizzy looking up at them.

Madame Hortense made him sit at the dining room table and drink another coffee. "I have a son a little older than you."

"Where is he?"

Her long face stretched even longer. "At school in Paris. I miss him terribly when I'm here." She looked him over while he drank another bowl of coffee. "You've hurt your hands." She made him wash them well in a basin of soapy water at the kitchen sink. Then she buttoned the top button of his jacket, tugged down his cap, and sent him off.

At home he had to do everything just right. He had to wipe his feet at the doorstep, fold his napkin in half, then thirds, not let it touch Marc's hand or plate next to him, keep his elbows off the table, not swing his feet, not scuff his shoes, and most of all, hardest of all, he had to stay away from Marc. A kiss for Mother. A kiss for Papa. Kisses for the grandmothers. Their mustaches tickled him, but he couldn't wince. Kisses for his little sisters. If they kissed him back, it was the best moment of the day. Then up to bed. On his knees at bedside, two Our Fathers, if he could remember the words, two Hail Marys, and then, with his eyes closed tight against the dark blue square on the quilt, his private time with God. God bless

Mother, God bless Papa, God bless the grandmothers and the sisters, but not God bless Marc. And finally, with the smooth sheets over him, cold at first but then warm when he put his head under them, he breathed down into the darkness, "Please, God, if you find me not a bad boy entirely, make them not notice me."

At school that week, he was successful in avoiding Maurice until Friday.

"Meet us in place Bellegarde tomorrow morning," Maurice said.

Whatever they were planning to do, it would be no more enjoyable than being with his brother.

"I can't. I have to do something for my mother."

It wasn't exactly a lie. He would be doing something his mother made him do.

"What would that be?"

"Just something."

His stomach turned with the fear that whatever Maurice was planning, it might bring him to Jas de Bouffan, and Maurice and the others would see him working there.

"Coward."

Anatole spun around, flung his strap of schoolbooks over his shoulder so that it almost hit Maurice, and hurried away.

"Hey!"

He ran all the way home.

On the second Saturday, he stood before the wall and looked at what he'd made the week before. It was ugly. Big rocks stuck out sideways in places and the top was uneven. He thought if he put the big ones lower, it might look nicer. After a while he stepped back. Yes. It was a little better. Also, putting the bigger rocks lower on the wall meant he didn't have to lift them so high. He shook out his shoulders. They didn't hurt as much as they had last Saturday.

It was a warmer day than it had been lately. Madame Hortense came out to sit in the sun near him and knit. After a while she held up a blue knitted piece.

"What will it be?" he asked.

She smiled, the first time he'd seen her smile. "A pullover for Jacques. My son."

"That's nice," he murmured.

He tried to imagine a boy somewhere in Paris wearing the sweater, not knowing that his mother had given another boy a bowl of coffee so rich with cream.

A great swell of feeling came over him, and he curled his fingers tightly. "I'm sorry I threw a fig at your husband. I didn't even want to be with those boys." His voice came out a thin squeak.

She lowered the knitting onto her lap and looked at him awhile, sadly, he thought. "I believe you."

Marc pulled the dining chairs away from the table for each of the grandmothers. When they sat, he pushed them in.

"Anatole, it's your turn to say the blessing," his mother said as she set down a platter of meat and potatoes.

In a few moments, he bowed his head and began, "Bless this food, O Lord . . ." He knew that wasn't right. "Bless us, O Lord, and . . ."

Before he had a chance to think it out, Marc whispered, "And these Your gifts."

"And these Your gifts, which we are about to receive . . ."

"From Your bounty."

"From Your bounty."

"Through Christ," Marc prompted, louder that he needed to.

"Through Christ, our Lord. Amen."

"That was a brotherly thing to do, Marc, to help him," Mother said.

"Anatole should know the blessing better than that." His father's voice was firm. "Marc, you help him with it, and with the rest of the catechism too."

"Do you know that they piled up stones in walls and mounds in Bible times?" Marc asked.

Why bring that up now? Anatole braced himself.

"Is that so?" his father said.

"I learned it in my religion class. They were to remind people of something important. Like obeying the commandment 'Honor thy father and thy mother.' "

It made him sick, the way Marc always said what he knew they'd want to hear.

"Father Tissot came to class to teach us about John the Baptist preparing the way for our Lord, and John the Baptist said that God is able of these stones to raise up children."

No one said anything. Mother set down her fork and raised her chin. Anatole wanted to slip under the table.

"Now, isn't that interesting?" Father said and took a forkful of green beans, long ones, pushing them all the way back in his mouth. In a moment he asked, "And so, Anatole, how are you doing on Monsieur Cézanne's wall?"

"All right." Anatole moved a potato on his plate and wouldn't look up.

"Have you apologized to him?" Mother asked.

"He hasn't been home."

"He's probably out painting the mountain again," she said. "What a queer creature. He's wasted more paint on that mountain year after year. Adrienne knows his housekeeper, who told her he's painted that mountain more than fifty times. The man's dotty, I say."

"He could have given the money he spent on paint to some Christian charity to feed the poor," Marc said.

One grandmother looked at Marc and nodded. The other wiped grease off her chin. "I saw him with that Hortense woman at the market picking over every peach in the stall," she said. "The fruit seller asked him nicely not to handle them. 'I'll handle them all I want!' he shouted. 'How else am I going to know what's on the other side?' "

"He paints them. That's why he has to see them before he buys them," Anatole said.

"He's an uncouth beast with no manners, and that woman with him is a guttersnipe," Mother said.

"Madame Hortense has a son in Paris."

"You're not to talk to her. You're just to work on the wall."

By the third Saturday, he liked coming to Jas de Bouffan. It was a time he knew he'd be safe from Marc. It was always quiet there in the garden except sometimes he could hear faint piano music coming through a window. He allowed himself to think Madame Hortense was playing for him while he worked. It was so beautiful, he cried a little, quietly. As before, she gave him two coffees with cream, only this time she added a piece of bread and strawberry jam, and that night, thinking of her long face when she spoke of her son, he added to his prayers, "God bless Madame Hortense."

On the Friday before the fourth Saturday, Maurice cornered him in the narrow corridor at school, and the two other boys edged up on both sides of him.

"He's got a donkey now," Maurice said.

"To carry his painting gear," Benoît added.

All three boys grinned at Anatole.

"Can't you just see it? Four rocks at the same time, smack in the donkey's ass, and he'll tear off like a shot."

Benoît smacked his hands together and flailed his arms. "All his painting things flying."

Anatole felt sick, but he couldn't let them see it.

"Tomorrow, nine o'clock, place Bellegarde," Maurice said.

Anatole nodded and hurried away.

The next day he was in the garden by eight. He worked more slowly on the wall, and at the end of the afternoon, it occurred to him that if he took down the first part he had done in order to make it neater, now that he knew how, he might be able to come back again. He was going to ask.

He burst into the kitchen, and there was the painter putting peaches around a rumpled dishcloth on the table. Before Anatole could back out the door, the man turned and saw him. His mustache drooped down onto his beard, and a fluff of long gray hair surrounded his balding head, without a single hair on top. His pale eyes weren't like eyes at all, only wet pebbles fished from a river bottom.

"And so, my stone-throwing ruffian, we finally meet."

Anatole lowered his gaze to the man's jackboots. "I'm sorry, monsieur. I'll never—"

"Promises. What are they good for?"

Anatole's knees were trembling and all he could think to say was what Marc had taught him when pretending to be a priest. "I'm heartily sorry that I have offended thee and I detest all my sins . . ."

"Do you mock me?" he bellowed. He flung his arm out and Anatole flinched, thinking he was going to hit him. Then he swung his other arm out away from him. "You and your hoodlum friends. A pack of wolves you are."

"They're not my friends."

"Worse than wolves. Demons tormenting a man just going about his work."

"I thought of you this week, monsieur," Anatole said. "When I dreamed I was eating an apple."

The man snapped his head around. "Boy, don't you make a game of me."

Anatole shrank back against the wall.

Madame Hortense put a hand on the man's arm. "He meant no harm."

Anatole looked only at the man's rough, stained fingers, not wanting to see again the man's eyes so close together and strange. "I mean your pictures made me want to eat an apple."

The man stepped close and bent toward him, a fierce look in his eyes. "You watch what you say, do you hear?"

Anatole gestured toward the dining room, meaning the paintings. "Or a peach."

The man slumped back. His bushy eyebrows drew closer together. He shuffled to the kitchen table, put his elbows on the oilcloth, and muttered, head in his hands, "I'm just a fool who feels like weeping."

Anatole's whole body became hot. That he should change so fast and say such a thing, in front of him!

"Do you have a donkey?" he blurted.

Cézanne lifted his head slowly. "Yes."

"Be careful, monsieur. Look behind you."

He turned to Madame Hortense, silently asking permission to leave, slipped out the door, and walked home slowly, thinking of the man so sad-looking.

"Repeat it again, this time without a mistake," Marc ordered the following Saturday morning. He slapped a ruler on the table between their beds.

Anatole flinched. He had been on his knees at his bed for an hour while Marc, sitting behind him on the other bed, drilled him on the Apostles' Creed for his Confirmation. He took a labored breath and began again.

"I believe in God, the Father Almighty, Creator of Heaven and earth; and in Jesus Christ, His only Son, Our Lord; Who was conceived by the Holy Ghost, born of the Virgin Mary, suffered under Pontius Pilate, was crucified, died, and was buried. He descended into hell . . ."

He managed to get through all of it, and was getting up when Marc shoved him back down with his foot. "Now in Latin."

"No!"

"You have to know it in Latin too, so start." He snapped the ruler on the table again.

"Credo in Deum Patri omnipotem—"

He felt the snap of the ruler against the back of his neck. *"Omnipotentem,* not *omnipotem.* Are you a dunce?"

"Omnipotentem; Creatorum Caeli et terrae; et in Iesum Christum, Filium Eius, Unicum, Dominum nostrum."

Marc put his mouth close to Anatole's ear and yelled, *"Qui conceptus . . ."*

"Qui conceptus est de Spiritu Sancto . . ." That's as far as he could go. He readied himself for another swat. "Just words. What are they good for, anyway?" he mumbled.

Marc let out a lion's roar and lashed Anatole's ear with the ruler. "You'll go to hell for saying that. Hell is made for creatures just like you, idiots who can't remember holy words, lost souls who scorn the Creed and pelt old men with stones. A hell so hot that it burns with tongues of flame inside the empty heads of those who cannot recite the Creed." Marc was pacing now, waving the ruler, shouting. "A hell so furious that flaming brimstones are hurled at the damned from every direction, breaking bones already broken, pulverizing the skeleton because the raining down of stones lasts forever and cannot be escaped."

Anatole felt Marc's hands rest around the base of his neck like cold eels, as if they were going to strangle him. "That hell gapes open for you unless you learn by next Saturday the Apostles' Creed in Latin, start to finish, without a mistake. Father says so too. Promise that you will."

Marc shook him by the neck until he felt his head rattle. "Promise your priest."

"I promise." But even as he uttered those words, he knew the senselessness of reciting words without feeling, and that because he thought this way, the hell that Marc described surely did await him. Considering himself a creature doomed to misery, he sank his forehead onto the edge of the bed.

"One more thing. Remember that Mother said you have to work at Monsieur Cézanne's every Saturday for a month?"

Anatole nodded.

"This month has five Saturdays."

Anatole swung around. "That's not possible."

Marc grinned in a wicked way. "It is. Today is the fifth Saturday, and you're late," he sneered.

It was a miracle. He'd never heard of such a thing. Trying to keep his face serious so Marc wouldn't see his happiness, he scrambled up, reached for his jacket, and ran out of the house. After he turned the corner, he let out a cry of joy, running the entire way to Jas de Bouffan. He couldn't stand to be at home with Marc, and he had to stay away from Maurice too, so where was he to put himself after today? Maybe Madame Hortense would let him pull weeds in the garden every Saturday.

The gardener let him in, and Anatole ran along the pathway to the back of the house, knowing he was late, and then he saw it, the wall, toppled in five places as though some great animal, a cow or a horse, had leaned on it until it fell, and Monsieur Cézanne bending over. Anatole wailed softly.

"You don't have to fix it," the man said, despair in his voice. "You've done enough."

Anatole walked the length of the wall. The way the rocks had fallen and rolled inside and outside of the wall, this was no cow leaning on it from one direction. Only one person beside his parents knew about his punishment. Marc. The stupid brother who couldn't imagine that he might *want* to come again. His heart soared. He fell to his knees and picked up a slab of rock.

"I'll do it again. I'll do it better."

"Look at their shapes," said the artist. "Everything has a geometrical shape. Here, this one's long like a cylinder. Some are almost cones or rectangles. The cones are the hardest. Let's see how they can fit together." Anatole watched the artist fit a roundish one snugly between two rectangles. "Just like arranging fruit on a plate." After a few minutes the man gave over the task to him, saying, "Build it up, stone by stone. There's no hurry. Make it stand for eternity."

Anatole worked a long while, liking the feel of Monsieur's presence behind him. He stole a glance at him, sitting on the garden bench smoking a small white pipe. With his long gray hair, the lines in his face above his big beard, his torn white peasant shirt with full sleeves, he looked like the men pictured in the Bible history book that Sister Thérèsa showed him at school. Like Noah. They thought Noah was a fool too.

Once he heard Monsieur Cézanne say, "Yes, that's a good fit," and his heart beat faster. When Monsieur got up to leave, he murmured, "Balance is a very good thing."

Anatole raised up on his knees. "Is Madame Hortense here?"

"No. She's in Paris this week."

"Oh. With her son." He sat back on his heels and sighed.

Cézanne bent forward, as if to get him to look him in the face. "What's on your mind, boy?"

Anatole spread his fingers on the speckled rock at his knees and squeezed. "Did she . . . ?"

"Speak up."

"Did she say anything about me?"

"Yes, she did." He took a few puffs on his pipe. "She said you aren't a bad boy."

Anatole breathed in a long breath through his nose and felt his chest fill with warmth and goodness. Still, it wasn't courage so much as fear that now, without Madame Hortense, this might be his only chance, which made him ask, "Why do you paint the same mountain again and again?"

Anatole watched him take another puff on his pipe.

"Why does a man pray to God again and again? To know Him better. I paint to know the mountain, the spectacle God spreads before our eyes. From every angle, in every season, in sunshine, in shadow, in every circumstance of our lives. It is never the same, yet it is always the same, and always good, like God the Father. Painters need to think of the world as their catechism." The man gazed off in the distance. "And I paint it to receive the Father's blessing."

Yes, that was it. Making something good to please God. Like a good wall. More important than words. Anatole waited without moving in case the painter would say something more.

"But then, I'm only an old fool."

"No. I think . . . I think you must be a saint."

He couldn't look at the man right then. Instead, he stared downward at a spot of orange paint on the man's boot. It seemed to him a cheerful color, like the bowl of coffee. If he could only remember that happy color shining there on the man's boot, maybe from some peach he painted, painted for eternity, then no matter what would happen, he'd be all right.

A Flower for Ginette

Giverny, 1907

Quickly Émile took out the green wooden rowboat so he could lift fallen leaves off the pond. When Monsieur came out of the pink stucco house at six in the morning, it had to be just right. With no breeze yet, the water lay like a liquid mirror, and Monsieur would want to paint the rosy clouds reflected among the water lilies. After considering them from several angles, Émile trimmed a few errant lily pads overgrowing the shapes Monsieur ranted about keeping just so. He knew what Monsieur wanted.

At the pond's edge, he leaned to the side of the boat to cut off agapanthus, irises, and azaleas that were spent, careful not to leave a blunt end visible. He couldn't reach the lily of the valley spilling over in bunches and sending its slightly acid scent out through its in-verted cups. He'd have to snip the wilted ones on foot, along with the rhododendrons, before he moved to the upper garden to do the same for the dahlias and Chinese lilies there. He let the other gardeners do the fertilizing, watering and transplanting of greenhouse seedlings, but never the pruning, for that was an art. Seventeen years had taught him how much Monsieur wanted left—a profusion of plants just short of the point of excess, a well-designed tangle of delights. He had to create anew, every day, that single point the master wanted between the presence and absence of a gardener's hand.

One enormous deep violet blue bearded iris thrust itself before a fan of sword-shaped leaves. He'd been watching it grow. No doubt Monsieur had noticed it too, on his twice-daily strolls through the gardens, but as far as Émile could tell, he hadn't begun a painting of it. Today would be the day. The bloom was at its bursting peak, puffed out like a dowager queen in regal velvet wearing a dewdrop jewel. He might be able to get it home and be back before Monsieur came out to paint. Ginette would think it spectacular. He imagined that round O her lips always made at the flowers he brought her, and then her hint of a sigh. Blossoms didn't last. No matter how moist the flesh under the velvet skin, the petals were dead the moment their stems were cut.

What would Ginette do for flowers after he was gone? The thought troubled him more this year since the pricks of pain had begun in his chest.

He listened for Monsieur's footsteps on the coarse sand pathways. Hearing nothing but the high trill of a kingfisher, he snipped off the iris for his wife, feeling only a fraction of the guilt he'd felt the first time. God would forgive him in the name of love, even if Monsieur wouldn't.

The veranda door banged. Soon rapid footsteps crunched on the pathway.

"Émile," Monsieur roared.

He felt a tiny pain in his chest, or was it his imagination? He hid the iris under the lily pad clippings.

"Clemenceau is coming on Sunday. For Jean and Blanche's anniversary, and to see the dahlias in bloom. Everything must be at its best. Transplant if you need to." Still in his dressing gown, Monsieur waved his arm toward the upper garden. "Nasturtiums are invading us. Keep the *sense* of it overgrown, though not actually. Leave space for two to walk abreast."

"Yes, I know. A sinuous path."

"Will you have time to repaint the rest of the woodwork?"

Émile had finished the green veranda railing and morning bench—Prussian green, Monsieur would call it—and, the day before, he'd repainted the underside of the Japanese bridge from the rowboat so that green would reflect in the water, and had lifted the wisteria to paint the rails. What remained were the clematis trellises along the wall and the large railed storage boxes for unfinished canvases situated in unobtrusive spots in the garden.

"Of course," Émile said.

"You can get one of the others to help if you need to."

"I wouldn't think of it."

Monsieur stopped moving and studied the spot on the bank where the giant iris had grown. A scowl darkened his face and his big fingers curled into a fist. Émile shifted his feet in the boat to hide the lily pads and iris better. A bee buzzing near it threatened to give him away. Monsieur snapped his head to peer at him for a long moment. How could he not know? Ever since they'd knelt together to plant that first pansy bed seventeen years ago and Émile had snipped off a yellow and violet pansy face and hid it up his full sleeve, he thought Monsieur suspected but tolerated his flower thefts, ignoring them for the sake of their good relationship. Maybe he was even amused by them, but this iris was no mere pansy. It was the grandest bloom in an Eden of blooms. Had he gone too far?

"Are you feeling all right?" Monsieur asked in a voice softer than his usual gruff tone.

"Yes."

"*Alors, bien,*" Monsieur said with an abrupt nod and strode back to the house.

The iris was safe.

Émile continued the daily trimming of the water garden and moved to the upper beds. He wanted to take special care with the dahlias, the one type of flower immune from his thievery—not because he didn't feel as strong a passion for them as Monsieur felt. He did. It was because of the happy hours spent with Monsieur in the greenhouse crossing the dahlia species, anticipating the new colors, worrying over them like two parents, sharing their excitement as their created varieties flourished.

Once, when he lifted off the pollen from a stamen with a tiny brush and twirled the brush in a pistil of another variety to get the pollen to stick, Monsieur said to him, "Doesn't it make you feel like a god, creating a new flower?"

"God's workman, maybe. Just like a bee."

"We're no more important than insects?"

"It's God who creates everything," Émile said.

"Everything? Even a painting?"

"He gave you eyes, didn't He? And hands."

Monsieur grunted and pursed his lips. "You're good to have around, Émile, to keep me humble—whether I want to be or not."

Now, as he snipped out single wilting petal points from the blossoms, he thought of how in their dahlia horticulture, they were equal partners, and because Émile cherished that, he could not steal Monsieur's joy in a single dahlia bloom, even though Ginette had never seen the new creations.

By noon, after a quick trot home midmorning to take the iris to Ginette, and a few minutes' rest to catch his breath, Émile had finished the day's pruning and had tied the clippings in burlap to lay out to dry behind the wall for burning. He was pleased, now, to put away his clippers and take out his brushes and paint can.

Monsieur's morning work apparently went well too. Émile heard no lion's roar through the willow trees. Monsieur was prone to fits of despair that often led to rash acts. Madame Alice always said the right thing to him, and so effortlessly, but Émile had to think out the words to say ahead of time in case Monsieur's wife wasn't there.

Once, painting from his floating studio on the Epte, Monsieur had bellowed a loud "Ooff." Hearing the clatter and splash, Émile had called to Madame Alice and rowed quickly on the narrow Ru, which ran through the water garden out to the Epte, thinking that Monsieur had fallen in, but it was his easel and canvas that were floating.

"I'm through, Émile," he cried and flung his palette, tubes, and brushes into the water. He stepped from the studio flatboat into Émile's rowboat. "I'm not a painter. Row me home."

Émile tried to save the canvas.

"Let it go, Émile! All the way down the Seine, if it wants to." Coming into the pond in the rowboat, they saw Alice at the gate which separated the flower and water gardens.

Monsieur hollered, "I'm not a painter, Alice." His voice set off the peacocks in a raucous answer.

"Today, maybe not. But tomorrow, yes," she called back. "In the meantime, this afternoon you've got to plan the colors for the new flower bed with Émile."

Émile could see the agitation leave his face as he rowed him across the pond and Monsieur gazed down at the reflections of clouds floating over submerged grasses. By the next morning Monsieur had a new idea and was calling for more paints.

To be so little at peace with one's work—Émile felt sorrow for him. Monsieur painted as a happy man would see things, but he wondered whether Monsieur was happy the way he was happy, hurrying the perfect iris home to Ginette, blurry-eyed with love.

Only last month, Monsieur had begun to slash for burning three stacks of water lily canvases. "Once I'm dead no one will destroy any of my paintings, no matter how bad they are," he'd said.

Madame Alice had stood on the porch and watched, gripping the railing with hands as white as her hair. "Help him, Émile. He can't be dissuaded. He'll paint more, and better ones."

With an aching heart, Émile had helped to lay the fire.

"Isn't there one of these you wouldn't mind if I took for Ginette?"

"No! Burn them all." With his razor Monsieur hacked another canvas out of its stretcher and threw it to the ground.

The bonfire rose into the dusk and Monsieur watched it behind the glowing tip of his cigarette until the work of a year was only embers. Émile took care to pour water on the mound before he went home in the gloom.

"You mean to say you've broken your back for him all these years and he wouldn't even give you one painting he didn't want?" Ginette had said. "You, who spent your best years on your knees to care for what he loved? Who was it who defended him against those farmers shouting that his water lilies would poison the water supply? Who created something that made him rich and famous? You! He'd rather burn them than give you a scrap!"

Émile shrugged and fell into bed exhausted, smelling smoke on his skin and mustache.

Early the next morning he found that they had overlooked one elongated triangle of sliced canvas. It was covered with ashes and dirt, but still intact. He swept it up and stuffed it under his shirt, apologizing to God for his disobedience, and only then looked around to see if someone was watching. No one was up yet. He'd hardly seen the thing, and as he felt it stiff and scratchy against his skin while he bent and stretched to examine the undersides of rose leaves for aphids, he was agitated with curiosity.

When the sun finally dipped behind the plum trees, he tramped home through the field of wild red poppies, his heart hammering in his chest. He didn't take out the slash of canvas until he had bolted the door behind him and caught his breath. Then he gently washed off the ashes and dirt. Brushstrokes of pink, lavender, blues, and greens swirled in what might be an oval if the piece were larger. Just colors, he thought, sinking into a chair, until he turned it upside down. Thick paint rose in ridges for part of a lily. Next to it, paint had been applied smoothly for willow leaves. It *was* something.

Breathless, he showed it to Ginette.

"What is it?" she asked.

"A hanging willow branch and half a lily. A flower that will last."

"He gave that to you?"

"No. If he knows I have it, he'll be raving mad."

"And you'll be fired for sure, and then what will become of us?"

"It's for you, Ginette. For our bedroom. Don't tell a soul."

That Sunday, he worked all afternoon to fit the joints for a little triangular wooden stretcher and frame. He sanded the frame smooth as satin and painted it with Monsieur's green paint he had taken in a pickle jar. Nothing else seemed so right. And every night since, before he turned out the light, he looked at the sliver of painting above Ginette's dressing table with satisfaction. Ginette would always have a flower, not a real one, but one made by God nevertheless.

Now, after the midday supper, Émile lifted a fragrant veil of blue, pink, and white clematis away from the trellis so he could paint it. The pale rose variety with a deep rose stripe down each of the seven petals looked to him like a bursting star.

"Painting again?" Henri, the youngest gardener, asked with a tone of derision.

"Clemenceau is coming. If you feed the geraniums on the veranda, they might open out by Sunday."

"Why paint the back? It's up against the wall. Monsieur can't see it."

"No, but I can. And you can."

Henri shrugged and went on by. He's too young to understand my satisfactions, Émile thought.

With the corner of his brush Émile lifted off a bristle that had stuck to the wood. He liked painting things almost as much as gardening, and so would not give it up to the younger men. He liked that creamy feeling of dipping the brush. He often said a little prayer, *"À la grâce de Dieu,"* before that treacherous moment of swinging the loaded brush from can to trellis, over the clematis, so not a single drop would mar a leaf or petal. Then there came the pleasure of the smooth spread of shining color until he felt a slight drag on the brush telling him he needed more paint. He loved all these feelings just as much as Monsieur did. He was certain of that.

"Ooff! It's maddening," Monsieur cried from somewhere near the pond. "It's a damned obsession."

The poor man's railing again, Émile thought, pained by his disquietude. He finished the trellises and started on a storage box. On this hot-heavy day, the spicy, clovelike scent of pink dianthus swirling with the balmy sweetness of roses was so intense it made him dizzy.

"I'm no better than a pig. I know nothing!" he heard.

Monsieur's *sabots* scraped against the coarse sand path. Émile smelled his cigarette and saw out of the corner of his eye Monsieur's fist hanging like a small ham. "Don't you ever find it hard to do what you have in mind?" Monsieur asked and lifted his slouch hat to wipe his forehead with his handkerchief.

"No. I just keep things in mind that are possible."

"Where's the joy in that?"

"Look around you. This garden. It's full of joy. We've always kept the possible in mind, even that first day of digging the pond. Now you want the impossible. You'll want to paint the scent of flowers next."

"Right now I just want to paint the reeds underwater, the water's surface, and the sky reflected, all of that at once. What's impossible about that?"

"Only God—"

"*I* want to do it."

"You will, God willing. You are."

Monsieur was looking at a pale rose clematis blossom as though he'd never seen one before. "My God, how exquisite. Look how the light bathes the petals, adding colors before the sight meets our eyes." He shook his head. "What a confounded profession. No matter what beautiful thing I see, it's too hard. It's beyond an old man's powers."

Émile dipped his brush and watched the bristles puncture the smooth green surface of the paint in the can.

"Hand me that brush," Monsieur demanded. "Let me paint something I can."

"No!"

The word struck like a deep bell in the quiet garden. He had never contradicted him before. Monsieur stood for a long time with his big hand out for the brush. The air thickened with the will of his temperamental genius. Émile took only shallow breaths.

He had come to work for Monsieur when the Japanese cherry trees were only spindles. Together they'd knelt to plant the first blue forget-me-nots to harmonize with mauve tulips and pink peonies. He'd been here before there was a Japanese bridge, before Monsieur had even bought the meadow that became the water garden. All those years. Never a disagreement.

Émile drew the brush across the wood. "This is mine to do," he said. "You do yours." He felt a ping in his chest. Even if he had to fight him, ridiculous at their age, he would not give over the brush. He tightened his grip, in case Monsieur tried to grab it.

A lark sang a short flutelike song and, after a long pause, did it again, as though he couldn't help it. They waited without moving for the third song, and at last it came. Monsieur turned and walked back to his canvas. By then the light had changed. Émile heard him shove the painting into a garden box. He didn't move until he heard him pull out another.

Something about the way he'd said, "beyond an old man's powers," touched him more than any of Monsieur's ravings ever had. They were both old men, but Émile was older, and likely to die first. And then what about Ginette's little scrap of painting? She might try to sell it—need might force her—and Monsieur might learn of it. He shook his head, trying to think straight. If he took the lily from her, what would she do for flowers after he was gone?

Still, Monsieur had a right to choose what remained of him, just like he did—the smooth green coating on this box, for example—and if Monsieur thought a single lily was beyond his powers, then it should not remain. He could not violate the man in that way.

Panic seized him. He forced himself to finish the box and clean his brush just as carefully as he always did, then hurried out the gate, across the field through closing poppies, praying that God would not let him stumble and break a leg and die in the dirt track, would not let his heart stop beating before he could get home to build a little fire of kindling in the grate and place on it the slice of both their masterworks. He knew what Monsieur wanted.

In the Absence of Memory

1939

She stood on the sidewalk. The Louvre at last. Empty and closed. Surely her father would have taken her *here*. She crossed the Seine at Pont Neuf and watched a boat slide past. That would have been a nice memory if he had taken her on such an outing. She walked to Notre Dame. Jeanne, a Catholic, would certainly have taken her here. She paused to watch workmen, in clothing the same dark gray as the March sky, stacking sandbags high against the façade. Not for fear of rain. No. Paris was waiting.

Giovanna crossed to the Left Bank and turned onto boulevard Saint-Michel. It was hard to believe she was really here. She had waited ten years and now she didn't know how long she could stay. Probably only as long as the Maginot Line held.

She snugged the itchy wool collar of her coat up around her neck and over her mouth, and fought her way against biting wind on boulevard du Montparnasse. Stepping into the street around a queue of women holding ration cards outside a *boucherie*, she continued on toward the Café de la Rotonde, the heart of her father's life.

She noticed the street sign on a building. Rue de la Grande Chaumière. His street. And Jeanne's. She turned right onto the one-block street strewn with flapping laundry and foul-smelling trash, so narrow that the four-story buildings seemed to lean inward precariously. A man wearing *sabots* carried a large painting down the middle of the street, muttering as he fought the wind, which soon snatched it out of his grasp. It cartwheeled over the cobblestones, smacked into a parked Renault, and broke apart. She wondered if the man had known her father, but it wasn't the right moment to ask, with his painting torn.

An art supply store. They would remember him there, but it was closed, the display window nearly empty. She knocked on the glass and waited. Three doors away, the peeling brown shutters at number eight, Father and Jeanne's *pension*, were closed. The door was locked, the concierge's lodge empty, the buzzer unanswered or not working. Disappointment choked her.

Back on the corner of boulevard du Montparnasse, out of the wind against the building, a woman in a shapeless black coat and carpet slippers stooped over a brazier, a frail bird of a woman roasting chestnuts. Giovanna bought some in a paper cone. She felt thankful in a small way because they warmed her fingers. Maybe Father had done the same. She saw herself here, a little girl holding his hand, stopping at the chestnut seller, who might have even been pretty then, her father holding the paper cone down low, she reaching for it, warming her hands. Not quite a memory because it never happened, he was dead before it *could* happen. It was only a fantasy, which was better than what she had, which was nothing.

At the intersection, six streets came together like the spokes of a wheel. On a point jutting into the traffic, the empty chairs and tables of Café de la Rotonde faced out in two lonely rows. So that's where he got drunk every night. Shabbier than she had imagined it, but then everything in Paris looked shabby. Maybe that was just her. Maybe it was the war.

As a girl in Livorno she had dreamed of coming to the famous Rotonde or the Dôme or the Closerie des Lilas to listen to the artists talk, and, if she was brave enough, to ask them if they remembered a painter named Amedeo Modigliani, to find out something good about him so she could love him.

She turned back to the chestnut seller. "Are you always on this corner?"

The woman glared at an army *camion* grinding its gears as she held one hand to her ear. "Ehh?"

"I said, are you always on this corner?"

"Mademoiselle, I was *born* on this corner. I've taken root here."

Giovanna smiled and caught the woman's eyes for an instant. It wasn't self-pity. The woman was just stating a fact, giving her credentials. She had a long sock wrapped around her neck inside her collar, making do.

"Did you know the artists here before the war?"

"*Certainement.* Before both wars."

"Who?"

"Zarate from some poor South American country. Chaim Soutine, the sloppy little Jew. He must have gone into hiding. I don't see him any more. Diego Rivera, the Spaniard. Picasso, another one."

"Modigliani?"

The woman pointed with her tongs. "He lived just down that street."

"What do you remember of him?"

"Street sweepers found him dead drunk in that dustbin right over there. A shouter, he was. Roaring drunk, spouting poetry in the cemetery," she said, pointing the tongs in the opposite direction.

"How do you know that?"

"Stories are thick as thieves around here. But I know this for sure." She struck the air with her tongs to emphasize her words. "He never let his wife come with him to the cafés. An Italian through and through."

"What was she like?"

"She was usually dressed in some bohemian getup, trailing behind him except when he was hanging on her. Once I saw him pulling her along by her hair. Most nights she had to fetch him home from the *Commissariat de police.* Oh, but he was handsome. Wore a red silk scarf. Always coughing." Her amber eyes turned vague. "He saw that I was hungry and gave me a tin of sardines once. A pig and a pearl, he was."

"What's your name?"

She chuckled. "They call me Geneviève. Patron saint of Montparnasse." Decisively she closed her grooved lips and turned her hand to accept a coin. One more word and it would have to be two coins.

Giovanna gave her a twenty-centime piece. The woman probably made more from selling memories than from selling chestnuts.

Giovanna turned to the intersection again, not sure how to get across. She stepped off the curb and a truck driver honked at her. She stepped back and waited, looking at the café across the traffic. There might still be a waiter there who had known him.

She turned to the woman. "Do you happen to remember anyone else who knew him? Maybe Leopold Zborowski?"

Geneviève's lips didn't move. She lifted her palm.

Giovanna crumpled the paper cone around the chestnut shells and stuffed her hand in her pocket. There was something pathetic about buying memories from street women. Losing heart, she turned to walk back the way she'd come.

Such memories as she did have tumbled through her mind while she walked down boulevard du Montparnasse. The Livorno Girls' Academy back home in Italy. Signora Leonelli. She was, what, twelve then. Ten years ago. Twelve and tormented. The year she found out.

Colette's taunts had hurt the worst because she idolized Colette for having lived in Paris, and for her name. Colette. She knew no Italian version of that name. It was entirely French, and therefore lovely. Her own name had a French version. Jeanne. The name of her mother she never knew.

"Your papa was a drunk," Colette said during a pause between lessons, a retaliation for Giovanna giggling at her accent.

"That's not true."

"He sponged meals off people in cafés and never paid his debts."

"How do you know?"

"Everybody knows. He picked fights in cafés."

"That's a lie!"

"He was a drug addict."

"You're a liar!"

"He was a Jew who died a drunkard's death."

"Shut up, *bruta.*"

"Giovanna! Silence!" Signora Leonelli commanded. "You will write an apology."

Fury boiled up in her. No one was going to make her write a word.

When Signora Leonelli turned toward the chalkboard, Colette passed her a note. *Bastarda,* it said. Giovanna crumpled it into a ball and stuck her pencil through it, breaking the lead.

At home that afternoon she let the door slam, and flung her book satchel onto the carved Moroccan chest in the parlor. Grandmother raised her head from the daybed. "Not there. You know better," Nonna said.

She pushed it onto the floor and went through the dining room without even glancing at her father's drawings above the sideboard. She leapt down the two stairs into the big kitchen. Nonna got up and followed her.

"*Dio buono,* you come into the house like a whirlwind," Aunt Margherita said from the sink where she was chopping onions. "What's gotten into you?"

Nothing had gotten into her. There was only a dark empty space inside her. She slumped at the kitchen table and dug a groove with her thumbnail along the checkered pattern of the oilcloth.

Margherita set some tomatoes and a paring knife on a cutting board in front of her. "Fresh from the garden. Wash your hands first. Small cubes. For *cacciucco.*"

"I hate school."

"Hmm. Why the sudden change?"

"No reason."

Aunt Margherita looked at her with a raised eyebrow.

"Colette said Father was a drunk and never paid his debts."

Grandmother positioned her two canes carefully on the first step and let herself down slowly. "That's only a rumor. Certainly he paid what he owed," Nonna said, preparing to step down again, warily, on the only steps she could manage.

"Did he drink a lot?"

"Yes," Aunt Margherita said.

"No more than other artists." Nonna hooked a cane over the chair back.

Giovanna felt Nonna's crooked fingers comb through her hair. "Did he sponge meals off people in cafés?"

"Your hair's getting long and beautiful. There's still some red in it."

Nonna's way to end a conversation. *You don't have to answer,* Nonna had told her whenever she'd had trouble at school. She pulled her hair free of Nonna's fingers and went to the sink to wash her hands.

"Was he a drunk or wasn't he?"

"Dedo could recite Dante by the time he was fifteen," Nonna said.

"So?"

"Better that she knows." Aunt Margherita took a breath that raised her chest. "He lived a reckless life. He was overbearing, swaggering, and aggressive, controlling everyone around him. A disgrace to the family, and yes, a drunk."

Every word pushed the truth she'd suspected farther down her throat.

Aunt Margherita didn't stop there. "You may despise me for saying so, but it was good that he died before you knew him."

"Margherita!" Nonna struck her canes together and turned her back on Margherita, her face screwed up like a walnut. "He was a captivating intellect, Giovanna, and a brilliant painter, and all the world will come to know that someday, even your friend Colette."

"She's not my friend."

She never wanted to see Colette again. The next morning she left for school on time but went to the Livorno harbor instead, to watch the steamships leave. A line of stern-looking men wearing black uniforms and tall boots guarded the gangplanks of ships leaving for Sardinia, Corsica, Elba. Finally one was about to leave for Nice. The horn blasted a last call to get on board, and she wanted to run right by those Black Shirts, up that gangplank, and keep on going—by train from Nice to Paris, where he had lived. The churning water behind the ship spread out and settled. The engine noise faded. The ship became smaller. All of it magical. All of it sad.

In the afternoon she went to the library to look for a book that might mention him. After not finding him in several armloads of likely books, she became discouraged. If there was a book about him, it wouldn't say what she needed to know anyway—whether he loved her, whether she could find something in him to love.

She looked up to the wall clock above the poster of Il Duce. Quarter to four. She ran all the way home, wheezing, doubling over with a cramp every few blocks.

When she opened the vestibule door she heard Signora Leonelli's voice. She froze.

"I can't protect her from the world, nor can you," Signora Leonelli said. "If the charges are incorrect, then give her information with which to counter attacks."

"We intend to. On her fifteenth birthday. When she's old enough to know things," Nonna said.

"She needs to know now. Twelve is not too young. It's an uncomfortable thing to have another person know more of your own father than you do."

Yes! Giovanna clamped her hand over her mouth.

"We thought the less we spoke of him, the less she would brood," Nonna said.

"Do you have any mementos or photos? Any articles? Reviews of his exhibitions? That would make her feel proud."

"Yes, of course we have. This chest is full of things." Nonna ran her hand over the carving. "She'll see them when she's old enough."

Always locked. How many times had she secretly searched for the key? She squeezed her hands into fists and stepped out into the parlor.

"I *am* old enough!"

No one moved. Aunt Margherita gasped. The wrinkles of Nonna's face took on a tortured look.

Aunt Margherita threw her shoulders back. "You ought to be ashamed of yourself. Where have you been?"

"Nowhere. The library."

Margherita and Nonna exchanged glances, signaling that they would deal with her later. She knew the look.

"There's going to be an exhibit of his work at the International Venice Biennale soon," Nonna announced, to change the subject. "It's intended to mark ten years since his death. We have a special invitation."

"That exhibit would be good for Giovanna to see," Signora Leonelli said.

"We have five of his drawings here. Would you like to see them?" Without waiting for an answer, Nonna leaned far forward on her two canes in order to get up, and led Signora Leonelli into the dining room.

The first one of a peasant boy wearing a slouch hat and vest too tight was all right for Signora Leonelli to see, but she cringed when Signora Leonelli looked at the three drawings of naked women. The idea of taking off your clothes for a man to draw you was a little disgusting.

"They're life studies," Nonna said, "drawn from live models."

"That's a stupid name."

"Giovanna!"

With Signoria Leonelli there, she felt braver. "Life study should mean learning about a person's life. Or learning how to live."

"Perhaps a drawing can show that," Signora Leonelli said as she came to the last one, done in colored chalk.

Giovanna held her breath and looked at it too—the woman who floated in her dreams trailing a river of red hair down to her ankles. *Petite Jeanne, jolie Jeanne, je t'aime, je t'aime beaucoup,* the woman sang as she pushed the baby carriage in a park. Or so Giovanna hoped.

If she was very still she could feel her heartbeat speed up whenever she looked at the woman's long curved neck, her thin oval face tilted at an angle, her small, pouty lips colored bright red. One eye was higher than the other. They didn't have any dark centers or any white. They were just solid aqua. What did that show about her? That she was blind?

"We think this last one is Giovanna's mother, Jeanne Hébuterne," Aunt Margherita said.

"*We think. We think.* We don't even know for sure."

"That's enough, Giovanna!" Aunt Margherita's voice sprang at her like a coiled snake.

"I'm sure that there's much to be proud of, Giovanna, in your father's life." Signora Leonelli gave Grandmother a sidelong look. "When you are permitted to look in the chest, I'm sure you will learn fine things about him."

Signora Leonelli stood so close, Giovanna could smell the starch in her white blouse.

"I shall see you in school on Monday. If you learn not to fight back, the taunts will stop." She nodded to Nonna as if to say, See the problem you're creating?

Aunt Margherita ushered her out and then spun around, scowling. "How dare you dishonor the family this way, not going to school."

"I deserve to see what's in the chest."

"Go to your room."

She stomped up the stairs, flung herself onto the bed, and wept. Eventually, she heard Nonna and Aunt Margherita arguing in whispers downstairs but she couldn't make out any words.

She traced a smudge on the wall next to her bed. Her room had been her father's. Nonna had told her that he had drawn chalk pictures on the walls when he was a boy. Sometimes she tried to make them out in the smudges. This one, she imagined, was a girl, maybe Margherita, at the harbor with steamships. Those drawings were how Nonna had known he had talent, so she sent him to an art school.

Eventually the stairs creaked, one by one, the sound coming closer and closer, so slowly she couldn't hold her breath that long.

She crumpled the bedsheet in her fists. Nonna never came upstairs any more. A sliver of yellow light widened along the floor and over her quilt, and then Nonna's head appeared in the doorway.

"Are you awake?"

"Yes."

"I have something I want you to see."

"You should have shown me before." She rolled toward the smudge on the wall and heard Nonna scrape the wooden chair against the floor and sigh as she sat down.

"I'm sorry I didn't. Will you look at it now? It's a letter from a friend of your father's."

She rolled back. Nonna's chest was heaving.

"I'll read it to you." Nonna held the letter in the shaft of light and waited until her breath became regular again.

"Today Amedeo, my dearest friend, rests in the Cemetery of Père-Lachaise, covered with flowers, according to your wish and ours. It was a moving and triumphant funeral for our dear friend and the most gifted artist of our time. He was a son of the stars for whom reality did not exist. Three weeks before his death, Modi—as if he saw the end coming—got up at seven in the morning, something very unusual for him, and went to see his child. He came back very happy.

Yours devotedly,
Leopold Zborowski"

Her eyes stung. "Why wasn't I with him?"

"You were in the country with a wet-nurse."

Did that mean her mother hadn't wanted her? She put a wad of her bedsheet in her mouth and bit down.

"Why doesn't Aunt Margherita like him?"

"He's been an inconvenience to her. She's always had to make allowances for him. I'm afraid I gave Dedo more attention than I gave her."

"He never did anything to hurt her, did he?"

Nonna leaned back out of the light.

She waited for her answer, but knew that waiting was useless.

"When can I look in the chest?"

"Tomorrow."

The next morning wings fluttered inside her as she knelt before the chest. Aunt Margherita inserted and turned the old black key, and then sat down to mend her stockings, as if the thing about to happen weren't important.

Giovanna peered inside, winced, and drew back. A ghostly plaster face stared up at her, lying on a brown corduroy cushion. Nonna bent to lift it on its cushion, and held it toward her. "It's your poor father's death mask. Made by a friend the morning after he died."

She could not take the thing in her hands.

"We had this and you never let me see it?"

She forced herself to look. Sunken cheeks. Thin lips, slightly open, leaving a dark space between them. Solid white eyes lying like little eggs in oval egg cups. How would she ever know from those eyes if he had loved her?

"Handsome, wasn't he?" Nonna lowered herself carefully into an armchair, and placed the death mask and cushion on her lap. Giovanni watched with a sickening feeling as Nonna lay her gnarled hands on both sides of the face.

"I made this little pillow from his last jacket," Nonna said. "I had the jacket tailored on his last visit home, and I bought him black wool trousers and a red silk cravat to go with it. He loved fine clothes."

"He abhorred them, Mother. Tell the truth. As soon as you gave him that jacket, he slashed off the sleeves, and said, 'All the painters in Paris dress like peasants.' "

"Why can't the two of you ever agree?"

Giovanna leaned into the chest, finding it less full than she'd imagined it, and inhaled the musty smell of old newspapers. It felt like she was entering a tomb. She lifted out clippings, envelopes, magazines in French and Italian, and spread them out on the rug. The top clipping said his work was "undisciplined, unhealthy, and pessimistic" and that "the eyes of his models have the kind of torpor which follows indulgence in drugs." She didn't want to ask what torpor meant.

An article in a magazine called *L'Eventail* had a drawing of a woman with a long nose and a tiny mouth pinched tight. She was wearing a tall hat with a rounded crown and a wide drooping brim. Under the drawing were the words, *À ma fidèle, Jeanne, 1919.* Faithful. The word in her mind sounded as soft as a dove's breath.

"It's the same face!" She took it to the dining room. "I'm sure it is."

"We think so too," Aunt Margherita said.

It *was* her mother, just as she had thought, her mother in the same room with her—not seeing her with those solid aqua eyes. Once she had wanted eyes like those—little window shades she could draw down when she didn't want anyone to see in. Behind them she could still be six or seven and not make herself sick wanting to know her father and mother, or even just ten and not go crazy wanting to go to Paris, to walk where they walked, and make up memories. A swelling in her throat ached.

She came back to the chest. In a stack of letters about painting sales was a handwritten note on gray lined paper.

Today, July 7, 1919, I pledge myself to marry Mademoiselle Jeanne Hébuterne as soon as documents arrive.

On the bottom were three signatures.

Amedeo Modigliani
Jeanne Hébuterne
Leopold Zborowski

"They weren't married?" Her own parents. No. It couldn't be. She felt her body crumple.

"He was going to."

1919. She was already born. It was true, then.

"You should have told me."

"We would have."

The way Nonna stroked the plaster face in her lap made Giovanna turn away.

"Why did he need documents?"

"It was wartime. He wasn't French."

She stared at her father's ugly note. *Bastarda,* it said, just like Colette's. The lines of his handwriting were wide and dark and slanted. She could write that way if she practiced, but that would not make her any more his.

"Here, Giovanna, look at this." Nonna handed her a large envelope.

She took out a newspaper, *Paris-Montparnasse,* which had a section of several pages about him. It was only a month old. "How did you get this?"

"Jeanne's brother sent it."

She read the return address on the envelope. André Hébuterne, 5, rue Amyot, Paris. She'd learned enough French to guess the headline: "One night when he was drunk . . . Homage to Modigliani." Her hands trembled.

"Did he die from drinking?"

"No. He had tuberculosis."

"Mixing hashish and absinthe didn't help," Aunt Margherita snapped.

"Which is true? Tell me," Giovanna demanded.

"He was a genius, and a passionate man. He just had a turbulent soul," Nonna said.

"What kind of a man would tell his lover on his deathbed what he told Jeanne?" Aunt Margherita's voice was low and mean.

"What did he tell her?" Giovanna braced herself.

Nonna covered her face in her hands.

"He asked her to follow him to the grave so he could have his favorite model with him in Paradise and enjoy her eternally. That's what geniuses are like—thoughtless and self-centered."

Giovanna felt sick to her stomach.

Nonna lifted her face to Margherita. "Opportunist." Then she closed her eyes. "He meant it romantically, *cara*."

"He meant it selfishly."

"What am I supposed to think?" Giovanna screamed. "You never say the same thing."

Nonna wouldn't look at her. Aunt stabbed the needle through a stocking stretched across her fingers.

Giovanna's body quivered uncontrollably and felt about to explode. With shaking hands, she gathered up the articles and letters and laid them back in the chest and closed the lid. "Don't lock it any more. I'll look again another time." She opened the front door, swayed a moment on the step, and then set out for the harbor.

"Giovanna, stay here." Aunt Margherita hurried after her, turned her around, and led her home.

"I want to be alone."

In a daze, she walked in a circle in front of the house and went to the narrow side yard. She sank down onto a low gardening stool next to the tomatoes. She held on to herself with her arms around her ribs until she heard the front door open and close. The plants in front of her blurred. She hugged herself and rocked, tipping the stool.

What right did he have to say that, when he wasn't even married to her? If they ever found out at school, she would die in one breath. Years of trying to keep it a secret stretched ahead of her. She reached out for a plump tomato and squeezed it slowly, feeling it burst in her fist and the pulp and juice ooze between her fingers.

She refused to go to school for a week. Nonna cried a lot. Aunt Margherita was quiet.

"I want to see the exhibit," she said. "I'll go back to school if I get to see the exhibit."

Two weeks later Giovanna and Aunt Margherita sat in a second-class rail carriage on their way to Venice. Since Florence was on the rail line from Livorno to Venice, Aunt Margherita had insisted they spend a night there in order to go to the Uffizi Gallery. "It's a proper preparation," Margherita had said, but Giovanna knew that it was really because Aunt Margherita wanted to see it herself.

"I still don't understand why Venus was standing on a shell," Giovanna said on the train, thinking about what they'd seen.

"That's how she was born. It's a myth."

"She was pretty, but I don't like her being naked."

"I prefer Tiziano's Venus over Botticelli's. Do you remember her lounging on a divan? She's a more mature beauty."

For the third time, Aunt Margherita checked her handbag to see if the Biennale tickets were still there. Giovanna was surprised at how happy and lighthearted Aunt Margherita had been in Florence, but now, the closer they got to Venice, the more she showed signs of nervousness.

"Don't be worried, Auntie. What else could I possibly find out?"

They checked into a small hotel near the train station full of mosqui-toes and canal stench, and immediately took a *vaporetto* down the Grand Canal in shimmering sunlight. "It's a fairy-tale kingdom," she said, and Aunt Margherita agreed.

"Dedo studied here, but I never thought I'd have a chance to see it."

Their *vaporetto* passed an enormous red, white, and green banner stretched along the Grand Canal advertising the exhibition at the Italian pavilion.

"I had no idea the Biennale was so important," Aunt Margherita said, which made Giovanni's heart swell.

Margherita let out a happy "Whooh!" as she stepped safely onto the Molo at Piazzetta San Marco. They bought a Biennale program at a magazine stand to look at later, and went into the cool Basilica. At the same instant they noticed the uneven, sunken floor. Margherita chuckled and said, "It feels like we're still on the water."

They linked arms and walked all day, pointing, telling each other to look at this or that beautiful palace or statue or loggia. They laughed whenever they found themselves on the wrong side of a canal with no bridge in sight.

That night at the hotel, they soaked their feet in the bathtub to-gether, Giovanna sitting on the edge of the small tub, and Aunt Margherita overflowing a stool. They wiggled their toes in the hot water, splashed a little, took turns soaping and rubbing each other's feet. Margherita winced when Giovanna touched a bunion, and Giovanna let go. It was red and swollen. More carefully, she patted Margherita's feet dry, and they put on their nightgowns and sat up in the double bed to look at the thick exhibition program together.

Aunt Margherita checked one more time for the tickets in her handbag. "They sent three tickets for us," she said. "Mother sent one back, saying it would be too difficult for her to make the trip. They sent it back to us again, inviting my husband."

The thought of Aunt Margherita married, loved by a man, jolted Giovanna. "They didn't know," she murmured, embarrassed for her aunt's sake.

"No. They didn't." Margherita reached over and touched Giovanna's knee in a soft gesture.

Resting her head against her aunt's shoulder, she felt closer to her than she'd ever felt before.

"What does it feel like to have a mother?"

"Hmm. It feels like you're going through life together, experiencing things together, big important things like deaths and marriages, and little things too, like that floor today, but maybe not at the same time or in the same way. It's having some of the same memories, and sharing the happiness and the hurt. And having someone to help you."

"Why didn't you ever get married and have a child?"

Margherita stuffed the tickets back into her handbag roughly and snapped it shut. "I had you. Already. So I didn't need to."

Her clipped words sounded false. What she meant was that she couldn't, because of her. Giovanna pushed herself back against the iron rails of the headboard. She had stumbled onto a secret sadness, a smoldering resentment that explained a great deal. The sharp snap of her spinster aunt's handbag told her it had been her fault.

She thumbed through pages of the Biennale program without seeing them, until Margherita said, "Look. A whole page devoted to Dedo."

Giovanna passed the program to her.

"They call him '*un pittore d'Italianità,* true to nationalist sensibilities of beauty dear to Raphael, of proportion as laid down by Michelangelo, of expression and character as taught by Leonardo,' " Margherita read aloud. "They certainly don't want anyone to think he was French."

Finally, here was something she could be proud of.

Margherita looked for a long time at his paintings of women printed in the program, and abruptly handed it back to Giovanna, put on her coat over her nightgown, slipped on her shoes, and picked up her handbag.

"Where are you going?"

"Downstairs to the desk. I won't be gone long."

In the morning, Giovanna put on her new dress, a lady's dress, not a schoolgirl's, sized down from one of Nonna's, but with cuffs and collar made of her father's brown corduroy jacket. She stroked the softness of one cuff with her thumb. Maybe Father had touched the same spot.

Their *vaporetto* was crowded with people, all going to the Biennale. They made their way through the vast, tree-filled park scattered with pavilions, one for every country, each built in a different style. A large striped banner on the Italian pavilion proclaimed, *Modigliani, Pittore d'Italianità.*

"I wish Mother could have seen this," Aunt Margherita said as they took their place waiting to get in.

Giovanna felt her heart beat with importance. All these people, and not one of them knew she was wearing cuffs made of his jacket. "They don't know who we are," she whispered to Aunt Margherita.

The moment the doors opened, people elbowed their way in. "Hold my hand," Margherita said, "so we won't get separated," but her grip told her it meant more than that.

A whole room, and another and another, full of Father. She slid sideways between people in order to get up in front to see each painting and read every card. She made herself go slowly and not look ahead. The paintings were hanging in the order he had made them. They were of real people, people he must have known—the same peasant boy with his vest too tight as the drawing at home, a lady wearing a green fan-shaped collar, a young gypsy holding a baby in a long knit cap, a silly-looking man wearing a monocle. She was seeing his life. She felt him very close.

"These must have been his friends, Auntie. Dozens of friends."

A man in a derby had one solid aqua eye without eyelashes and one solid black eye with eyelashes. Papa was funny, in a way. She'd never thought of him that way before.

"They seem fragile, don't they? And a little absurd," Margherita said.

"No. They seem alone. With eyes like that, you can't see in."

In most of the paintings he outlined the noses with a black line. He liked noses. She could tell because he exaggerated them and made them swoop up. Maybe he was searching the world over to find the perfect nose. She wondered what he would think of hers. She thought he would like it. It was long and turned up just enough.

She allowed her eyes to roam over a nude lying on a fuzzy maroon spread. Her skin was painted in shades of peach, orange, yellow, and rose. She had real eyes with black pupils and white around them.

"Giovanna! She's like Tiziano's Venus in Florence, looking right at us. Remember?"

"It's Papa's own Venus." She gazed at it a long time, feeling a new womanhood growing in her. "Papa was one of the great Italian painters."

She looked at all the people studying, admiring, talking about Papa's paintings as if they knew him, or claimed him in some way. He didn't belong just to her. He belonged to Italy. Even this minute, this most important minute of her life so far, she had to share him with strangers. There wasn't anything other than her cuffs to connect her with him. No gift from him. No painting made for her. No day spent together. Not even a single memory. If she had one memory of him, holding her high in the air, or tickling her, or kissing her, that would be something no one else had.

And yet Papa had come to see her in the country just before he died, maybe even on a day when he didn't feel well—she had that, and the letter from his friend telling her so. It wasn't a memory, but for that day, he did belong to her more than to the people around her now. What did they claim anyway? Pride in his paintings maybe, but not love of the man. She knew as a certainty, if he had lived, she would have loved him.

When they came to the paintings of 1918, the year she was born, she found a small sign on the wall introducing Jeanne Hébuterne:

Modigliani had found in this young, slim girl with the widely set eyes and slow gestures a madonna worthy of his brush. He immortalized her in fresh colors, in various outfits, her face a pure oval, her naked shoulders a tender line, lying down or seated, naked and adorably pure, with her orange skin tones against a background of a perfect blue. What a noble character Modigliani must have been.

"Noble! Humph." Margherita was about to say something else when Giovanna looked at her and Aunt Margherita closed her mouth.

Jeanne's long nose and tilted head were everywhere in the room. Jeanne in a blue dress and red bordered scarf. Jeanne in profile with her hair piled up in a cone. Jeanne standing next to a bed. Jeanne sitting sideways on a chair, with aqua eyes and sad, sloping shoulders, and cheeks the colors of a peach. Giovanna wanted to engrave each painting in her mind. *A madonna. Adorably pure.* Beautiful words.

"He must have loved her a lot," Giovanna said.

"Yes, I suppose he did, in his way, painting her so often. They're all so similar."

Her mother on all sides of her, a real woman with reddish brown hair like hers. A hot wave passed over her. She didn't want to leave the last painting, Jeanne in a tall drooping hat. The frame faded and Mother stood before her, away from the wall, in textured blue fabric and round flesh smelling of lavender talcum powder. Mother, coming toward her, reaching for her. *Petite Jeanne. Jolie Jeanne.* I was once inside her body, she thought. She felt me there in the innermost part of her.

Under this last painting a bouquet of peach-colored roses lay on the floor.

"Who do you think did that?"

Margherita smiled. "Even a small hotel with mosquitoes has a concierge who will go out at night."

She wanted to wrap her arms around Auntie right there, but something held her back: her mother on all sides of her looking at her daughter hug another woman. Instead, she just squeezed Aunt Margherita's arm, and read the next card on the wall.

In despair, Jeanne Hébuterne leapt from a five-story window of her family's home just before dawn of the second day after Modigliani's death. Her private services made use of some of the flowers left over from Modigliani's well-attended funeral the day before. She was twenty-one. She left a daughter, Jeanne Modigliani, fourteen months old. Within a week she would have had another child.

The paintings quivered and spun. She felt faint, saw only blotches of color, felt like she was falling, a long, heart-stopping plunge. Auntie caught her and folded her in her arms. A new feeling, a kind of welcome, like landing in a plump cushion of bird's down. She cried, as softly as she could, against Margherita's big, comfortable breast. She could not remember Aunt Margherita ever holding her before. Auntie knew, had known all along, that last cruel act of her mother, and had tried to save her from knowing.

Her stomach cramped. She would have had a sister, or brother. Too much. It was too much.

"She was distraught, Giovanna. And somewhat imbalanced, I have to say. She loved your father too much to go on living."

"No. She did what he told her to. Knowing that she was pregnant, he said that! And I thought I loved him!"

Standing in the wind on the cobblestone sidewalk in front of number 5, rue Amyot, next to a sparsely supplied greengrocer's shop, she looked up to the fifth floor. Only a narrow balcony. The wrought-iron railing waist-high. She shuddered. A person had to be determined.

She hugged her ribs, burrowing her gloved hands up opposite sleeves, and waited. A boy bolted out the door, and she caught it before it closed. The first flight of stairs was carpeted with a dark red runner. The rest were bare wood. She smelled garlic cooking on the third, and heard radio war news on the fourth. "Italy joins war with Germany, invades Albania. Thousands die." Her hand went up to her mouth to stifle her gasp. Would Italy invade France next? Her heart would not slow down as she climbed the last flight of stairs. She pressed the buzzer.

A thin man opened the door a hand's breadth and gripped its edge.

"Pardon me for bothering you, but are you André Hébuterne? The brother of Jeanne Hébuterne?"

"I don't answer any questions." He started to shut the door.

"I am Giovanna Modigliani. Jeanne Modigliani."

He straightened his posture. She straightened hers while his eyes picked over her coldly, from the features of her face down to her worn shoes. She felt her illegitimacy more sharply than ever.

"I knew there would be a day when you'd come."

"I knew I'd come sometime too."

He allowed her to enter two steps, but didn't invite her to sit down in the small parlor cluttered with books and magazines. Over his shoulder she could see on top of an upright piano a violin case next to a thin bronze figurine of a woman. Her?

"You have her hair," he said, a little more softly.

All of her rehearsed courtesies vanished. "What can you tell me about . . . how it happened?"

She waited. His eyes seemed to look inward.

"I stopped her three times that night. I knew she would unless I watched her." His voice leapt to a higher pitch. "I tried to find the right thing to say. Tried to stay awake until the danger passed." His forehead lines deepened and he turned away. "The scraping of the window woke me. Rain always made it stick. I rushed." His voice quavered with ash gray guilt. "Too late."

"It wasn't your fault."

"I gathered her up before my mother would see her. Wheeled her away in a grocer's wooden handcart to his studio. Imagine it. All the way down boulevard du Montparnasse." He shook himself violently, took out a crumpled handkerchief, and wiped his nose. The lines around his narrow eyes tightened. "My sister would not have killed herself if he had married her."

She reached for the doorframe, and it was all she could do to keep standing in front of him.

The man, her own uncle, moistened his lips, as though relishing what he would say next. "Our father, you see, was unsympathetic. And shamed."

"Apparently there were documents to obtain in order for such a marriage—"

"They could have been purchased," he said curtly. "There were ways."

She gave him time, wanting any shred of information, hurtful or not. "Anything else?"

"She played the violin."

"I didn't know."

"Bach was her favorite."

She nodded, grateful, knowing she would invent a memory of that. She drew in a breath of air just exhaled by him, her mother's brother, to say the words forming recklessly in her mind: "Can you tell me one thing? The last thing he said to her, did it . . . did it *make* her do it?"

He made a wheezing sound, inhaling. "Let's say it invited her. Thoughtlessly. That's all I can say. All I want to say." Irritated, he waved his trembling hand, brushing her off, holding himself in, or back, it seemed, from giving vent to bitterness or condemnation.

She had opened a wound, and felt sorry she had done so. "Thank you. I won't bother you any more."

She turned to go.

"It was selfish of him," he blurted.

"Of her too."

They stood for a long time in a dumb stupor, and it seemed to her, at least she hoped, that he was thinking about her, his own niece.

"What are you going to do if the Germans come?"

"Go home, if I can. Or hide."

He looked alarmed.

"Oh, I didn't come here for that."

"Wait a moment."

He rummaged through a drawer, and handed her a small, bent photo.

Jeanne's half-closed eyes did have that unfocused, unseeing film, as though she couldn't see beyond her narrow love for a man, to summon any love for a child.

Giovanna wanted to ask more, but her uncle grasped the doorknob. "Take it with you. Go."

As she approached the Cimetière du Père-Lachaise on the Right Bank, a light snow began to fall. Sharp dry pellets the size of birdseed stung her cheeks. Bare limbs of ash trees stretched upward as though in supplication. For what? Peace? Paris had given her no peace. Nor had André Hébuterne.

Numb, not just from cold, she knocked at the concierge's cottage just inside the gate, and heard, *"Entrez."* Inside, a one-armed man sitting behind a chessboard struggled to pin a gray muffler around his hanging stump of an arm. The first war, no doubt. Wounded in action. She didn't want to look closely. It would be ugly. She pretended not to notice, but the cloth wouldn't stay in place.

Twenty years he'd had to struggle since his war. Twenty winters of struggling to wrap his arm. The sock that had been around Geneviève's neck would be better for him; his muffler better for her.

"May I help?" He grunted his assent, and she took off her gloves. His cold flesh was flaccid, like an eel. She wound the scarf and pinned the end in place.

"Can you direct me to the Jewish section?"

"Second sector. Ninety-sixth division." He gave her a map. She didn't even know how to hold it. He took it from her and set it the right way in her hand. *"Allez, allez,"* he said, pointing the way and waving her out, impatient to close the door against the cold.

She dropped a fifty-centime coin into his ashtray, more than she could afford.

She walked quickly down Allée Principale, trying to avoid muddy places. Snow would cover the inscriptions soon. She passed elaborate Greek sculptures streaked black with soot, Gothic spires above ornate tombs, angels with snow collecting in their curls. She shivered. It was a grim city of the dead.

She came to an iron sign which read *Partie réservée au culte Israélite*. Row after row of flat, plain tombs, hardly a foot above the ground, in no apparent order, left little room to walk between them. In an area where they seemed newer, she found his, *Amedeo Modigliani, pittore giunse alla gloria*. She brushed snow off the granite, feeling a cold colder than the air through her gloves. She let the pellets remain in the letters. Inscribed below his dates on the same tomb were the words, *Jeanne Hébuterne, La compagna di Amedeo Modigliani devota fino all' estremo sacrificio*.

"You got what you wanted, Father."

And Jeanne. For her to throw her life away, and her baby's . . . Ever since the exhibition, from the moment she'd fallen into Aunt Margherita's arms, she had struggled to make the act seem noble. But it wasn't. She could tell, even André Hébuterne didn't think so. In this, her uncle and her aunt would agree.

Papa threw his life away too, only more slowly. Life was so cheap to them that they flung it away, while others were struggling in battlefields, then and now, for one more day of it. Neither of them considered the injuries they caused in others' lives. They were without conscience. Didn't their own war teach them anything?

No, she didn't have memories. She would never have memories of her own. Memories would never make her parents hers. Instead, she had imaginings—of his suffering, what Nonna called his turbulent soul, and Jeanne's suffering, and Margherita's and Nonna's. André suffered too, tormented by memory, and so did the concierge of the city of the dead, and Geneviève standing on that cold corner day after day, year after year—and though she hadn't recognized her imaginings as offering any recompense until now, they had enlarged her soul and stiffened her backbone. That was what she had. And that, not love, was what would serve her in the uncertain days ahead.

She let the snow collect until the letters filled in and the tomb was covered cleanly, until all that lay before her was a smooth rectangular plain, a patch of the earth not even marked with their having been here.

Interlude

The Adventures of Bernardo and Salvatore, or, The Cure: A Tale

On long summer evenings in the garden of the *osteria*, the old villagers of Pienza gather to tell the tales of old. Never does such an evening go by without their recounting the story of how Salvatore cured his friend Bernardo. No sooner does someone say that it happened a long time ago than Guido, the village tax collector who is always a stickler for truth, interjects, "It was sometime in the 1600s, two generations into the century."

The first teller resumes, saying that Bernardo, the bachelor cobbler, had a scare, which meant that his friend, Salvatore, who made the best *pecorino* cheese in five hill towns, had a scare too. That is the way between Tuscans. In spite of his body being as sturdy as a cask of Tuscan wine, Bernardo was sick, but he knew it wasn't any old sickness lasting a week, or the plague, lasting three horrible days. It had started in his heart as he worked at his bench, and then went to his head, pounding behind his eyeballs. Salvatore's wife, Bianca, told him to go to bed. She brought him soup, she brought him purgatives of buckthorn and rhubarb, she made a mustard poultice and applied it over his heart. Nothing helped.

"He lay abed three weeks," Guido adds at this point in the telling.

"I am dying," Bernardo finally told his friend.

"You will do no such thing," Salvatore said. "I'll be needing new boots soon, and then where am I to get them?"

From his bed, Bernardo gazed at his workbench with a pitiful look. The dimple in his hairless chin quivered in a way that had annoyed Salvatore ever since they were boys. "And who am I to play *un gioco di carte* with?"

"Ten years and you haven't beaten me yet. What are you waiting for? If you're ever going to do it, you'd better hurry up about it."

"What makes you think you're dying?"

"A man knows such things. There's nothing inside me but ache. Sometimes it's my heart, sometimes my belly, sometimes my head. I've got no energy. There's nothing ahead for me."

They had this conversation every day—"for three weeks," Guido butts in—until Bernardo said, "There are two things I want to do before I die."

"*Madre di Dio,* what are they? Quick, man, I have sheep to ruddle."

"I want to have a religious experience so I'll know . . . you know."

"No, I don't know."

"What's wrong with you? Don't you have a brain in your head? So I'll know what it'll be like in Heaven."

"Assuming, of course . . ." Salvatore rolled his eyes upward, and then dropped his head and looked at the ground.

"And I want to see the world's great art."

"Phuff. You expect it to come to you?"

Bernardo's round face sagged at that, and there was real pain in his eyes. "No. That's just it. How can I?"

Later that day Salvatore thought about Bernardo's dilemma as he went about grinding the red ocher to mark his sheep. Bernardo had never been farther than Montepulciano on market day. Neither had he. Weren't Pienza and Montepulciano beautiful enough? And the Madonna painted behind the altar of the church they had been christened in? And her statue with *Gesù bambino* just inside the door? And how the light from the votive candles made her look so beautiful and so sad? Wasn't the sight of cypress trees along the stream coming down from the hill all golden with wheat and his sheep bleating in the valley below—wasn't that more beautiful than a painting? Wasn't there beauty in his ewes' eyes, dark with fear and deep with trust at their first lambing?

He'd seen that same dark-with-fear look in Bernardo's eyes lately. A look of need. It was a horrible thing, to die without having done the one thing in life you wanted to do most. Taking long, slow strides, Salvatore walked in circles around his sheepfold, thinking that if Bernardo had something ahead of him, and something to do . . .

Suddenly thunder cracked the sky. He looked up and saw clear blue. Not a cloud anywhere. His sheep did not bleat in a frenzy as they always did at thunder. He scratched his forehead. Another clap of thunder roared, louder and closer. The Idea burst forth in Salvatore's head: What Bernardo is longing for before he dies will actually make him live!

He climbed the hill to Bernardo's house after the evening milking and said, "Here's what. After olive-picking, I'll go with you to Florence or to Rome, wherever you want, but I'll need new boots to make the journey."

Bernardo raised up on his elbows, which made his belly jiggle. "You crazy man. How can I make boots when I'm sick unto death? And why after olive-picking? I may not live that long."

"You will. I know it. I have an Idea."

"An Idea, maybe, but you have no olive trees to pick."

"I'll hire out to old man Granacci. He can't do his picking any more. He gets dizzy and falls. Then we'll have enough money to go."

Here, after a quick swallow of wine, Guido interrupts. "According to the tax records of Pienza, Granacci paid a picker eighteen lire a season."

Salvatore could see The Idea moving around behind Bernardo's eyes.

"Have you told Bianca?"

"Yes. She agrees."

He went home that evening and asked her, "Do you think a man has an obligation to do anything he can to save a friend's life?"

She eyed him warily, feeling a trap was about to be sprung. She set down his wooden bowl of hot *busecca* so roughly that it splashed his hand.

"Ai!" He dried his hand on his pant leg. "Well?"

"Well, yes. Eat your supper."

He told her of The Idea. "Humph," she said, and went to bed.

In the morning she said, "If he shows any sign of getting better, tell him I'll make him a new suit of clothes. He can't go to Rome or Florence in those rags he wears."

Salvatore didn't visit his friend for three days. Three days was all he was going to give him to show a sign that The Idea would work A Cure. In the meantime, he found Granacci in his barn repairing his olive press and told him The Idea to cure Bernardo.

Granacci scowled and let a winding key fall to the ground. "It's foolish to go off in search of the world's great art."

"Why?"

"It's not outside." Granacci pointed to his heart. "It's here."

This worried Salvatore, because he respected the old man.

And because Granacci was a Tuscan, Granacci worried for Bernardo too.

"Do you really think going somewhere to see art is a cure?"

"Yes, I do. It's doing something," said Salvatore.

"Hmm. There's plenty of art in churches, but how are you going to get into *palazzi* and villas? Those cardinals and magnificos don't just stand in their doorways saying to every passing bumpkin, 'You want to see some great art? Come right in.' "

"But I've promised Bernardo."

The Problem presented itself.

"You'd better know how you're going to wheedle your way in before you go off like a headless chicken. And you'd better take Pellegrina."

As if a donkey was going to solve The Problem.

Salvatore thought about it, "for three days," Guido declares, holding up three fingers. Salvatore couldn't sleep, he thought about it so much. He was thinking about it when he was milking Fleecia, his eldest, wisest ewe. She knew he was thinking about something very important because his hand just stopped working. Fleecia looked at him and he was sure she said with her dark, sympathetic eyes, Let me help.

Phuff! What could a sheep *or* a donkey do?

On the fourth day Salvatore still didn't have a solution. He would have to tell Bernardo it was only a fool's dream. He ducked into Bernardo's doorway.

"You are a good friend," Bernardo said before Salvatore could say a word. "The finest friend a man could have." He got up out of bed and laid a hide on the floor. "Put your foot here," he said and pointed with his finger that looked like a boar sausage, and drew around Salvatore's foot with a sharpened piece of charcoal.

Salvatore knew—now he'd *have* to find A Solution.

As the grapevines turned gold and red, Bernardo worked on softening the leather for his friend's boots, a little every day before going back to bed. Lying there one afternoon, drumming his fingers on his belly as though he were testing a wine cask, he thought of the beauties he might see—paintings and sculptures, villas and cathedrals, fountains in grand piazzas.

At this point, any of the villagers listening at the *osteria* who have had the good fortune of visiting Rome or Florence or even Siena murmur about beautiful things they've seen. "It feeds a person's soul, such heavenly things men have made," a grandmother says.

And now, because of his good friend, Bernardo was going to see such things with his own eyes. He got up out of bed the second time that day and worked a little more on the boots. Long, narrow feet, his friend had. Long enough to stretch to Florence *or* Rome.

Salvatore took five wheels of *pecorino* to market in Montepulciano and while Bianca was buying muslin and a new needle, and while he sold all five cheeses, he thought of Fleecia, his wisest ewe, wanting to help. He hurried home to the sheepfold for the evening milking. He looked into Fleecia's eyes again and she nuzzled him in the stomach. She looked up at him and said with her wise eyes, I told you I can help. I'll give you milk so sweet that you will make cheese so fine that people will do anything to taste it.

The Solution crept into his brain. He hummed a tune of rejoicing as he milked the other ewes, taking care to keep Fleecia's milk separate.

In November, when Bernardo heard the *chuk, chuk, chuk* sound of the olive pickers from the valley below, he threw his blanket over his shoulders and walked downhill to Granacci's orchard, not knowing how he'd get back up. There was Salvatore, lanky and awkward, wielding Granacci's wooden picker's staff, with his head tipped back looking up, and a leaf caught in his beard. Wheezing, all Bernardo could do was to sit in Granacci's cart and watch. A few days later, Bernardo came to help for half an hour. He worked slowly, resting after each branch, and complaining of his neck aching.

"That's nothing compared to Michelangelo's neck ache every day for years painting a ceiling," Salvatore said. "Sometimes a person has to suffer for great art."

Bernardo picked another branch without complaint, then lay on the ground to rest. "How will we know where to go?" he asked. "Florence or Rome?"

Salvatore didn't know. Every Tuscan, whether he'd been to Florence or not, was proud of the great art in the Tuscan capital, but Rome had the Vatican. "Something will tell us. Maybe your religious experience will tell us."

They waited through the winter, watching for a sign. Salvatore gazed into Fleecia's wise eyes every evening, hoping she would tell him, but on this question of direction, she was silent. Bernardo grew stronger and finished the boots. One evening, Bianca presented him with the pants and shirt, and Bernardo gave Salvatore the brown boots, and at supper three pairs of eyes looked aglow in the rushlight.

They drank wine and Bernardo raised his glass and said, "We will see the pope too."

"And if we go to Florence?"

Bernardo shrugged. "Eh. We will see the bishop."

One fine morning—so fine that the orange sun peeked over the Tuscan hills early to see the events in Pienza, so the villagers say—after lambing and weaning, Salvatore bade his sheep goodbye, and gave a special tap on the head to Fleecia, who seemed to smile at him. This time her eyes said to him, Don't forget me when you're gone. In the piazza he and Bianca met Bernardo wearing his new suit of clothes. Bernardo's grin made mountains of his cheeks. Granacci presented Salvatore with a small bag of coins for the olive-picking.

"Twenty, to be exact," Guido explains. "Because the tax collector was a Tuscan, he had charged every villager seven piasters more on their taxes that year, and gave it to Granacci to give to Salvatore." Guido winks, thinking himself the hero, or at least the descendant of the hero who made the journey happen.

Granacci also handed over Pellegrina's reins to Salvatore, who hummed the song of rejoicing as he wrapped in straw and sackcloth two of the biggest wheels of *pecorino* the villagers had ever seen, and wedged them into Pellegrina's two canvas saddlebags, giving each one a good-luck pat.

"When in Rome, it's as good as coin," he said.

"Good? Good and ripe by the time you get there," Bianca said, shaking her head at her fool of a husband.

Salvatore looked down at his new boots. If he rode the donkey first, they'd stay clean longer. He looked at Bernardo, more ample in front and in the rear than necessary, and chuckled because Bernardo was looking at Pellegrina like a heartsick lover. Pellegrina was looking from one to the other of them and saying a little prayer that it would be the thin one to climb on. No such luck. Salvatore motioned for Bernardo to climb up.

Bianca kissed them both and made the sign of the cross.

"May the Holy Virgin permit you to find whatever it is you're looking for," Granacci said and slapped Pellegrina on the rump to start her off. Everyone in the village turned out to wave their hats in the air, yelling out as they passed, "Good luck! Good journey!" and the bellringer climbed the bell tower and kept up the ringing until they descended the hill and could hear it no longer.

At Chiusi, the village where they'd have to turn north to Florence or south to Rome, they learned at an inn that a bridge on the road north had washed out.

"*Bene.* For us, all roads lead to Rome," Bernardo said.

"That means you'll have your religious experience in the holy city," Salvatore said. "What could be better?" They savored their last full-bodied wine from Tuscan sangiovese grapes before they entered Umbria to taste its different vintages.

In the morning they turned south, and traveled many days, trading off turns riding Pellegrina every couple of hours without comment, because that is the way with Tuscans. Salvatore worried about Bernardo feeling sick, but Bernardo didn't talk about it as much as he had in Pienza, and each day they were able to travel a little longer before he couldn't go any farther and had to stop at an inn for the night. "We're going to Rome to see the world's greatest art," Bernardo said to every taverner or his wife or daughter, and their eyes widened, and the closer the travelers came to Rome, the more they learned about what to see.

In one tavern, when Salvatore gave the taverner's wife a wedge of cheese, she put it to her nose. Her eyes opened wide. "Santa Maria! *Pecorino* from the Lord's own table in Heaven!" She said her brother was groundsman at the Villa Farnesina on the banks of the Tiber in Rome. If they would take this embroidery for his wife, she said— "giving Salvatore three folded handkerchiefs," Guido adds—her brother would show them the paintings there. They agreed heartily.

Salvatore watched Bernardo looking over the taverner's daughter. "That's not your religious experience," he said and cuffed him on the jaw. "And she can't be had for a cheese."

Bernardo's wide nose flared, and the dimple in his fleshy chin quivered in that pitiful way, and in that instant Salvatore realized part of The Problem behind his bachelor friend's sickness.

Finally, Porta del Popolo, the northern gate to the city, came into view, and beyond it, a large oval piazza, a sign of the grandness to come. They entered the Church of Santa Maria del Popolo to give thanks for having arrived without misfortune. In a side chapel they saw their first painting. A priest told them it was Caravaggio's

Conversion of Saint Paul. Bernardo looked at Salvatore and made a face. Saint Paul was sprawled on the ground, having fallen off his horse in his moment of enlightenment, and the huge horse, from edge to edge of the canvas, was headed away from them.

Slowly Salvatore sniffed and made a face too. "The rump of that horse is so close I can smell it."

"I hope that the greatest art of the world will be something more beautiful than the fat ass of a horse," Bernardo said, worried, and because Salvatore was a Tuscan, he worried too.

"I don't feel so good," Bernardo said and then groaned.

This was not what seeing the world's great art was supposed to do. Salvatore let him ride Pellegrina through the city, which had more magnificent buildings and more fine horses and women than they'd ever seen before. Salvatore had to shake Bernardo's foot for him to notice a beautiful girl pouring out a chamber pot at an open window.

"She looks like a painting there in the window, doesn't she?" Salvatore said.

"Huh?"

"Why, man, wake up your senses! We're in Rome!"

Bernardo sniffed a breath of air. "I am." He nearly careened off the donkey and Salvatore had to push him back up.

Bernardo learned quickly. Later that day, Salvatore had to poke him in the stomach so he wouldn't miss a statue while they were passing three women with their skirts hiked up washing clothes in a fountain. Bernardo began to like asking questions, especially of women with their skirts hiked up, and eventually they found the Villa Farnesina. The groundskeeper accepted the handkerchiefs for his wife, and Bernardo explained why they had come.

"You sound like Tuscans. Tell anyone here who asks that you're fresco plasterers come from Florence. Follow me."

He showed them a fresco of a naked woman riding on a shell pulled by dolphins, a man coming up from the sea grabbing another naked woman, and sea creatures playing love games under a sky of cupids.

"Now, this is more like it," Bernardo murmured, his eyes as round as his belly.

Salvatore nudged Bernardo in the belly. "Look at her you-know-what."

Bernardo slapped Salvatore's hand. "I see. I see. What do you take me for? A dolt?"

"Raphael painted it," the groundsman said. "The woman's Galatea."

"*Si,* of course," said Salvatore, nodding, but he'd never heard of Galatea. "*Che bella,*" he said, and felt a movement in his loins he'd only felt before at the thought of Bianca. He pressed against it with his hat. That colors on a wall could make him churn so—he was surprised at the power of it. He glanced sideways at Bernardo, who held his hat in front of him also.

Embarrassed, Bernardo dismissed the painting with a wave of his hand. "Nobody can ride on a shell," he said.

"That's not the point. Beauty's the point," Salvatore said.

As the groundsman took them through the villa, they gaped at other paintings, fine furniture, and sculptures of Roman heroes and nubile women. He told them where to stay—an *osteria* with a stable called Inn of the Three Jackasses near Saint Peter's Basilica—how to get there, and what to see in the city. "You'll have to have more than a handkerchief to give the brethren in order to see what you came for."

"We do!" Salvatore said, and cut him a wedge of *pecorino.*

The next morning, they went into every church they saw, saving the best for last, Saint Peter's Basilica. The huge space inside stunned them. Salvatore dropped a coin into a friar's upturned hand and he led them, shuffling in his sandals, on a circuit of the church, up the left side, down the right, explaining the mosaics, the monuments and tombs, the statue of Saint Peter, and the great bronze altar canopy of Bernini, ending at Michelangelo's grieving Mary with the crucified Christ on her lap.

They stared, unable to move.

"How he can make a dead man beautiful and a grieving woman peaceful," Salvatore marveled.

"It's not just the dead man who is beautiful," Bernardo said dreamily.

Awe filled Bernardo's belly and prickled Salvatore's spine.

"Where is the Cappella Sistina?" Salvatore asked the friar.

"Prohibited. It's the pope's private chapel."

"We have come far," Salvatore said.

"On one donkey," Bernardo added, holding up one pudgy forefinger.

The friar looked them up and down, especially Bernardo, and his holy eyes opened wide, and his thick bottom lip protruded.

Salvatore shook his bag of coins.

"Too much for one day. Go at dawn." He told them where to wait for another friar. "Instead, today go to the other San Pietro, the smaller one, San Pietro in Vincoli, to see Michelangelo's Moses."

They got lost in narrow, crooked streets, but after Bernardo asked two Roman beauties, they found it. The church was small enough that they spotted the huge marble Moses immediately. With his muscles bulging like a blacksmith, and the raised veins of his hands following the veins in the stone, Moses glared in holy rage at the Israelites' worship of idols. Salvatore thought he was about to bellow a curse and hurl a thunderbolt right at them.

"*Terribilità*," Bernardo whispered, sounding genuinely frightened. "What we felt—you know, in front of that marble Madonna and Christ from the Cross—was that worshipping an idol?"

Salvatore raised his shoulders, not knowing. "Such a thing," Salvatore said. "It's only stone. This Moses is a thing made from the artist's mind, just like a boot is, Bernardo. You think it first, then you make it."

A boot. Just like a boot, he told himself. That made Bernardo feel better than he'd felt in a year.

Soon after dawn the next morning they found a different friar at the gate in the wall surrounding the Pope's residence. "My friend is certain that he will have a religious experience if he can only stand in the Cappella Sistina," Salvatore said. "You wouldn't deny a man a religious experience, would you? That's close to heresy for a friar. Enough to shame your order *and* endanger your immortal soul."

Salvatore could see the friar's Adam's apple rise and fall. Salvatore pressed into the man's hand the largest of old man Granacci's coins, pressed it hard so the friar would feel its size.

"You can tell anybody that we're Florentine fresco plasterers come to inspect for cracks," Bernardo said hopefully.

"Come with me, but don't make a sound."

They shuffled quickly through corridors and the friar opened a plain wooden door into an enormous, high-ceilinged room, the walls and ceiling painted with hundreds of figures. Their eyes seized on one panel after another, each telling a story. A drunken Noah. The flood. The creation of man with God and Adam nearly touching their outstretched arms. Temptation in the Garden of Eden. Banishment from the Garden. They bent back their necks and walked the length of the room. Salvatore became dizzy. Bernardo went weak in the knees.

Bernardo walked back to stand again under God sparking life into Adam with a touch of the divine finger. He saw himself there, on the cloud, listless, ready to die, then touched and brought to life again by that powerful, white-bearded giant with the wise, kind face.

Overcome with gratitude, he wept in silence, and felt a strange pleasure in his weeping. The ache in his heart lessened. He was seeing
the greatest of the world's great frescoes, yes, but more than that. He
was seeing the intention of God Himself.

Salvatore noticed that the friar was pacing, so he asked him a
question to keep him occupied: Who painted all these wall scenes
from the lives of Jesus and Moses? The friar reeled off a string
of names: Botticelli, Ghirlandaio, Perugino. Salvatore looked at
the huge and horrible Last Judgment with the grotesque agonies
in Hell, and knew that Bernardo had better not see it. It was too
fearsome.

He walked toward Bernardo but stopped when he saw that his
friend was having his religious experience. Salvatore looked up to see
what made Bernardo weep, and noticed this time a young woman
nestled under God's arm. Just then Bernardo turned toward the Last
Judgment wall.

"It's Eve," Salvatore said, to draw his attention back to the ceiling. "Up there with God." He pointed above them.

"It's Mary," Bernardo said, looking up again.

"Eve, yet to be created," Salvatore said.

"Where's your brain, man? It's Mary, the Holy Virgin."

"It's Eve, the reason for Adam's fall. Look at the next panel, the
creation of Eve."

"What are you? An idiot? It's the blessed Virgin with the holy
bambino at her knee."

Their voices echoed in the large space, and the friar accosted
them, waving his arms in panic, and shooed them to the door. Salvatore wouldn't cross the threshold, so Bernardo didn't either.

"Show us something else," Salvatore said, and let him see another coin.

"No, I cannot."

Salvatore let one coin fall on another in his palm.

"What do you take me for? A man of God can't be bought with coin."

"Ah! Not with coin," Salvatore said, reached in his sack, and cut a quarter wheel of *pecorino*. As soon as he unwrapped it, the whole Cappella Sistina smelled like *pecorino*. "The finest in all of Tuscany." Salvatore remembered Fleecia's last look. "From a blessed sheep named Fleecia, the direct descendant of a lamb present at the birth of our Lord and Savior in Bethlehem."

The friar's eyes nearly popped out of his head. *"Madre di Dio e tutti gli angeli del Paradiso!"* He crossed himself.

Salvatore passed the cheese under the friar's nose. The man of God sniffed and screwed up his face so that the mole above his upper lip touched his nose. *"Allora,* perhaps a little peek at the Residence of His Holiness."

The friar hurried them through a long corridor painted with maps. Pieces of sculpture passed quickly beside them. The friar opened a door. "Be quick about it. And don't talk."

Before them stretched an enormous fresco, the size of five donkeys head to tail. In it, about fifty figures stood or sat in groups conversing under a wide arch, on steps and in alcoves under a painted ceiling.

"Philosophers," the friar whispered. "By Raphael, the master of idealism."

They heard deep voices from the next room, soft at first, then thunderous, saying, *"Formaggio, formaggio!"* Immediately the friar hustled them all the way out onto the street.

"In that painting, each one was talking or listening or writing or figuring," Salvatore said, puzzling it out. "They were debating, exchanging ideas. Exchanging ideas, Bernardo. What a noble thing."

"There were too many people in it. I didn't know where to look."

"That's only because we were rushed. It's a magnificent painting. How long do you think it took him to do it?"

"*Che stupidata.* How long does it take to make a fine boot? Two weeks to make it. Ten years to learn how."

The old villagers of Pienza shake their heads in amusement when they relate The Solution, how Bernardo and Salvatore got inside the Pope's apartments, the great villas and *palazzi* of the cardinals, with wedges of Fleecia's "holy" cheese. They were blocked sometimes, and once Bernardo was kicked in the ass, but until their cheese ran out, they saw their fill of the world's greatest art.

At the Inn of the Three Jackasses on their last night in Rome, wine warmed them and made them imagine again, in the glimmer of a tallow dip, all that they had seen. Salvatore's mind was reeling. Bernardo's soul felt rich and full. They felt intoxicated in a way they'd never been.

"Life is good, eh, Salvatore, to see what we have seen?"

"Just think when we tell Granacci and Bianca and everyone at home."

"The smoothness of Bernini's marble," Bernardo said. "Months of polishing."

"Slick as Granacci's olive oil on a plate," Salvatore said.

"Beautifully shaped," Bernardo murmured, thinking of two of Bernini's sculptures in Cardinal Borghese's villa—Daphne turning into a tree the moment Apollo grabbed her, and Proserpina's thigh indented by Pluto's grip just as if it were flesh. "Round as our sangiovese grapes," he said.

"Smooth as our Tuscan wine," Salvatore said.

"Bernini's Daphne, don't you think Bianca's niece looks like her?" Bernardo made a point not to look at Salvatore when he asked this.

"Ah, yes, my friend. She's just come of age too." He turned away so Bernardo wouldn't see his smile. "What is beauty?" he asked, thinking that would be a question Raphael's philosophers might ask.

"Beauty is what brings me pleasure here." Bernardo pointed to his eye. "Or here." He pointed to his heart.

"What about here?" Salvatore pointed to his head. "Or here?" He pointed to himself beneath the table.

Bernardo scowled in puzzlement. All four were the places he had ached. Could beauty be felt in so many ways?

And because they were Tuscans, they eventually talked of love. "What do you love more? Sculpture or paintings?" Salvatore asked.

"Where's your head, man, to ask such a thing? Can a man answer when some fool asks him which child he loves more?"

"What do you think those paintings are worth, just what we saw yesterday?"

Bernardo rolled his eyes. "They're not things that cost like a cart full of cheese. They're things that do the invisible. You know, what they do inside you. To make you better."

"Feel better?" Salvatore asked, hopeful that The Cure was working.

"Not only that. To be better too. A better man." He finished off the wine in his glass. "It was Mary there on the ceiling," he said, having trouble getting his tongue to work.

Salvatore let him say it even though he was wrong. After all, he was the best friend a man could have.

The tavern girl brought them another jug of wine, and trailed her fingers along the back of Bernardo's neck. Bernardo snapped his head around to see her hips sway and her breasts move beneath her blouse. "That's great art too, my friend."

"You've already had your religious experience, remember?" But because he was a Tuscan, Salvatore chuckled and let him imagine, though he preferred that Bernardo imagine his wife's niece. Bernardo poured himself another glass, which was unfortunate for his amorous fantasy because it was just enough to make him limp.

"So who was the greatest artist who ever lived?" Salvatore asked.

"Not Caravaggio, painter of a horse's ass." They had a good laugh at how worried they'd been.

They slept the next morning, Sunday, "until the ringing of twelve chimes," Guido says, nudging the old man next to him who had fallen asleep during the telling.

Salvatore nudged Bernardo with a strong kick on his straw mattress. Bernardo's flesh jiggled.

"Eh, Bernardo, wake up. We missed the blessing of the Pope."

Bernardo drew his new shirt over his head to keep out the light, and continued snoring.

By midafternoon, Salvatore had roused Bernardo, and they passed under Porta del Popolo heading north, squinting against the sun as it beat on their throbbing heads.

A few hours out into the country, Bernardo got off the donkey and gestured for Salvatore to get on.

"I have seven male sheep, Bernardo."

"So?"

"So I had always thought I would name them after the disciples when my flock grew to twelve, but no. I have names for them now." He counted on his fingers. "Michelangelo, Bernini, Ghirlandaio, Perugino, Botticelli. The eldest, the prettiest one, will be Raphael, and the fat-assed one I'll call Caravaggio."

"So which one is named for the greatest artist in all the world?" Bernardo asked.

Salvatore swung his leg up over the donkey's ass. "Raphael, of course."

"Puh. Where were your eyes, man?"

They rode in contemplation for a while until Salvatore said, "Raphael painted like an angel. Any fool can see that."

"So did Michelangelo. He even has *angel* in his name."

"Raphael *is* an angel!"

"Haven't you got a brain in your head? Michelangelo is greater. Didn't you see the agony on Adam's face when he's leaving the Garden? His people *feel*."

"He learned it from Raphael," Salvatore said smugly and slid down off Pellegrina and handed Bernardo the reins.

"You mean Raphael learned it from Michelangelo." Bernardo climbed on.

They passed through a village, and watered the donkey at a stream on the other side.

"Raphael painted that beautiful woman—Galatea," Salvatore said.

"So did Michelangelo paint beautiful women. Eve and Mary, for example."

"Raphael can make a man turn to butter out of love for beauty."

"Michelangelo can make a man quiver in his soul." Bernardo spat in the road. "And Michelangelo was a sculptor too, and sculpting is a higher art. Any Tuscan knows that."

"How can you say such a thing?" Salvatore said in an offended tone.

"Because a sculptor makes a man, like God making man." Bernardo held out his open palm, as though he were cupping something solid. "Just like He makes olive trees and grapes. Just like a man makes a boot." Pleased with himself, he sat tall on the donkey and looked straight ahead over the donkey's bobbing head for a long time.

"But to make a man feel like there's flesh and blood and a beating heart on a flat wall, that's the highest genius of all," Salvatore said.

"Spreading paint is easier than hammering stone. It doesn't ask as much of a man."

"That's ridiculous."

"It's easier on the back," Bernardo said scornfully, looking down at Salvatore walking in the road. His long ears looked just like the ass's ears.

"Then who's better between Bernini and Michelangelo?"

"Michelangelo," Bernardo snapped.

"I say Bernini."

"You've got pebbles for eyes."

"You've got pudding for a brain."

"Eh, *porca miseria.*" Bernardo stretched up and yanked a thin branch from a tree and switched Pellegrina with it until she trotted ahead, leaving Salvatore in the dust.

Salvatore looked at the two big asses' asses ahead of him. He pulled up a stalk of dried grass from the side of the road and broke it in two, one longer than the other. "Wait ahead, you mongrel." He caught up and held up to Bernardo the two straws, their ends even with each other so that they appeared to be the same length, and grinned. "You choose the long one, then Michelangelo is the greatest. He's got the longest name. You choose the short one and Bernini is."

Bernardo snorted and made his choice, which turned out to be the shortest. "For today." He shook it and let it blow away. "For today only." He got down off Pellegrina and thumped Salvatore on his chest so he would get on. "Sometime, when the bridge to Florence is repaired, we'll decide for all time."

Salvatore smiled. The Cure had worked.

Now

The Things He Didn't Know

They'd come to Christmas on the Promenade in Balboa Park because she wanted to, which was okay with him. He wanted to please her, and the museums were free tonight. Every hundred feet or so there were carolers in old-fashioned clothes, or bagpipers, or here now, as they were walking, a brass band.

"Steve, wait! They're playing 'Good King Wenceslas,' " Kathy said.

How did she know that? He stopped and she looked up at him with such a bright, happy smile it made him want to grab her right then. Just like a storybook character in that Red Riding Hood cape and black beret. Not every woman would wear something like that. He hadn't bought her a Christmas present yet. If he gave her a ring after knowing her only five months, that'd bowl her over and show he had balls—if he really intended what a ring meant. If he watched himself, if he was careful, this Christmas might prove to be the best of his adult life. If he screwed up, it might be his worst.

Next to him a little kid riding on his dad's shoulders beat on the man's head in time to the oom-pah of the tuba. The man put up with it. Amazing. The wife reached up to make him quit, and the boy grabbed his dad's chin. Steve imagined himself and Kathy with a kid. He could even see himself letting a kid, their kid, beat a tuba rhythm on his head.

He had met her the summer before on the beach where a person's background wasn't obvious by the clothes a person wore. Otherwise, he probably wouldn't have tried to talk to her. Nothing had kept him from looking, though. She was all legs wading in the shallow water in a purple bikini. When a wave was about to soak her blanket, he ran over and dragged it out of reach. It was only later, after they walked the beach and were eating dinner in a Mexican restaurant a couple blocks away, that he knew he was outclassed. He was doing construction work, and she, well, she had some kind of art history degree and worked for a magazine.

"I'm a hands-on kind of guy," he'd said, thinking for an instant of the exact framing job he'd done on a condo complex that week. "A guy with cracked fingers and a sore back who really works for a living. Well, not that you don't."

He felt like a jerk for saying that until she said, "The age of commensurate educations is over." She threw up her hands as if she were tossing off a weight. "Other things are more important."

"Houses have to be built more than paintings painted."

"That wasn't exactly what I meant." She let him sit there and wonder what she *had* meant. Instead of explaining, she'd surprised him by asking, "You know what I like about you?"

"You like how I saved your blanket."

"I like how you listen to me."

He'd listened more than talked only because he didn't know what to say. When he opened his wallet to pay for dinner, a piece of paper fell out, his scribbled notes.

"Girls' names and phone numbers?" Kathy asked.

"Things to do. I'm a list maker, I guess." He flipped it over so she could see.

> Bailey's storm drain
> Dad's fence
> Call Bud about City Heights job
> Pick up blueprints, mud sill bolts, laundry soap

"I can't remember otherwise."

"No? Then you better add this: *Call Kathy.*" She rustled in her bag for a pen.

He wrote it down, *Call Kathy,* drew a line next to it for her phone number, and slid it across the table to her.

Smiling one of those enough-to-make-you-crazy smiles, she wrote the number and put a double box around it.

"Make me a list," she said and smoothed out a paper napkin in front of him.

"Of what?"

"Whatever you want to tell me. Things you *want* to do. Things you haven't done."

"Not now."

But a few days later, he did. Two lists. So he'd have something to show her when he saw her again.

Things I've Never Done:

Gotten my contractor's license

Gone skiing

Drunk cappuccino in some fancy dancy resort

Gotten knocked out in a fight

Dumped a woman

Pretended I was somebody other than who I am

And Things I Have Done:

Pitched a no-hitter against the cross-town rivals

Worked on a fire line in the Big Sur fires for fifteen straight days

Crawled on my belly in the desert behind an automatic weapon

Thought I was going to die

Prayed

When he showed them to her across a table in a coffee shop, she placed her hand on his arm. "My father was a career Army man." Her eyes became moist.

"You must love him a lot."

"I don't remember him much. He rescued me from a tree when I was six. I'd climbed too high and was afraid to come down." She stroked the hair on his arm sideways, just once. "Your arms remind me of his." She balled up her fist and tucked it beneath the table. "He was killed in Vietnam."

"I'm sorry."

"My mom still puts red roses on his grave."

Since then, whenever he came to her apartment, he always brought her a red rose. It was all he knew how to do to show respect for what she'd told him. Now, tonight, there had to be something in one of these booths he could get her, some Christmas tree ornament or a wreath or fancy candle.

He made a detour to the Danish booth for two plates of some kind of round puff pastries and hot cider.

"Oh, abelskivers! I love them," she said. "How'd you know?"

"I didn't. They just looked good."

He tested the drink first so she wouldn't burn her tongue. They listened to four or five carols in the organ pavilion until Kathy said, "There's a lot more to see. Let's go to the Museum of Art."

"Whatever you want." He'd never been in an art museum. He chuckled. "I'll have to add it to my *Haven't Done* list, cross it out, and then add it to my *Have Done* list." On the way he bought a ginger-bread man and aimed its sugar-coated head into Kathy's pretty red mouth.

Inside the museum he looked up at the fancy ceiling and let out a soft whistle of appreciation. "Hell of a lot of work. I wonder whether it's carved wood or molded plaster. Nobody builds like that now." He wondered if the work was done on the ground and then set in place, or actually worked on the ceiling.

Kathy smiled just as though she'd designed it herself. "I want to show you my favorites," she said and tugged at his arm, acting like it was her own house she was showing him. "Let's go into the Nineteenth Century Room."

"It's hard to believe that so many pictures can all be valuable," he said, stopping in front of a painting of a barefoot country girl tending her sheep. The laces on the back of her dress were so real he felt he could pull apart the bow and it would all loosen. What his hands would feel if they could actually roam over the painting—stone to sheep's wool to leaves to fabric to laces to skin. The girl gave him a flirty look over her bare shoulder, as though she were inviting him to follow her, yet the painting was only one moment. What would happen next was left to the imagination. He imagined Kathy in the painting, in the dress, and him unlacing those laces.

"It should be called . . ." He tried to think of something racy.

"Not an important painting." Kathy dismissed it with a wave of her hand.

"Then why is it here?"

"As an example. The French academy was turning out hundreds of paintings like this." She pulled him by the arm toward a scene of two haystacks in a field at sunrise. "Not nearly as important as *this*." She stepped back to show off a small painting of a farmer's field. Her eyes glistened the way he wanted to see them glisten at him. "See how the mauves and greens spread harmony and peace across the landscape?" She hugged her arms and waited, smiling up at him. "Well? What do you think of it?"

The painting had no clues. There weren't even any people in it. Most of it was just sky. He'd say anything she wanted him to, if only he knew what it was. He didn't like being put on the spot.

"Isn't the point just liking it? Enjoyment?"

"Yes, but what I love about this is that it's 1865, twenty-five years before Monet started his famous haystack series, which was the epitome of the Impressionist style, but here he was already beginning to get interested in the properties of light. In a moment that pale sunrise is going to explode into light and color just like the art world was about to do with Impressionism." Her fingers flew apart like birds let out of a cage.

Something seemed cockeyed if a painting had to be talked about before it did what it was supposed to.

She was slipping away, and he had nothing to say. He had to remind her, right now, of their best times, when there was no one to impress and they were naked alone together.

It almost always started as play—with teasing, chasing, ambushing. They were like excited kids who couldn't wait for something they knew would be good. Once she wrapped them both in sheets, and they ate grapes on the floor and drank wine in bowls, all of it leading to sex. Kissing the pulse of her throat, closing his mouth around her nipple, or working his hands up between her legs—the play turned serious, and they rocked on until they exhausted themselves.

He stepped behind her as she looked at the painting, buried his face in her dark hair, and squeezed her shoulders, feeling them lower and give in to him. He whispered, "Picture us there, right by that haystack on the grass. I want to take you down. Right there in the open field. Like peasants."

She nudged him in the stomach gently but didn't move away. Standing close behind her in the crowded gallery, he reminded her with his hands how his fingers felt moving up the back of her thigh underneath her short skirt until she stepped away, trailing her hand behind her, which invited him to do it all over again a few feet away.

He did.

"My place or yours?" she whispered.

"Ours."

The word bursting out of his mouth surprised him. Too many times he'd gotten his hands moving before his mind. He had a sneaking suspicion that it was happening again.

He'd never been this crazy about a woman, never had a girlfriend who wanted him like she did. The closest was the only girl he had dated in high school—Karen, who was beautiful, sophisticated, smart, and deaf. He'd chosen her because he didn't think he could ever have a classy girlfriend who didn't have something a guy would have to ignore or settle for. Karen would be grateful for anyone, he'd thought. And then it got fun, finding ways to communicate with his hands. But when she figured out he was settling for someone flawed, she was gone.

Things I Didn't Know:
> How girls can read your mind
> The difference between love and convenience

Now, in the museum, he followed Kathy upstairs. With her, he wasn't settling for someone flawed. In fact, it was just the opposite. He was amazed that she seemed to be settling for him.

He noticed the woodwork of the balustrade passing smoothly beneath his hand. It had been sanded and polished with great care. They came to a wall of large Italian canal scenes. All those buildings and bridges and boats. He paused to look at them closer.

"I thought you'd like those buildings," she said. "These Venetian paintings served as travel postcards for English aristocracy making the grand tour." She giggled. "Amazing, huh? Bringing home one of these huge paintings as a souvenir?"

"Canaletto! Look," he said. "The guy's named after what he painted."

There was applause coming from another room and she darted ahead. He caught up with her in the crowd and grabbed her hand.

"Let's go to Venice," he said. "See the real thing, not just a painting. For New Year's Eve. A honeymoon."

She pretended to ignore him, but he could tell by the puckering of her lips that she heard. She heard and liked it. He'd chalk that up to *Things I Did Right,* along with *Saying to her "make love" instead of "fuck,"* and *Knowing how to enter.*

The sound of a harp and a woman singing came from the Renaissance Room. In the center was a large painting with wise men and shepherds kneeling in front of the baby Jesus like he was king of the world. "It's called, *Hail to the Pudgy Kid,"* Steve said.

Between songs Kathy leaned in to him and said breathlessly, "See Mary's robe? You can see in the draped fabric the folds where it had been stored in a chest. That shows she brought out her finest robe to meet the Magi. Isn't that interesting?"

How did she get all that out of the painting? He had no idea what she saw.

"And she's wearing the traditional red and blue. Painters crushed lapis lazuli to make that blue. In the Renaissance, blue stood for heaven, and red for the blood that Christ would shed." Her words tumbled out in a bubbling stream.

"But do you *like* it?" he asked.

She shrugged and smiled at the same time. "I like it because I know things about it. That's why I'm telling you—so you'll like it too."

Things She Doesn't Know:

Guys don't like to be lectured about shit they don't know about

"He looks dead. No, I guess he's only sleeping. Such a good little kid. He'll grow up to be polite and eat everything on his plate and say only what he's told to."

She puffed out a breath of air and pursed her lips in exasperation. He seized the opportunity and kissed them quickly—to keep things smooth.

He'd have to learn to appreciate what got her so excited. Could he ever? How were you supposed to look at a painting anyway? A sick feeling came over him that someday she'd get tired of slumming around with him. He might just be a convenient boy toy before some fruity intellectual with a pansy in his buttonhole would come along and talk art to her.

He wanted out of there. He took her hand and sidestepped between people, past paintings of pale, skinny Jesus hanging by his hands with thorns digging into his forehead, blood squirting everywhere.

"Helluva thing to be looking at just before Christmas."

"The Spanish paintings are the ones with more agony. Northern Renaissance figures are resigned."

She jumped at this chance to tell him one more thing, some fact she learned from a wormy old textbook.

He stopped at a painting of an empty stone tomb, more like a cave. Three women at the opening of the tomb looked in or at each other in disbelief. *Gone. Three Marys Grieving the Loss of their Lord,* the sign said, by an Italian with an -ini name he couldn't pronounce. "It's called *Escape of Houdini,*" he said.

"Steve!"

"Okay, okay." He held up his hands in apology. He'd be serious and not make any dumb jokes. He wouldn't even try to say what he thought she wanted to hear. He'd be entirely truthful to what he saw, take it or leave it.

He turned back to the painting and studied the women's faces. What *was* there? Confusion? Worry? Joy? It was hard to tell. The face of the Mary closest to him revealed a longing for something she couldn't have. He felt that yearning too.

He started slowly, feeling his way. "This Mary's eyes have something the other women don't have, a spark of knowing," he said. "This one loved him differently. This one knew all along he wouldn't be there. He'd be gone."

His own thoughts astonished him, and gave him a momentary high. Kathy's mouth went slack, and something important shifted between them. Scored one, for once. Like a surprise fly ball soaring over the fence. He wasn't ready to walk on and let that feeling go.

The Mary nearest him was so full of feeling that the skin of her face might be warm under his fingers. His hand reached out to imagine it and stopped an inch from her cheek.

"Steve! Don't!" Kathy raised her voice. "You're not supposed to touch anything here."

"I wasn't going to."

"Don't you know that the oils from your hand will damage it?" She glared at him.

"What did you think—that I'm some kind of retard?"

She did, of course. Not that bad, but in that direction.

She looked like he had hit her.

A tall guy wearing a sport coat noticed them. Steve could tell by how she straightened her back that she was embarrassed. Good.

She walked a few paintings away. Steve didn't follow her. He'd never seen that sharp, disgusted look in her eyes. Before this he'd seen only playfulness and love there—at least what he took for love. Not love like this Mary felt, though. That dart that shot out of Kathy's eye just then was real. He'd see it again. There'd be other mistakes, other shortcomings. He could make a list. If only they could freeze their relationship like a painting freezes a moment in a life, he could pick a terrific moment and keep living it and living it.

He turned back to the three Marys. Nothing could be so totally, meaningfully empty as that tomb. The look on the other women's faces was more than confusion and worry. It was fear. But not his Mary. Her look was something else he still had to figure out.

He couldn't stay there any longer. He had to make amends. He found her, and made an extravagant gesture of holding up his hands and locking them behind his back to show he wouldn't touch anything. She was standing in front of a small painting of a naked man all stuck through with arrows and leaning against a tree.

"The Wrong Place at the Wrong Time?"

Her mouth twitched but she wouldn't look at him.

"I know! It's *Saint Stephen Punished for His Sins.*"

Her tight smile told him she hadn't forgiven him, yet, but was on the verge. "Saint Sebastian," she said. "He survived this persecution, so they beat him with clubs and threw him in a Roman sewer."

"Terrific. The envy of every martyr. Something cheery to look forward to."

He'd never make it in her world, never get off like she did over paint on cloth. And when she found someone else who could be depended on for genius conversation at some gallery cocktail party, she'd be gone. It only had to be lived out.

He'd had enough of stuffy rooms full of paintings. On the way in, they had passed a *biergarten.* "Let's get out of here."

"But I haven't shown you all of my favorites."

"Another time."

Outside the museum they were caught in a procession of girls in white dresses, singing. One had electric candles in her hair.

"Oh, Steve, it's 'Santa Lucia,' " Kathy cried, clapping her gloved hands together. "It's a Swedish tradition."

There it was again, nerve-racking, the things he didn't know.

Away from her, in line for his beer, he felt his fingers uncurl, and thought of the empty stone tomb. He realized what his Mary's look was all about—gratitude. He felt it too, a little seed growing in him, for something inevitable and similar. He wasn't going to hang around like that poor fool saint, to be peppered with arrows like a dartboard. There were things he'd forget someday: The name of that punctured saint. The difference between northern and southern Renaissance paintings. Kathy.

Uncommon Clay

I smack the clay onto the wheelhead and begin to center when Mom calls to ask again about her new hearing aid, the second time this morning, the second time I have to wash my hands to pick up the phone.

"We have an appointment Thursday," I say. "I'm taking you. Look on your calendar. On the wall behind the phone. February fifteenth. You see it written down?"

I wait while she sets down the phone, then picks it up.

"Oh, yes, here it is. Thursday. This Thursday?"

"This Thursday. In three days. Today's Monday. It's all arranged."

When she hangs up I start the wheel again. The cool clay whirls under my hands, and the centering goes well. I get a lot of height out of each lift so the pot rises as if by magic, politely complying with the shape of the ginger jar in my mind. It's finished in a matter of minutes. That's when I know I'm throwing well. I begin another. The phone rings. Kita-oji, the master potter in the co-op, makes a move to answer it.

"I'll get it," I say. He is making glaze compounds, an exacting process, and any interruption can make him forget what minerals he's already measured and added. I wash my hands again and catch the phone on the fourth ring.

"You know, my hearing aid is giving me trouble these days," Mom says.

"Mo-om. I just told you—"

"Oh." A pause. "I'm sorry I'm so dumb," she says and hangs up. The injury I've done her stings me, but in a quarter of an hour all she'll remember is a vague malaise.

Twenty minutes pass. I try a larger ginger jar with wider shoulders and a narrower base than I usually make, the shape in my mind more graceful but a greater risk. Feeling confident, I change from stoneware to porcelain. I search for the essence of balance, that moment when effort is no longer necessary and the clay lives, orderly and independent. Kita-oji raises both eyebrows in approval as he passes by. For him, the epitome of subtlety, this is praise, and I am gladdened.

The phone rings again. I'm at a critical moment, and have to lift again to thicken a thin place in the wall before I leave it, even for a few minutes. Porcelain that thin can sink if you just breathe on it. "Let the answering machine take it," I say to Kita-oji. "It's my mom." Her message is the same, and there's another, fifteen minutes later, more distracted, more intense. "I don't know what I'll do without my hearing aid."

I wonder if the effort of her calls wearies her, or if, because she forgets, there is no tiredness.

I used to visit her twice a week in the kindly-enough repository for the shrunken, the sick and the baffled where she lives, until she looked at me with a strange curiosity once, wonder in her face tipped sideways. "Hello again," she'd said, which seemed to me an effort to cover for not recognizing me, but I couldn't be sure. Now, despite the co-op's semiannual show only a few weeks away, I visit her every other day, to ensure the connection, to forestall the inevitable.

Still, it sneaks up on me. When I arrive on the day of her appointment, she points and says, "You have flour on your pants."

"No, it's glaze powder or dried porcelain."

"Whatever for?"

"I make pots. I'm a potter. That's how I make my living."

"Imagine that. You mean bowls and cups?" she asks.

All my preparations for this moment of loss are burned away in an instant. "Yes. Remember I brought you a vase once? Cobalt blue glaze?" I make the shape with my hands, not that I think it will make her remember, but because doing so, carving space into line, is natural for me.

"Well, you must be very special," she says.

"And you are too. Do you know why?"

"No."

"Because you're my mother."

"I am?"

Only a soft chuckle escapes her, and I realize that chaos can be a quiet, gentle thing. I take her hand in mine, her hand that had braided my hair, written funny notes in my lunch sacks, whacked me when I did wrong, and I stroke the fingers one by one from knuckle to nail. The curvature of the white moon following exactly the curvature of the yellowing tip sweeps me with a sea surge of the past. I don't know what is worse—Mom not knowing who I am and what I've done for her, or her not knowing what she's done for me, shaping me from babyhood.

The silkiness of clay spinning on the wheel soothes me, and responds to my slightest pressure. Its shape is the visible record of the history of its influences, of how it has been touched. I'm working on teapots that are perfect rounds, that have perfect integrity, shoulder matching shoulder, the languid spouts curving upward just so. I need to get them absolutely right. Over the next couple of days, I make a dozen identical ones so the process will become instinctive and natural. Only their spouts and handles will be different. I try to imagine and understand the shape of the blackness held within, like a lung, or like the space where memory should reside, but that mysterious inner realm, as plastic as the clay itself, eludes me, as my mind turns again and again to Mom. I can only wonder what her present thoughts might really be.

When I see her again, the ache of her not recognizing me is replaced with the ache of my not recognizing her. She is wearing a mint green sweat suit, just like the other patients. And tennis shoes. Tennis shoes! She's never worn them, always said they looked like men's shoes. All the patients, I notice, have them now.

"Do you like wearing tennis shoes now?" I ask.

She looks down curiously at her feet, lifts up her legs, heels together, toes outward, wiggles them, and shrugs. Apparently the answer isn't important. Reaching for a shred of identity, I say, "Yours are cleaner than the others." She laughs as if I've made a joke.

Because "Where is everyone?" has become a refrain, I've brought some photos. I spread them out on the table and tell her the stories that match them.

"All these are the family. See, here's Jane and Dave on my last birthday."

"Oh, yes, what ever happened to her?"

"She's in Alaska. She married a fellow who works on the pipeline."

"Where's Jennifer?"

Her memory of my sister's name shocks me. "She died when she was six. Remember? Scarlet fever."

Mom's face doesn't even cloud over, and I have to swallow back my amazement.

I point to a photo of Mom at the state fair. She lifts it, is distracted by a fly, sets it down. The photo shows her elated smile, her quilt hanging behind her, and the blue ribbon pinned to its edge. It hurts me that she doesn't remember winning first place. Another photo shows the church choir standing behind her, the soloist, when she sang with the voice of an angel, "There is a balm in Gilead

to make the wounded whole." Her singing always took me to that
elusive place called Gilead, a beautiful mountain where peace,
gentleness, and order reigned.

"See, Mom? You're someone special."

"I am?" Her hands go up to touch her cheeks. She looks incredu-
lous and delighted. She touches another photo with a cautious index
finger. "Who is that man?" she asks, her curiosity apparently more
powerful than any shame of not knowing.

"That's Dad. He was your husband."

Her eyes widen, she leans toward the image, scrutinizing its
mystery, but she says nothing.

Neither can I.

Losing a past seems to her only mildly annoying, like losing a
sock, an earring. No. A key.

I pack up the photos; there are some she didn't even look at. The
one with the quilt I tape to her wall so the nurses will see, and
know—she is no common woman.

The round teapot shape is instinctive in my hands now, and I can almost work without engaging my mind. On the second teapot of the
morning a sense of loss consumes me and I become reckless,
stretching the form, distorting it. I make the shoulder overbroad as if
to hold the heaviness of massive sorrow, but the attempt leaves more
lateral unsupported clay at the rim, more weight than the clay can
usually hold. I dent the walls and push out bulges from the inside—
to show the effects of stress on a living thing. By twisting the spout
so it's unpourable, I strive to create something uncommon, where
function bows to sculpture and the piece is hardly recognizable as a
teapot. That realm beyond the common and functional, into the uncommon and dysfunctional, must be where craft becomes art.

For days we glaze our finished bisque ware and load the kiln.

Kita-oji says a little prayer in Japanese and lights some incense before he lights the big burners. Everyone in the co-op works restlessly and frets. The surfaces of the pots have memories, and their colors and textures will bear evidence of the swirling gasses released from the glaze minerals in the firing. Those that survive will show that they have been tempered, tested, threatened with destruction, yet have withstood the heat. Why one survives and another perishes is a mystery.

After a day of cooling, we open the kiln. Kita-oji murmurs something in Japanese. I hold my breath. We caress the pots, our own and others', as we lift them out, warm as newborn babes. It is a good firing. Only one is lost, my distorted teapot, caved in and sunken, its shape too wide, too wild for the clay to bear, its thin shoulder surrendering to the weight of gravity.

"Sometimes the fire takes even the best, to keep us humble," Kita-oji says quietly.

I consider, for a moment, letting Mom see it before I toss it out. For all my thinking, I cannot find the effects in Mom of her having lost my sister, of her having sung solos for a decade, the congregation uplifted by her voice clear as a thrush at daybreak, and in that moment I feel the cold emptiness of negative space. I lay the teapot in the trash bin, and begin to miss her while she is still here, before she takes her leave.

I've brought Toblerone chocolate and Mom and I eat it in the calming, celadon-colored common room.

"You know when we lived in Vienna, I always used to make you hot chocolate at night."

"No, Mom. I never lived in Vienna. You did, but only as a child. It must have been your mother who made you chocolate."

"She's coming for me, you know. We're going home."

"No, Mom. This is your home. California. You've lived here forty years. I was born here. Remember how you got here? After the war? With Dad?"

Slowly she squints her eyes. Her cheeks lift and her face becomes an eroded hilly landscape.

"Please please please don't make me think it out." Her forehead reshapes itself and her eyes glisten wet like transparent glaze for a moment before she buries her face in her hands. "I don't know where I'm supposed to be."

I hold her awhile, her face against my shoulder, which is all that I can do. I wonder, for the hundredth time, how it feels to rummage through shards of shifting memory.

I go back to the loft and smash the teapots that are imbalanced, the imperfect seconds. The crashing sound is strangely satisfying. Kita-oji rushes inside from the kiln patio. His face is white. Quickly I look from him to the rubble. "Well, you said that Hamada cut through his first five hundred pots."

"That was when he was a beginner." His voice drops. "The show is three weeks away."

We run out of red iron oxide, and Kita-oji needs another load of clay. It's my fault. I should have ordered it, so I go with him in his rattlly truck to our supplier across the city even though it's my visit day with Mom. I help him load his clay so the work goes quickly and I ask if he wouldn't mind stopping at the home on the way back. "I'll make it quick. You don't have to come in."

"Of course I will," he says.

I introduce him. Kita-oji Yanagi. "I share his studio, Mom, and learn a lot from him."

He extends his hand, makes a slight bow.

"Are you from Japan?" she asks.

"Yes, I was born in Shigaraki, the pottery village, but I am an American citizen now."

"So is . . . she," Mom says and points to me. "A citizen. Now. But she was born in Vienna."

I cast a sideways look at Kita-oji. The discomfort of untruth gnaws at me.

"Yes, a country full of mountains," he says. "Like my own. My town is in the mountains, near the clay."

"Mine isn't, so much. But when she was a little girl we took her to the mountains. To Lech. It was a long way. She cried in a tunnel, it was so dark and long."

"I never—"

A lovely soft shine glassing her eyes makes me bite back my conviction that it is condescending not to correct her, that letting untruths pass is the easy way out.

"Yes, you did, and on the way back too," she says. "But you loved the wildflowers in the meadows, especially the cream-colored ones that smelled like vanilla—what are they called? Stra . . . straph . . ." She shakes her hands at not remembering, but goes on. "And the air so clean and sharp inside your nose, and the streams still frothy with winter, and the cowbells echoing high and low, and the mountains, oh, the mountains, they were like . . ." She raises her arms and looks up, uplifted by their soaring.

She doesn't finish, but the bravery with which she launched the sentence, trusting that she'd land somewhere on solid ground, warms me with pride.

"Don't you remember?" she asks. Urgency makes her shake her hands again and a tightness threatening her euphoria forms around her mouth. It is a critical moment.

"Each one a different shape," I say. "White as porcelain. Yes, Mom, they were magnificent."

For that instant, living in the moment with her is freeing, buoyant. Perhaps she is more centered than I am. The world may be spinning around her, mountains, people whirling in and out of rooms, but she is at its center, knowing those are her hands at the end of those arms, that that is her breath moving in and out of the dark center of her being.

Afraid that truth will suddenly crash and splinter, I say we have to go.

"I am honored to meet you," Kita-oji says, and my vision blurs at his kindness.

As he opens the truck's door for me he says, "She is full of poetry."

I close my eyes and nod in agreement.

Back at the studio I throw with a spontaneity and freedom I have not known before. The mound of clay is unwieldy on the wheelhead. I open it and lift anyway, with hardly an effort at centering. I work blithely, with the cylinder wildly out of round. I don't fight it as it rises wobbly, one side wider than the other, lurching with a life of its own. All my practiced skill has vanished and I am a novice again, a witness to a mystery.

I curve the sides out and in and out again, bring in the lip, and practically close it off, to make its dark interior shape unknown, leaving only a breath-wide opening. I cut the misshapen pot off the wheelhead, a vertical wavy egg standing precariously on its narrow end. The marks left by my pressure are oddly interesting, and its struggles to be upright, full of grace.

Kita-oji stops his unloading to look. "Exquisite," he says. "It has uniqueness and mystery."

"Really?" I turn it to examine its lines. "If it survives the fire, should I exhibit it?"

He nods. "What will you call it?"

As I gaze at it, an acquiescence settles over me. *"The Balm of Gilead."*

Respond

To Cynthia, the art supply store was an exotic place. It had everything you'd ever want. Brushes soft as a loving whisper, or stiff as need. Watercolor paper textured like the skin of a man's throat, right next to those darling little carving knives. Small unisex figures made of polished wooden shapes connected on wires, moveable so that they could assume any position. She raised the head of one and lifted the arm and little flat hand to wave a greeting. Then she laid it on its side on the shelf, crooked the elbow, and bent one knee provocatively. She picked up a second figure and was nestling it against the reclining one when she stepped back to assess the effect, bumped into someone behind her, and dropped it.

"Pardon me," the man said. He stooped to retrieve it and placed it deliberately in her hand, smiling under his healthy mustache. "*Mea culpa.* I shouldn't have come up behind you." He looked at the figures. "What you were doing, very interesting." There was a glint in his eye.

He was a funny little man, with bronze skin and a swoosh of longish gray hair. He sidestepped past her to put up a card on a bulletin board. After he left, she read it: *WANTED: Sculpting Model.* It gave his name, Mr. Gianni, and a phone number. She chuckled. Signor Mea Culpa Gianni.

She drove home by way of the tennis courts, listened awhile to the *bonk, bonk* of returned volleys, people responding instantly to each other, and forgot to stop for salad dressing. They'd eat their romaine undressed. Brad wouldn't notice. His mind would be on glasnost, unaware that exchange started at home.

She charged through the front doorway to the phone, "Ride of the Valkyries" surging in her mind to fuel her nerve. She'd do it now or not at all. She had to do something startling to break out of the stagnation she'd been living in.

"I'd like the job of sculpting model," she said when a taped male voice answered. "I practice yoga so I can assume any position you'd like. You won't be getting any other calls. I took your card." Her bluntness appealed to her. "My name is Cynthia Harris, but don't call me. I'll keep trying."

She was about to hang up when he came on the line, the same solicitous voice, the same deliberateness.

"Maybe you want to inspect me or something," she said. "Like beef. USDA choice. I'm the woman who bumped into you today."

"Ah!" His voice rose in recognition. "I'm delighted. Yes, well, surely. I'm delighted. You'll do just fine, but there's one thing you must understand."

"What's to understand? I stand there and you carve me or something."

"You stand there, and students study you. Nude, of course, in a mixed class."

She enjoyed the fluttery contraction in her stomach when she said, "Of course."

He told her the place, time, and payment. She didn't care about being paid, but it seemed more professional to accept it.

Picking out the correct robe took the next week of lunch hours. Terry cloth wouldn't do—too homey. Neither would nylon and lace, for obvious reasons. At an Oriental import store she bought a jade kimono, and hid it in her lingerie drawer for Tuesday night, wishing she had someone to tell, to imagine with her the delicious terror of standing peeled in front of strangers and declaring with her body: This is me. Respond.

On Saturday she went with Brad to the university library. "Just to be with you," she said, even though she knew he'd be immersed in research for Tuesday's panel on "The Future of a United Europe." He was host of the University Lecture Series on World Affairs, and being the campus expert took up most of his nonteaching time.

He shrugged. "Suit yourself."

"More a matter of desuiting myself," she said, but it didn't register.

"I followed your suggestion," she said in the car.

"What suggestion?"

"Don't you remember? You said I should take up a little hobby to keep me occupied—tennis or watercolor painting, race car driving or sword swallowing." Something that might involve me while the world is made safe for domesticity, she thought. "I went to an art supply store to find out about watercolor classes, and signed up for a sculpting class."

"Good. I hope you enjoy it."

In the library, she headed for the art history section. When she came to the books on sculpture she stopped and lifted out a heavy volume, *The Female Form in Western Art.* There was *Venus de Milo* with her arms sawed off just below the shoulders. No thanks. That was going too far. So was *Nike of Samothrace.* No head, though the rest of her looked terrific. Long body, full but firm, chest high, leaning forward like one of those bowsprits on old sailing ships. She could do this. *Crouching Aphrodite* from Rhodes was nice—torso turned sideways, hands in her hair. What was she doing? Scrubbing? Did the women who posed for the Greeks have the same skitterish flow of blood she felt just below her skin?

She took the book to the back of the stacks and crouched like

Aphrodite, with her feet and arms in the same position as in the photo. She turned the pages slowly and imitated the poses, drew stick figures and labeled them. Here, in marble and bronze, women were fluid, strong, some even defiant. *Psyche Abandoned* caught her attention. Alarmed and forlorn, about to rise from a bench, Psyche was portrayed at the moment of desertion. "Her flesh palpitates with distress," the commentary said, "and her despair gives her a languid pose not only touching but seductive." She had no idea how to make her flesh palpitate but she still practiced the position. Rodin's *The Kiss* sucked all the air out of her chest. The pair's tender responsiveness, their intensity. She sank down to the floor and stared, envious of the white stone. After a while she wondered if her position right then would work, would be despairing enough to create a good pose.

On Tuesday morning she took too long in the shower, shaving meticulously, making overlapping passes over each swath of skin, practicing Psyche. She looked down at her stomach and wiggled it with her hands. Vanilla pudding. Maybe she should have chosen an exercise class instead of a sculpting class. At least she was tall and moderately curvaceous, which might make them think she was statuesque. Should she wear her hair up or cascading over her shoulders the way Brad liked it? Up, to show her neck. That's what Venus did.

She was late for work, and all morning at the bank she caught herself making tiny errors, transposing digits or adding an extra zero.

At dinner she looked at the birthmark on Brad's cheek, and traced his jawline with her eyes, down his neck to the curve of his Rodin shoulder outward and then down, reversing ever so slightly where it became his arm, shapely enough to make her cry. A sculptor would see these things. Early on, just the sight of that shoulder had been enough to set her off.

"You know, you had a good idea, Brad. My class starts tonight." Although she hated to admit it, she had often needed his encouragement to try new things.

He made a sound rising to a slow question mark.

"The sculpting class at the community college."

His eyes bore down onto the page. "Hmm." He was editing his opening remarks for the evening's panel, his papers spread out between the broccoli and the salad bowl.

If he had asked her what they would sculpt, she would have told him.

In the center of the empty studio loomed a platform accessed by four high steps. A fist reached down her throat and clutched, the sensation satisfactorily electrifying. She stood immobile at the door.

"Come in, come in. I am just preparing." Mr. Gianni came toward her with both hands outstretched. His smile was a deliberate stretching and scrunching of his cheeks, and a lifting of his bushy eyebrows. "Thank you. It's hard to get a model, and I am glad, so glad you are come."

"Where are the students?" The thought flashed through her: It could be a trap.

"Ah, they come. They come. I get enraged when they are late. Tonight, they will be on time. I have called each one to say you will be here. It is a terrible behavior to come late when we have a model." He motioned her to follow. "They work in wax on small *maquettes* to be cast into bronze. Four weeks to sculpt, four weeks to cast and polish. You will come three more times?" She nodded. "This is not a beginning class. They already know the basics of proportion. This class is about expression."

He padded toward another room and held the door open for her. "I am sorry I can offer you only the ceramics damp room as a changing salon, but I assure you it's warmer in the studio. I came early to turn up the heater. You have some robe to put on? Yes, that's fine." He began to close the door. "I will stand here. No one will come in."

It was clammy in the dim room with all that clay, and gooseflesh rose pebbly and white. Damn. She was tapioca pudding now. She rubbed her arms and thighs to make it disappear. Voices of arriving students and scraping of stools against the floor struck her as suddenly and profoundly real. What if one of them was a neighbor, or the sandwich-maker at their corner deli? She wondered—should she take off her robe at the side of the classroom and climb the steps naked, or disrobe on the platform? There was something too dramatic in that second choice, but something sleazy about the first.

She tied the sash, drew her shoulders back, and came out to meet Mr. Gianni's kindly nod. He had on a work apron now, with tools sticking out of the pockets. The cement floor was cold against her bare feet. Moving through the students, vaguely registering a range of ages, she focused only on the platform, mounted the steps, and undid her sash. She would not let the robe fall to the platform. This was not a stage. She was no stripper. This was artistic business with a three-thousand-year history.

History. The first time she had stood naked before Brad, he had floated his fingers down her side, her hip, her thigh, looking like a blind man worshipping at a shrine. The sight of him, vulnerable before her, had sent a hot thrill right through her. Don't think of that now, she told herself.

Now, she felt the silk against her flesh, then loosening, then only air. She concentrated on breathing, on folding the silk neatly, aligning the shoulder seams the way her mother taught her to fold her T-shirts. She laid it, a jade square, on the edge of the platform by the steps and stood up, looking at lockers, draped shapes on shelves, tops of heads, anything but faces. Here, in the country I come from, she thought, this is what thirty-eight looks like. Thirty-eight and tactilely deprived. If they don't see me as beautiful, she thought, could they still create beautiful art? She felt a weight of responsibility.

"Tonight we are engaging in what Giorgio Vasari said four centuries ago was the best thing for an artist to do—the prolonged study of the nude. We are all grateful, so grateful to Miss Harris for allowing us that opportunity."

Mr. Gianni's words fell like petals on her skin. Feeling part of a continuity that stretched from antiquity, she assumed the *Venus de Milo* stance—weight on the left foot, right knee bent forward over the other, torso a slight twist—but she didn't know what to do with her arms. Venus, poor Venus didn't give her a clue. Mr. Gianni stepped onto the platform and nudged her foot into a position less perpendicular to the other. "Easier that way," he whispered. He guided her arms, touched her left shoulder gently, and in response she dropped its stiffness. "Better, yes?" She told him yes with her eyes.

He turned to the students. "The marvel about sculpting a figure, and the reason artists return to it again and again, is that it's always different. Every person is an individual. It's the sculptor's job when doing a life study to find that individuality. Observe until you see a quality that makes her individual, and intensify that."

The scar on her knee from a bicycle accident the summer before? Had they noticed that? She'd wanted Brad to wash it tenderly, kiss all around it, bandage it with feathery hands instead of so efficiently handing her the antiseptic. His subcutaneous love, not without merit, but . . . Or had they noticed her left breast slightly smaller than her right? Or the tight, aching heart beneath that breast?

As people looked at her she saw nods of approval and heard murmurs, at first just soft sounds that conveyed appreciation, then definite comments about line, proportion, shapes, planes—all oddly objective yet intimate. To stand pared, shelled like an almond, all imperfections visible, body and soul, and have them murmur, not leering but studying, was strangely, airily uplifting. That same airiness she'd felt—her mother delighted in reminding her—when, at four, she had kicked her swimsuit off in the lake and climbed onto the boat dock at the big Fourth of July picnic, raised her arms overhead, and announced, "Look, I'm wearing a waterdress."

No. This was deeper than elation. It had more potential.

"We will do four short poses before we settle on one for the evening's work," Mr. Gianni said, his voice soft in the quiet room. "So work your wax quickly but not too quickly, just for exercises of proportion, keeping in mind that individual quality you observed." He came around so she could see him. "Are you warm enough?"

She gave a tiny nod.

A young man came late, flinging wide the door, letting in chatter from the hallway. She felt the movement of air through the hair below her belly. Mr. Gianni sputtered angrily, something about the young man's disrespect for the model. She willed herself not to twitch an eyelid—Venus hadn't for more than twenty centuries—but to look out the doorway into the corridor of people, like an immortal work of art. The discovery of control when the truth of her body was laid bare allowed her to float above the room.

Moving her eyes only, she looked down with a hint of scorn at the latecomer, and felt a growing awareness that her expression could render her naked or nude. By her attitude, she could show herself or clothe herself with the aura of antiquity. At the next pose, which Mr. Gianni also let her choose—one of *The Three Graces*, left foot back, with only the toe balanced against the floor—she gave the latecomer her back.

Unevenly placed weight was a mistake, she discovered. A thin line of pain traveled up the arch of her left foot and the back of her calf. Trying to control its quiver only made it spread. That alone would have told Mr. Gianni she'd never done this before, but she was sure he'd surmised it from the start. There was more than one kind of grace, and he had the grace not to let on. Her next pose was more even. And the one after, *Dying Niobid*, almost down on her left knee, brought her eye to eye with the students, into a more intimate relation. She realized the four short poses were not for them, but for her, to decide which was comfortable enough to hold for an hour and a half. Standing was actually better, she decided. No wonder Niobid was dying. The cramp in her right thigh was *killing* her.

By then, Brad's panel had probably delivered their first remarks and he was directing the questioning. He knew every subtlety of how to lead a discussion. She'd watched him. He was a fine teacher, the kind that students come back to see five, ten years later, or write letters to from all over the world. He'd do anything for them too. She remembered the sight of him on the South Lawn at Founders' Day flipping eight hundred hamburgers in a sweltering heat wave, his arms and forehead burned crimson, sweating like a blacksmith in the barbecue smoke, clacking two hamburger turners together to the music and grinning.

Mr. Gianni drew his arm through the air as if to trace some line, and then stroked the *maquette* of an older woman who tipped her head to the side as she looked up at her. The thrill of being so intently regarded awakened a thrill of hatred for Brad's self-absorption, his abstract world concerns, his single characteristic gesture of affection, absently tousling her hair as if she were a boy child or a puppy. Second by second, standing there, she saw the naked truth that for years she had wrapped herself in awe that he knew so much, that he could speak on perestroika, the threat of neo-Nazism, coups in countries whose *names* she'd never heard of. Once upon a time, when she was younger, she had learned from him, the older authority on the world, even while she felt diminished by his accomplishments, and those of his more worldly parents too. His father headed an organization called Biologists for a Humane World. Hers died in a machinery accident when she was seventeen. His mother volunteered as a museum docent. Hers did data entry for a CPA. Her friends marveled that she married such a smart man, his that he married a beauty so much younger than he. That double awe had kept her silent. Maybe that's what she really hated—the awe that had made her passive.

A foreign-looking woman with olive skin and heavy eyebrows had been studying her from the front. Cynthia tried to study her too, as much as she was able to without moving. She noticed her cheekbones, large full lips, her long neck so slim that her tendons gave it shape. The woman finished working from the front angle, gathered her tools, and looked up at her. "Beautiful. Thank you," she mouthed.

Cynthia blinked her eyes in response and the woman nodded. How much such a little bit of attention can mean.

Mr. Gianni chalked her position on the platform so she could take a break. She enjoyed the feeling of his hand brushing against her feet. As she released the pose, pain and pleasure of movement washed over her. With unwilling muscles, she bent stiffly to pick up her robe and put it on. Slowly, leisurely, she told herself. A model must always exhibit controlled grace. Below her now, Mr. Gianni held up his hand for her to take when she stepped down. He must have known that after an hour of stillness, her descent would be shaky. She rolled her shoulders, shook out her legs, and circled the room looking at the wax figures. So this was what she looked like. Not entirely bad.

One man offered to get her coffee or tea from the vending machine. Tea seemed more graceful. Coffee would make her restless.

After the break she resumed her third position, that little number from Macedonia, and people moved around to get a different perspective. She could see them preparing their wax, larger lengths this time, heating them in their alcohol flames to make them malleable.

"Remember, students, all art is a matter of receptivity," Mr. Gianni told them.

So is life, she thought.

"Don't be in a hurry to start. Observe. Walk around her. Let the model awaken an emotional interest in you. It will be there. You just have to slow down to find it. Then, when you are sure of it, seek to express it by objectifying it in line, protrusion, and depression, even exaggeration if it suits your feeling."

With the class absorbed in serious work, a thin film of purpose settled over her skin and she felt artful. She was supposed to be there to awaken an emotional interest in them? She was the one feeling the awakening.

Eventually Mr. Gianni told them they had to stop. It was time. "Thank you, Miss Harris, thank you," he said and they clapped. Amazing. He assigned Ed, the man who had come late, to walk her to her car, a man curiously boyish now, so suddenly bashful under the streetlight that she felt like a teenager being deposited on her doorstep by a blind date.

"I apologize for being late and opening the door," he said.

She chuckled. "Mr. Gianni sure lit into you."

"I guess it can get to a man when someone else doesn't think of something as passionately as he does." He swung his backpack onto his shoulder and glanced at her. "Why are you doing this?" he asked. "Do you need the money that much?"

"No. But what if I did?"

"I'm sorry. I guess I'm just curious about what would make a woman—"

"It was the first thing that presented itself that might make me whole. It has to do with being put on hold until the world is healed."

"Don't hold your breath."

She got home before Brad did, feeling light-headed. When he came in, he turned on the late news. Of course. Something might have happened in some struggling revolution somewhere in the world since six o'clock. She sat next to him on the sofa, ready to talk about the class after the news.

She thought how they'd gone through all the classic stages—the private emptiness, the mounting tension, disclosure of the problem, her appeal to him, the discussions, the rehash, the therapist, and then the failed new efforts. So here they were, existing in that pendulous state as a water drop or a tear gathering fullness for the plunge into midair, when all is known but no move is made.

If she should say it tonight—"I am leaving you, I am leaving you," twice, the way Mr. Gianni said things, just to shock him into talking to her—Brad wouldn't hear. It would be as though she'd said, "I'm going to bed now," or whatever he thought she usually said this time of night.

He turned off the television and the light.

"I want to tell you about my class."

"In the morning. I'm exhausted."

She would hold her breath, even though Ed told her not to. She would wait.

"Do you think that people's personal lives have to be put on hold until the world is healed?" she asked him at breakfast.

"If more people felt that commitment . . ." He bit into his toast and got up to rifle through a stack of journals. He handed her one, opened to an article. "Read this. By a former student of mine in 'The Individual and the World.' "

"I meant *our* lives. Do *we* have to?"

For a moment their gaze intersected as if on an invisible wire. The birthmark on his cheek was brighter rose. She'd never seen it that way and it gave her hope.

"Do we always have to be concerned with 'The Fate of the United Nations in the Next Millennium'? What about the fate of our union? Do I have to give a State of the Union message?"

He opened his mouth to say something but stopped himself and spooned in the last of his cereal. "I'm late," he said and took his toast on the run.

During the next class she discovered she could be more naked for some than for others. She could control it, just by a look. By looking directly at the young man in paint-smeared jeans who kept pulling in his chin to study her, she could get him to meet her eyes. She could command an acknowledgment by the arch of an eyebrow, the subtle lift of one corner of her mouth, less than a half smile, less than a quarter smile, a minuscule fluttering of her fingers just when she saw someone studying them. In some students there was a response to her offering, a kind of silent conversation. In others there was nothing.

That Saturday night while Brad was reading in bed, she stood brushing her hair and, by looking at him intensely from the bathroom doorway, tried to get him to glance up and meet her eyes. She wondered, what if she managed to get him into an art gallery someday, and there she was, a figure on a pedestal? She imagined him staring at her bronze limbs with curiosity and then, finally, and with a shock delectable to her, recognizing his wife.

Or would he?

Before they were married he told her that he'd mapped every inch of her outline. It was at L'Auberge du Loire. Just after he said it, he walked his fingers across the tablecloth and lay his hand out waiting for her to place hers over his. And later in their relationship, those hands had eased her, kneading her, unfurling her.

At the beginning, lovemaking had been natural and joyous, nothing dark and dusky, just breezy laughter and some languid stroking before their bodies' impulses took over. Now it was as if he thought members of the U.N. Security Council were tapping their collective knuckles outside the door waiting for him to get back to the conference table. Was it a sin to love one's own private world when some were starving?

A tangle caught and the hairbrush spun out of her hand. The clatter on the bathroom floor made him look up.

"Do you remember when we had a picnic in the bathtub?" she asked.

A slight smile passed over his face as if he caught sight of a simpler world, fleeting, gone too soon, a world impossibly naïve now that he'd matured. The picnic had been his idea, from the time of his innocence, that and their first anniversary in the hot air balloon, and on their fifth, the trip to Pamplona. But the bulls crushing those running men, slam, face down on the street, had reminded him of the Spanish Civil War, and they took no more self-indulgent pleasure trips after that.

His eyes dropped back to the page.

There it was—plain. A whole new meaning to attention deficit. Her own. Her well of attentions given her had run dry a long time ago. Maybe bathwater would help fill it.

"Would you like to do it again? The bathtub picnic?"

"Someday."

"How about tomorrow?"

"I'm not ready for Tuesday's panel, I have sixty hours between now and then, four of which are in class and some of which I'd like to devote to sleeping, and I have forty-two exams to read by Friday."

"Sorry. Maybe next summer."

She mounted the platform and looked at the clock. Seven-thirty. Brad, who made it a practice to be punctual, would be opening the panel on "Economic Sanctions in Relation to Human Rights Issues" right about now. As a commensurate gesture in his honor, she fluffed up her pubic hair as she took her pose, the Macedonian Muscle Torture.

The robe slipped off more easily and she allowed Mr. Gianni to take it from her. He folded it into a square just as she had done and laid it on the platform by the steps.

She felt keenly her desire to give them what they needed. She savored it, in fact, and as a result, she felt valued. Maybe that was the beginning of feeling whole. And who did she have to thank for it? Brad. It was lovely, the gift of this class he'd given her. Lovely and wise. She wanted to tell him so. The bathtub picnic would have been a nice time to do it.

It was the third Tuesday, and he hadn't asked about her class yet. Unbelievable. She'd tried to lead up to it without sounding so needy, which always irritated him. "Look at the moon," she said one night. "A thin crescent, like a sculptor's marble chip." He barely looked. "Do you know what tapioca pudding reminds me of?" she'd asked as she served it to him. Another night she asked, "Do you ever feel stiff? I mean when you stay in one position too long?" Somehow the conversations, such as they were, always got diverted.

She'd brought home large books of sculpture and laid them around the house, open to photos of Rodin's *The Kiss,* and Bernini's *Ecstasy of Saint Theresa.* No reaction. She was sliding down toward the end of her rope with nothing below to catch her. Desperate, she changed the pages to Bernini's two rape sculptures, Pluto abducting Persephone and carrying her down into the underworld, and Daphne turning into a tree when Apollo grabs her. Nothing stimulated a chip of curiosity. This man had focus, and it wasn't on Cupid.

She observed the students' work with detached interest. Ed's *maquette* was wildly disproportionate. He hadn't looked past his imagination. She felt like telling him that if he was after accuracy, he'd have to pare down her breasts—she wasn't one of those outlined girlies on the rubber mud flaps of diesel trucks—but maybe he wasn't after accuracy.

The olive-skinned woman, Yseulte, brought her strawberries to eat at the break. "Look at the variety in their shapes," Yseulte said, and Cynthia saw them as individuals, each one.

"It's like eating art," Cynthia said.

She liked it that Yseulte had laid out the strawberries in a flat container so that they could see them all at once.

"You take a class like this," Yseulte said, "and everything you see in life becomes sculpture."

"Or the other way around," Cynthia said. "You wish that sculpture would turn into life. Whichever way you look at it, there's art to living, and those people who trudge through life unaware of it are missing one of the best parts."

Getting ready for her last class, she crossed the bedroom naked from the bathroom to her dresser to get clean underwear, walking right in front of him sitting in the leather easy chair. She asked her standard question: "What are you reading?"

"About the crises in Somalia and Rwanda. This week's topic is 'Successes and Failures of World Reaction to Crises in De-colonialized Africa.'"

She looked down at his magazine on the ottoman. Dozens

of thin, bare forms, knees protruding from shrunken legs, starving children's bulbous tummies. Sculpted grotesques. Each one an individual, to somebody, a world away. She was supposed to feel they were her sisters and brothers. She held her breath and tried, genuinely, to feel it, did feel it deep beneath her breast for a throbbing second or two. How long did most people?

"Life—so naked," she murmured.

He raised his head slowly, pain reshaping his mouth into a thin line drawn down at one end, and regarded her as if she'd said something inordinately stupid. "Of course they're naked. Somalia's destitute."

"I didn't mean *they* were naked. I meant their life is. Raw and bare."

She pulled on a pair of jeans and a sweatshirt and grabbed her bag containing the jade robe. "I'll be home late tonight. The class is going out for coffee afterwards."

She went out to the garage, almost late, turned on the ignition, turned it off and came back inside.

"This will only take two minutes. Something occurred to me today. Something very important to us."

She got down on her knees right before him and didn't move, a pose of supplication. Looking at him steadily, she leaned toward him minutely, and he looked up.

"Your birthday is in two weeks, May eighth. It's 1995. You're going to be forty-nine years old."

"Why are you telling me that now? To make me feel old?" He reached to gather his papers.

She thrust her hand out, knocking them out of his grasp. "Count back nine months and forty-nine years." She paused. "You were conceived roughly between August sixth and August ninth, 1945. *1945,* Brad."

Almost imperceptibly, the muscles in his face went slack. "Between Hiroshima and Nagasaki," he murmured.

"Your parents made love right after the world knew. Think about it."

She gave him what felt like a full minute to respond, and then got up and left.

Sweet sadness rose in her as she looked down at the students working the wax. It was the last session for her, but they would, in the next weeks, make plaster molds of her form, pour in molten metal, polish it until she gleamed. Each student would have something solid from their encounter.

Mr. Gianni moved from student to student, commenting on their work. She held the pose twenty minutes longer at the end of class so they could finish.

Afterward, in an Italian café attached to a gallery, colors, shapes, and music surrounded her. A small bronze figure, no more than a girl, rose on tiptoes above a circle of red begonias in the entryway. "Tiptoes! Not even the Niobid could pose like that," she said. They laughed.

"Too perfect," Ed said. "Needs some interest."

Mr. Gianni tipped forward on his toes, then back on his heels, smiling in a knowing way.

"It reminds me of a fountain in my village back home," Yseulte said.

The figure's belly was rounded with the lingerings of childhood, her breasts mere buds.

"It reminds me . . ." Cynthia couldn't finish. The child's protruding belly reminded her of the naked children in Brad's magazine.

They drank raspberry mochas and passed around gooey layered

desserts, rating each according to artistic merit. They gave her daffodils, and Mr. Gianni slipped her the check inside a card with a drawing of her in her last pose. Everyone had signed and written something personal. Yseulte had written, "Your grace and generosity have given me the courage to create." At the bottom were the words, "You are more whole than you think. Ed." She felt like she had just burst through the surface in her waterdress. She had done something useful. She would show the card to Brad, put it on his pillow. She floated home and thought now she was strong enough to tell him—"I'm leaving you." To tell him twice, the first to clear the fog, the second he'd hear. If she wanted to.

She found him hunched on the edge of the bed, his shirt and socks off, an illustrated article open on the floor between his feet. His eyes as he looked up to her were wet brown stones, melting. Then his head dropped.

"Senseless. Fundamentally, pathetically senseless," he said. "The repetition of human failure. Why can't we learn?"

Her breath caught. She felt flushed. If she could sculpt his beautiful shoulder overburdened with too much weight, his lowered head, his hanging hands, she'd call it *Atlas Defeated*.

The agony of his knowledge streamed down his cheeks, the potential for feeling always there, yet only for the large, the distant, never for the skinned knee of a wife. The efficient thing would be to hand him a handkerchief. The gracious thing, the responsive thing, would be to hold him.

"The speaker tonight," he said. "Habigali, from Rwanda. Whole villages slaughtered. Families, husbands and wives, torn apart."

Her heart opened up and filled with wonder. She sank down next to him and her arm went around his shoulder. He looked at her with recognition and yearning before he laid his head on her breast which had recently borne the gaze of people trying to create something meaningful out of a human being. It seemed one country trying, finally, to speak to another, to acknowledge what she'd always known but never admitted, that his heart—yes, he did have a fine heart— was too large. That her own, too small, might grow, if she fed it right.

She started slowly: "This man. Habigali. Did he have a wife?"

Crayon, 1955

One summer, when the raspberries along Miss Haskin's fence hung down all ripe and ready and I didn't know what to do with dolls any more, Gramp came to our house to die. That meant I had to move out of my bedroom and set up camp near the living room sofa. It was the same day Miss Haskin, our neighbor, asked me to water her plants when she went on vacation.

We had just moved and I didn't have any friends yet, so I stayed at home, played "Doggie in the Window" on my record player about fifty times a day, and waited for fourth grade to start. Daddy worked late most nights, so it was just Mom, Gramp, and me. And, beyond the raspberry fence, Miss Haskin's house.

"Go in, talk to Gramp," Mom said that day, but I hardly knew what to say. He was so old he seemed like someone from another country. I pretended to get something from my room to do on the back deck, drawing or embroidery or a book, but my things were hard to get to. Daddy had set up Gramp's easel right next to the bed and a card table for his brushes and paints. I felt cramped with his things on top of mine. Even if he wasn't dying, I didn't want to look at him lying there in my bed in his stringy old-man's robe the color of raw chicken liver. But he was watching me so I had to say something.

"I have a job," I said. His gray eyebrows popped up, kind of like he was glad I was talking to him. "Taking care of Miss Haskin's plants."

"Who's that?"

"Just the gray old maid next door. She walks like a flamingo. Honest. She has long legs like one too, and she plops her big feet down, smack, on the sidewalk. She has a cube for a head."

"Jenny!"

"It's true. Her mouth's too big, and her eyeballs are in scooped-out holes, and she blinks a lot, but other than that, she's okay."

Gramp's mouth tried to smile. "Jenny, Jenny, look a little deeper," he said.

What was I missing? Once Mom called her an in-tel-lec-tu-al. She made it sound bad, but I always thought that being smart was a good thing. I felt sorry Miss Haskin had to live alone, and wondered what she did with her life.

"She's going on vacation," I said to Gramp. "But not a normal trip, like to the Grand Canyon or Yosemite. She's going to Guatemala, just to stay in one place and dig. Something called arc—"

"Archaeology."

"Is that like a search for buried treasure?"

"I suppose you can think of it that way."

The day after she left, I marched out to the sidewalk with Miss Haskin's key on a rubber band on my wrist. I turned left into her driveway and flapped my feet down toes last and lifted my knees high like she did, then looked back at our bay window. Mom would give me a talking-to if she caught on. I opened the door into a dark entryway. It smelled cool. When my eyes worked right, I could see it was our house, only flip-flopped. That was creepy. Where we turned right to go down the hall, Miss Haskin turned left.

In the entryway shelves where we had Daddy's bowling trophies, she had wild carvings made of stone and clay. Some had lips that pouched out and giant circle earrings. Others had potbellies. A woman's breasts were round bulges like marbles barely stuck on. A man's thing stuck straight out in front, like a small third arm, pointing. I hurried by it and tripped over a rug in the living room.

Gramp said to look a little deeper, so I did. Her shelves were filled with Indian pots and shiny black boxes decorated with polished stones or tiny fairy-tale paintings. I wanted to pick up a gold paper Chinese fan, but was afraid. It looked like it might tear. A globe sat on a stand in one corner. I looked for Guatemala. It was orange. In another corner, a carved tusk curved toward me, taller than I was. I felt sorry for the elephant, having that heavy thing growing out of its face. There wasn't any television. Thick picture books of paintings, not *Reader's Digests* like at our house, were spread out on the coffee table. On the cover of one called *Pre-Columbian Art* was a carving just like the woman in the entryway with the round belly. Inside there might be pictures like that man figure, so I didn't open it.

I watered the inside plants and was careful not to drip water on anything. Outside, I turned on the sprinkler and waited out in the patio in a hammock under a yellow honeysuckle vine. Maybe Guatemala was like this. It was an enchanted house. I wanted to memorize it, and in the darkness before I fell asleep, to walk around in it again and touch everything and open the books and boxes. I felt badly that I had called Miss Haskin a flamingo and a cube.

"What's pre-Columbian, Mom?" I asked while drying the dinner plates.

"Before Columbian, I suppose."

"But what's that?"

"Well, you can look it up, honey."

She meant in the *Encyclopedia Americana,* a big-deal purchase that year. It didn't have any colored pictures like the *Junior World Book* at school did. After it arrived in its too-tight bookcase, any question of mine got the same answer: Look it up. But I could barely pull out the books. I don't remember my parents ever using them.

Volume 21, the *p*'s, said that pre-Columbian meant "Indians of Mexico and Central America in the pre-Hispanic period," whatever that was. The encyclopedia always made you look up something else to understand the first thing. Maybe in Guatemala Miss Haskin would dig up a little clay Indian with his thing sticking straight up out of the dirt. If pre-Hispanic was old, I figured Gramp would know about it. He could discuss it with Miss Haskin when she came home. Maybe they would like each other, and while they talked I could look at more things. I went in to ask him, but his eyes were closed and his mouth was open and his loud breathing made me tiptoe back out.

"Jenny," he said the next day. His voice scraped like a Popsicle stick across the sidewalk. "Let me teach you to paint."

I wasn't sure I wanted him to. The room smelled bad, but not just because of his cigarettes and paints. Once Mom said Gramp's blood ran with turpentine, which I thought was what made his skin waxy and yellow.

Practicing a secret style of shallow breathing, I sat on the edge of the bed and he held my hand inside his spidery one while I held the long brush. He squeezed so tightly, directing where my hand should go, that his long yellow nails jabbed into my palm. I curled up my toes and kept quiet. Like a miracle, in front of me appeared an un-rolled white flower with an orange finger inside. "There's nothing so cheerful as a calla lily," he said as we worked. "They grow tall and graceful just like you, and one day, they open themselves to the world."

"Miss Haskin has lots of pictures on her walls," I said. "No flowers, though."

"Pictures of what?"

"Stone villages and pointy churches. Kind of like castles. Maybe you can see them someday."

I gasped, thinking I shouldn't have said that.

"Maybe."

Now I had to go on. "And talk to her about them."

I finally had to let go of my breath before he said "Maybe" a second time, softly, looking out the window.

Each day I explored more of Miss Haskin's house. In the den, which in the flip-flop was actually my room, books in tall bookcases were alphabetical, by author. I followed the names: Anderson, Browning, Cather, Dickens. A pink book had gold letters down the edge that said *Canterbury Tales*. I thought it might be children's stories or fairy tales. I lifted it out carefully so it wouldn't leave a pathway in the dust. It wasn't even English but almost was. I knew it would be useless to ask Mom what it meant. She'd only say, "Look it up, honey." In another bookcase, sitting right out there next to an atlas stood *The Communist Manifesto*. I didn't know what manifesto meant, but I knew the first word well enough. I sure wasn't going to tell that to anyone. Miss Haskin could count on me.

After a few days the mail piled up below the slot in the door so I carried it over to the dining room table and stacked it according to size. Then I thought she might want to know what order it came in, so I rearranged it. Her first name was Harriet. I felt I knew a secret. Even Mom called her Miss Haskin. One letter called her Dr. H. Haskin. Two letters had foreign stamps. Scotland and Mexico. I could hardly believe she knew people there.

I moved the sprinkler from the ivy to the grass, and settled in the hammock with a giant book. *Picasso*. The name reminded me of piccolo. The book was full of paintings of people, but all stretched out, with the faces rearranged. On page 107 was a picture of a crazy woman. She wore a crumpled red hat with a blue flower, and her hair hung in long purple and green ropes behind petals for ears. Her skin glowed the bright yellow-green of honeysuckles where the blossom joins the stem, but her nose sat crooked and her big mouth was a bunch of angles. Her fingers clutched at her teeth. She looked about to explode. Under it was printed, "*Woman Weeping,* oil, 1937."

Her mouth reminded me of Miss Haskin. I wanted to bring it home to show Gramp but I thought it might make him not like her. His paintings weren't like that at all. He only painted countryside and mountains that didn't make the world so jangled.

Inside, the telephone rang. I slammed the book closed and turned off the sprinkler, but didn't answer the phone.

"You were gone a long time," Mom said when I came home.

She gave me the narrow-eyed, Eleventh Commandment look. I had already been taught the Old Testament Extensions. Honor thy father and thy mother included thy grandfather. After my cousin's family got a new car, the Tenth was, "Thou shalt not covet thy neighbor's house nor his ox nor his ass nor anything else in thy neighbor's garage." I knew it also meant anything in Miss Haskin's living room. Mom's look told me the Eleventh: "Thou shalt not be nosy."

"I was watching television," I muttered. Oops. Maybe Mom knew that Miss Haskin didn't have one.

"Go in and talk to Gramp, will you, Jenny? He needs some company."

Gramp wobbled his head when I came in and squished out another cigarette. It smelled like a teepee over a campfire, not like my room anymore. "Hi," I said, trying to make one breath last as long as I could.

His hand, like a spiky leaf all dried up, reached out under my

Dutch girl quilt and clamped on to my arm. "You did your lessons good today, Jenny?"

"Gramp, it's summer. School's out."

"Oh." His fingers loosened, but he didn't let go. "Where were you, then?"

"Miss Haskin's." He looked flat under the sheet. I didn't understand how he could have a pointy thing or where it went. I looked away. On his easel was a small painting of a mountain lake with tall needle trees, a flock of sheep, and clouds. "It looks peaceful," I said. "Where's that, Gramp?"

"Gilead."

I'd never heard of it, but thought it might be in Montana where he went on a painting trip once.

"It's nice." He looked at me, almost into me, as if his greatest wish were that I had meant what I said. "I like it. Have you ever heard of Picasso?" I asked. He nodded. "What do you know about him?"

"Paints like a crazy man." The way he sliced out the words surprised me so I didn't say anything more. It made me worry that when Miss Haskin came home, they wouldn't like each other, and then I wouldn't be able to go over there any more.

In the middle of that night Gramp snored differently, with wheezing breaths, sometimes sudden and gagging. I put the pillow over my head to make a soft, cool cave. In the darkness I saw Gramp's face rearranged, his ears upside down, his eyes at weird angles. His face was yellow.

His breathing sounds that night frightened me and made me go to Miss Haskin's earlier the next day. Her mail was a postcard invitation to something at a gallery and a letter from Maine. I looked it up in her atlas and found it wasn't close to Montana at all. The states didn't believe in alphabetical order. I started the sprinkler and took a fat book called *Romantic Painting* to the patio and sank down in the hammock. I thought I'd see pictures of couples in old-fashioned clothes holding hands in parks or on sailboats.

There weren't any sailboats, but one lady had on a long dress and two men wore tight, shiny knee pants. When I turned the page my skin crawled cold. A man with a rag wrapped around his head hanging sideways was lying in a box or a bathtub with a board across it like a table. He held a letter in one hand and a feather pen in the other, but he was dead, or maybe just dying. *The Death of Marat,* it was called. A tiny maroon cut in his chest leaked a trickle of blood. The bathwater looked like raspberry juice. The way light fell on him, the sheet behind him, his head rag, and his skin all glowed with the same color, a pale greenish yellow. My stomach cramped. It was like Gramp's skin. It gave me the chills, it was so real. I knew it wasn't good for me to look at it, I would be sorry later, but I couldn't stop myself.

In the corner of my eye I saw a trickle of water, like the bloodstream, running across the cement under the hammock. I'd forgotten the sprinkler and flooded the ivy.

"How did you learn of Picasso?" Gramp said one morning when I went in to get clean clothes.

"From one of Miss Haskin's books. She has books with paintings in them that I look at sometimes."

He watched me with a weak smile. "Good. You do that, Jenny."

"Why are you mad at him?"

"At who?"

"Mr. Picasso."

"I'm not. He just caused a lot of changes, and it was hard for me, that's all." I gathered underwear, socks, my plaid shorts, and a red shirt. "What else does Miss Haskin have?" he asked.

"Lots of things. Carvings and pots and boxes. I wish you could see them." I glanced toward the door. I didn't want Mom to hear how nosy I was. "Do you think someday you would feel good enough to go with me?"

"No, Jenny. That wouldn't be right."

"Then after she gets back?"

"Yes, maybe then, if—" He stopped, right like that.

"If what?"

"Nothing."

It was Miss Haskin's den I wanted to explore most. That afternoon I just stood there and stared, in case she came back early. It was confusing knowing what to wish for—Miss Haskin to come back so Gramp could know her, or her to stay away so I could keep going there.

A plaque awarded to Harriet Haskin, Ph.D., hung on the wall. "For Excellence in Teaching, College of Arts and Letters, June 1951," it said. A school just for writing letters. No wonder she got so much mail. On a small table there was a typewriter, something we didn't have.

I walked slowly to her desk. She had folded a newspaper section back to show the baseball scores, just like Daddy always did. It made me laugh because baseball was so different than everything else here. In a gold frame there was a photo of a young couple sitting in a skinny boat. A man wearing a striped shirt was standing in the back of the boat holding a long pole. I bent over to get a close look. The man wore a squared-off straw hat and the woman a flowered dress. I'd never seen Miss Haskin in a flowered dress, but that stretched-out smile had to be hers. Her teeth were whoppers and her jaw jutted out at an angle. She looked happy, but she wasn't pretty. Just young. It made me sad for her.

I wondered if there was more. I opened the desk drawer about four inches, slowly, so it wouldn't make any noise. I didn't breathe. It creaked and I froze. The Eighth, Thou shalt not steal, pounded in my head. I shoved it closed. It wasn't that I wanted to take anything. I just wanted to know.

Practically the only sound in our house all day was Gramp's wheezing and sometimes a weak little cough that scraped at my ears. Miss Haskin wasn't due back for a week and every day Gramp seemed further and further away. I hated it.

"What's archaeology really?" I asked him after I'd waited an hour for him to wake up.

"Just what you're doing next door, Jenny. Digging up things. Then putting them together."

"Why do they do it?"

"To make a picture of a world." The words came out in scratchy spurts, as if it hurt, and I had to lean close to hear through the whistle in his chest. "Archaeologists are scientists who do it for whole civilizations, and you're doing it for one person." He choked but it seemed like he wanted to keep talking. "Or maybe you're doing it for a civilization too, come to think of it."

If I memorized what he said, maybe someday I'd understand it. I waited for some sign, for permission to ask one more question. I touched the back of his hand and the skin felt unconnected to the bones. His milky eyes lifted and looked directly at me. "Do you think it's wrong that I'm nosy?"

"No, Jenny. Look at everything. Always," he whispered.

I said hi to the pre-Columbian figures when I let myself in the next day, and took a closer look at the man. As usual, there were letters on the floor. One square blue envelope was pretty lumpy so I squeezed it a little. I gasped. It was addressed to Peaches Haskin. This was something I knew I shouldn't see. Who would dare call her that? R. Chenin, the return address said. From Canada. Nobody like Gramp, I was sure. Maybe R. Chenin read *The Communist Manifesto* too. I crept back home as if I'd stolen something, but my empty hands were only sweaty.

Gramp held a brush and stared out the window to the back yard. It didn't look like he had done anything on Gilead. Since he didn't notice me, I looked long, to remember him for all time. The whiskery skin of his throat hung in loose folds like a turkey. I wished he looked nicer.

I went outside to Miss Haskin's back fence and came back in. "Here's some raspberries," I said, and laid a bowlful on his bed. "They're Miss Haskin's. I just picked them." As if from a faraway country, he turned to me slowly and hardly smiled, and in that moment I was afraid. I watched his long fingernails grasp for the berries, watched as he laid them on his tongue, watched as his eyes got wet. He ate like a robot, concentrating on each one, and left one in the bowl.

"For you, Jenny." I shook my head. He pushed the bowl toward me and his mouth did a little jerk. My tongue found the soft hole at the top, and the sections of Gramp's last berry sprang apart in my mouth.

I took a piece of notebook paper folded in my pocket the next day. After I set the sprinkler going, I went into my room, her den. The typewriter was still there. The chair creaked when I sat down but I didn't even jump. My paper rolled in crooked. I stared at it, and didn't know what to type. It took a long time to find the letters. They weren't in alphabetical order. "Jenny Cochran," I typed. The keys went down a long way before they printed, and I pressed them unevenly. Every so often it skipped a space. I started again. "Miss Jennifer Cochran." Then, "Miss Harriet Haskin." Underneath that, "Peaches Haskin." "Dr. Peaches Haskin." Then, "Miss Jennifer Haskin."

I rolled out the paper and on the way home I tore it into tiny pieces.

The next morning when I woke up, Gramp's door was closed. Mom usually opened it a little first thing in the morning to hear him if he needed anything. I suddenly felt hot and cold at the same time. It couldn't be. It was too soon. I found Mom in the kitchen, just standing there holding on to the sink. She nodded, then told me to go to Miss Haskin's and stay until she called me on the phone.

In Miss Haskin's dark entryway, the pre-Columbian figures went all squiggly. He didn't wait. Through the blur of the hallway, I saw his turkey neck and Miss Haskin's flamingo legs and the woman with the purple hair and the man in the bathtub and Mom and Dad too, who probably didn't even know the bathtub man. I used up about six tissues. I tried not to because she only had a few left on her sink. Then I didn't know what to do with them. I didn't have pockets, and I didn't want to leave them there—she'd find out I was in her bathroom—so I stuffed them in my Keds.

I knew why I'd been sent here—so I wouldn't see, but that was just what I wanted. I had to find out if Gramp's arm was hanging over the side of the bed, like the man in the tub. I snuck into the house through the back door. Mom was on the phone, talking in a low, serious voice. Who did she think would hear? I held my breath and turned the knob at Gramp's room and cracked open the door just enough to see him. The yellow color of his face had leaked out his open mouth or evaporated or something, and his skin looked like crumpled wax paper. His arm was under the covers. I ran back to Miss Haskin's and dove onto her bed.

I lay there sideways for a long time, until the wet spot on her bedspread was cold and clammy next to my cheek. I rolled onto my back and looked around, and realized I hadn't been in her bedroom before, the most inside place. Of course, it was filled with treasures. Probably each one had a story. On her dresser there was a little china bowl. The lid was painted with a soft-colored scene—a stream flowing near a cottage and flower garden. I think Gramp would have liked it. That made me break into sobs, gagging like a little kid. He didn't get to know her.

He'd seen a lot of things—Montana and Gilead, places I didn't know anything about—and I hadn't even asked him. I hoped I hadn't annoyed him with my questions. I hoped that in some small way, I made his going easier. Then I was ashamed for thinking I could do that, and I buried my face in her pillow again.

When Mom called me home, hours later but too soon, he was gone. Our house didn't breathe. The bedroom door and window were wide open but the curtains weren't blowing so I still smelled turpentine and death in that room, my room I guess it was now. I still felt I should tiptoe around in it. Mom had the bed stripped and was putting on clean sheets—my favorites, the ones with the daisies. But he had slept in them the week before. His easel was gone, and the unfinished Gilead was propped against the closet door. I wanted to keep it in my bedroom, just like it was. His jar of brushes stood on the bedside table. When Mom left, I took the longest one, wrapped it in a tissue, and hid it in my bottom drawer.

That night I sat a long time on the living room carpet. Mom knew why and made up the sofa for me again.

Several mornings later, while I folded the blanket in the living room, I watched out our bay window as Miss Haskin flapped down the pathway to our front door. Too late. I hugged the blanket to my chest and didn't breathe. Maybe she'd forget to ask for the key. She had oxfords on, just like mine, but she was a lady of the world. When Mom called me outside to the porch, I felt suddenly shy, afraid Miss Haskin could read on my face what I knew about her.

"Did you have a good time—digging?" I asked, looking at her hands which were scratched and scabby.

"It was wonderful. I mean full of wonder."

I knew what she meant, and was able to look up at her face smiling down at me. "Did you bring anything back? Any treasure?"

"No, Jenny. We found many things, but they'll all be kept in a museum."

I was disappointed. Mom told her that Gramp had died. My throat tightened into a double knot. Miss Haskin's voice was deep when she said she was sorry. It wasn't her fault. Nobody said anything for a minute and I noticed she tied her oxfords with four loops just like I did.

"Death can be a rich experience," she said.

Mom's back straightened into her I-don't-quite-like-what-you-said posture. I guess it was a strange thing to say and I would need time to figure it out. For anyone else to say that, it would be weird, but not for Miss Haskin.

She thanked me for watering and said I did a good job, that the plants looked healthier and had grown a lot. She held out three new dollar bills. My hand would not go up to take the money. "Take this, Jennifer. Please." Her low voice floated down and surrounded me like the honeysuckle in her patio. If I didn't take it, she might think I didn't like her. I forced my hand toward her. For a second, both our hands were on the stiff dollar bills.

"Gramp wanted to see your picture books." The words spilled

out before I thought them. "On pre-Columbian art." My face got all hot. I turned so I wouldn't see Mom. Miss Haskin didn't look at her either.

"I'm sorry," she said again. "But you can. Anytime."

I looked at her shoes and let out a breath.

That night I stood on the back deck and knew I would not spend the three dollars for a long, long time. I think Gramp would've agreed that they would make good bookmarks. Beyond the raspberry fence, light from the den window next door shone out on the ivy. Inside the window I could see Peaches Haskin reading her mail. I went into my bedroom, turned on the light, and opened the curtains so that light from my window spread over our back yard, too. I took one of Gramp's sketchpads, climbed into bed, and drew a jumbled orange face with a giant, crooked mouth and purple hair. I didn't make the eyes match. Below it I printed, " 'Miss Haskin Reading,' crayon, 1955."

At Least Five Hundred Words, with Sincerity and Honesty

Dear Sister Wilhelmina,

I haven't forgotten that the last time I had to write you two hundred and fifty words with sincerity and honesty, you said my reputation here was "fast descending to the pit." I know it'll all hit the fan in chapel on Good Friday, so this time I thought I'd get a jump on it, sort of as a way to <u>redeem</u> myself. (Vocabulary word this week. Look for others. They'll be underlined.) And because the stakes are higher, I decided to double the amount.

Please remember when you read this that even though I'm an A student, I'm only in eighth form. We haven't been assigned *The Confessions of Saint Augustine* yet, so I probably won't get it right, the wording and all, but here goes:

I, Josie Carmichael, do hereby confess to the crimes explained below, and declare that all my words are truthful, so help me Mother of God.

I have to start way back with the drawing taped to the wall behind your desk which Sister Eleanor pointed out to you when we were doing vocabulary. I only made it because I was bored once and staring out my window at two guys skateboarding in that cement ditch thing outside the school fence. I know it wasn't up to my artistic <u>potential</u>, as you've said before, but just the thought of the Holy Mother and her sister Elizabeth watching their two boys, Jesus and John the Baptist, doing tricks on skateboards made the other girls on my wing laugh, and that made me feel cool for a change. (Denise especially liked the pointed little beard with a few scraggly curls.) (Oops, I'm sorry. I know how you <u>despise</u> unnecessary parentheses.)

You might have noticed that John was doing a kickflip, but Jesus got more air on his ollie. Now just think about it. Jesus was totally airborne, with his knees all bent up to his chest and his long hair flying and his board hanging in the air right below his feet. Airborne. Isn't that a neat way to picture him, spiritual and all? Like the Ascension. Or is it the Assumption? Remember, I'm new here, and I still get things confused. Anyway, it looked way cool. Even better from a distance than up close. Especially with Mary and Elizabeth off to the side cheering like Little League mothers.

I might as well admit that I was the one who wrote "Sign of Tricks to Come" as a title under the picture. You'd know it was me anyway because my i's are dotted with sacred hearts which I know <u>irritates</u> you. That'd give me away big time if I actually meant to let you see it, but I didn't. Somebody stole it and put it there.

You could have guessed as much b'cause my face was probably red when Sister Eleanor came into the room, and by the way I looked around to see who might have done it. Maybe your eyes were busy drilling holes through my vocabulary workbook in front of my face and so you didn't notice Carol snickering or Denise sitting up straight with that smartass look on her face that you always think is politeness.

I was hoping then that you wouldn't recognize who the drawing was of. (A bad sentence because it ends in of. Oops. Sorry.) All I did to Mary and Elizabeth was to put long scarves over their heads and shoulders. Jesus had on baggy cutoffs which any kid could wear. Then, seeing it again on your wall, I remembered. The halo. And John's skimpy fur rug he always wore. What an idiot I was. But you gotta remember it wasn't for you to see.

I know you went right on with the lesson after Sister Eleanor left just to make us all squirm, but didn't you notice Anita mimicking you? Saying, "Josephine, you will remain after class," in that prissy way of hers? I guess you didn't hear them snickering when they filed out, but how could you have missed Carol shoving me as she went by and Denise with her nose in the air?

After you told me I'd created a "crude defilement of the Holy Family," you said my foster mother didn't teach me respect.

Which one didn't do her job? Maybe you didn't know that I've had three foster mothers.

I'm writing more than two hundred and fifty words, which is the punishment I'd expect, because you said, "There are two sins here, Josephine, one the blasphemy to conceive of such a drawing, the other to put it up behind my desk, as if to suggest that I approved. Would to God we could direct your talent toward more suitable subjects."

That was a key sentence, which I'll explain later, but first I want to tell you something about Denise, Miss Queen Bee. She's hated me ever since Sister Eleanor made her family take me over Christmas holiday. Those snobby parties at Hampton Oaks when her mom made her let me wear her clothes, she treated me like a reptile.

Which is about the same way I felt when you yanked my picture off the wall and ripped it into pieces and let them fall into the waste-basket real slow, to torture me. I felt like someone punched me in the stomach.

Now the explanation for The Big Sin. Here's another five hundred or more. This time it wasn't just to be stupid or a troublemaker. There was a reason. I needed money. Here's why.

Ever since the drawing episode, the girls snubbed me and hud-dled around Denise which didn't surprise me. Carol warned me I'd be hating life if I told. What's it to her? She's just a wannabe anyway.

No way was I going to tell. I know how this place works. All the girls would stick like honey to their Queen Bee. For two weeks I stayed in my dorm room except for classes and meals, and except for after lights out. I didn't talk to anyone, and that ticked them off more, that they couldn't get to me. Then the names started. Freckle Face I could ignore, but not Charity Slut. I'm sorry, Sister, but I have to blow this place.

Only thing is, I kind of like it here. The quiet way you sisters slither, and singing in chapel, and all the paintings. Public schools don't have paintings. And the food's way better than the foster farms. But no way would I ever get the Bee and her hive to like me, or even tolerate me, and no way would my foster mom put me in public school when Our Lady would take a charity girl so the foster family wouldn't have to have me sitting in their living room every night and taking up time in the bathroom. Only my real mom would put me in public. Which was why I took the risk. One way or another, for better or worse, I'd be outa here. I had to come up with a way to get to her. That's why I needed money.

So, I organized a pledge drive. Once I thought of the idea, it was a piece of cake. When the Queen Bee and her hive saw that it would get me into deeper trouble, they dumped their money on me. I didn't let the day girls in on it though. Too much chance of them opening their mouths at home and some do-gooder mom tipping you off.

The pledge was that I would do something outrageous. If I did it by Good Friday, they'd have to pay what they pledged. If I didn't, I'd have to pay all of them double what they pledged by end of term, in the order they pledged it.

For me to earn the big bucks I needed, it couldn't be something boring like stealing wine from the vestry, or puny like stealing paint from the art room. I want you to know that I rejected the idea of painting Sister Eleanor with a cigarette hanging out of her mouth. Now that would have been disrespectful.

It took me a week to think of something, and I don't mind telling you I kind of prayed about it. Then one morning in chapel when we were singing the Canticle to Mother Mary, I had a vision. It had to do with that painting behind the altar of the Madonna and Child that Sister Eleanor says is a copy of one by Fra Filippo Lippi. I've had problems with this Madonna ever since you taught us the Canticle where we sing, "O sweet Virgin Mother, in you no joy is lacking." No way does Filippo's Virgin have any joy. The corners of her mouth just sag and her eyes are all droopy and half-closed. Most mothers smile at their kids, but she looks so bummed out and <u>miserable</u>, like she already knows he's gonna be nailed up there, it didn't seem right or <u>appropriate</u> for a church. If she's happy while she's looking down at her son, that might make us feel worse about what's going to happen to him. Isn't that the point?

I know for a fact that not all madonnas are so <u>melancholy</u>. Just go to www.louvre.fr and click on "Paintings," then click on "By Subject," and then "Madonna and Child." "Holy Family" will work too. There's a ton of madonnas going all the way back to the eleventh century. (If you have all the lights off in Sister Eleanor's office and turn the monitor away from the doorway, it doesn't show any light under the door. You know, nobody locks any doors here. It's a little <u>naive</u> to depend on "the rule of the order," if you ask me.) (Oops. Sorry again.)

It wasn't like I put a mustache on her, or fangs. I just thought she needed to look happier. It's only poster paint so I'm sure you can wash it off. I tested it first. Don't think I don't know the rule against using lipstick.

I'm sorry about the teeth, though. I got carried away, not as <u>excessive</u> or kinky as The Ecstasy of Saint Theresa, that painting hanging in your refectory, but I was definitely wired.

When we did our charity work at St. Vincent de Paul last month, I saw a mom carrying a baby in a sweater and I said to her, "Nice baby." She broke out in this allover toothy grin. She was kind of homely, but she was totally happy to hear me say that, which made me happy too. We've got to find our happiness where we can is the way I see it. I guess that grinning mom was on my mind when I went to work on Filippo's Madonna, on her teeth, that is. I knew right when I did it I was going to get up close and personal with the root word <u>outrage</u>, but I couldn't help myself. You got to give me a little credit though. At least I didn't touch the Christ Child, even though I think he looks like one of the Rug Rats. So fat he'd roll down Fourth Street hill like a beachball.

The wages of sin were $73.21 to be exact (Sister Eleanor always tells us to be exact) which you've got to admit is a pretty good haul considering there are only nineteen eighth grade boarders. If a miracle happens and Holy Mary Mother of God smiles on me and I'm allowed to keep the money, minus the cost of the paint I used up, I'm going to buy a bus ticket to Elster Township where my real mom lives now in a place called Barnaby's Trailer Park. I found that out on Sister Eleanor's computer. I guess I got sidetracked from looking up madonnas. It'll surprise the heck out of her to see me, and I don't know if she'll like me being there face to face, but hey, you've got to do what you've got to do. Please remember my <u>motive</u> when you decide on my punishment. If it's <u>expulsion</u>, like that painting of Adam and Eve in the Garden of Eden (an awful sad-looking pair—what is it with the church and sadness?), I guess there's no <u>alternative</u> but public school. I'm going to miss those Jesus stories. He sure could do some kind of moves.

When and if I feel <u>contrite</u>, I will confess to Father O'Connor, but for now, this'll have to do.

This and another picture which I'm gonna start as soon as I sign off. This one'll be for you. No weirdness. Just a nun sitting alone at a desk looking like Fra Filippo's Madonna before I got to it, with a wastepaper basket on the floor.

I want to say one more thing. A person doesn't always have to like every piece of religious art to be a good Catholic.

With all due respect,

Josie Carmichael

P.S. Please forgive me for dotting my i's with sacred hearts. I know how it <u>annoy</u>s you. A person can have blacker habits, I guess, no pun <u>intend</u>ed. The fourth verse of the Canticle says, "O blessed Lady, deign to set us frail ones free from evil habits." I'm sure you're doing your best.

Gifts

Charles felt dampness between his heat-swollen fingers as he placed them carefully at the edge of the counter in the bus station's eight-stool coffee shop.

"Another cup?" the waitress asked. She had stringy hair and looked trod over, an expression Mame used to say after a night of not sleeping well, a little like he felt.

He nodded, staring downward. It was his third.

As she poured, he noticed the clean, even semicircle of her thumbnail.

"Where you going, Bub?"

"It's not Bub. It's Charles."

"Where are you going this morning, Charles?" Her voice was softer.

If he said Wanoka, then she'd know.

No one went to Wanoka wasn't visiting somebody in the pen.

The waitress refilled the bowl of sugar cubes in front of him, and he noticed that all her fingernails had that clean crescent-moon shape. A woman could do that, he thought. A woman who don't have dresses or face creams can still keep her nails nice. Not painted, just nice. If she had one a them sandpaper sticks, she could. They'd let her have that, wouldn't they?

"Excuse me, ma'am. Do you know a drugstore open this early?"

"Nearest drugstore's three blocks down, but it don't open 'til nine."

He looked at the Coca-Cola wall clock. 7:25. His bus would leave at 8:10. If he told her that, she'd know where he was going.

"Is there any place else a body can get one a them things women use to—" The idea excited him. He pretended to file his nail, and his fist knocked his cup and splashed coffee over the counter and into the sugar bowl.

He grabbed the napkin to sop up the counter and then looked up at her. He felt like a kid expecting a swat for spilling his milk.

"I'm sorry," he said.

Calmly, she removed the sugar bowl, swabbed the counter with a rag, and poured him some more coffee. He put his elbow on the counter, rested his forehead in the heel of his hand, closed his eyes and thought of Mame. He couldn't even visit his own wife without doing something wrong. Couldn't even talk to Mame right without her going off and doing some fool thing.

Can't you get that kid to shut up! His own words scraped for the millionth time inside his skull. Then, in his mind, he heard again the slap, and the horrible crack coming a split second later, the sound that riled up his guilty feelings so fierce that they had kept him from seeing her in that place until now. But if he didn't find out what she was thinking of him, now that she was in that place, he'd turn crazier than a bedbug.

When Charles finally opened his eyes and lifted his head, there was a glazed doughnut sitting on a plate before him. He looked at the waitress but she had her back to him. After a while he tore off a section of doughnut and ate it. The sugar coating broke apart against the roof of his mouth and melted into sweetness. Once he started, he couldn't stop, even though he tried to eat it slowly. His hands were sticky when he was through and he had no napkin now, but the waitress had gone into the kitchen.

He emptied his pocket of coins onto the counter and went into the men's washroom. He looked at his hands scrubbing each other. If they let him touch her . . . They might let him touch her.

In the warm water he dug under his fingernails even though he didn't really see any dirt there. "Wash your hands first," Mame always told him when she put a plate of food down in front of him. She told the grandchild the same thing, probably even told him the last day of his life. He watched his hands working. He could bring her that. Clean hands.

Three people were already sitting in the bus when he got on at eight. There was no secret about where any of them were going. None of them spoke. Charles headed for a seat behind them all.

He passed a woman big as a Buddha stuffed into a gray uniform. She probably worked there. Maybe even knew Mame. Her round of purple-black flesh spread out like a melting pudding.

Next was a Mexican boy slouched with earphones on. Charles could hear Tex-Mex music when he passed. The boy had pulled his Levi's jacket over him like a blanket even though it was blazing hot.

The third was a girl with skin the color of molasses and her hair in rows of braids tight to her scalp. She was pretty now, being less than twenty, he figured, but in ten years, she'd only be ordinary. She pulled out a tablet, the kind with a spring holding the pages together, and as soon as they got out on the highway and the going was smooth, she started drawing.

After a while she set down her work and went to the head in the back of the bus. Charles stood up and pretended to stretch, and there on her tablet was drawn the aisle of the bus and the seats and the backs of the heads of the woman, the boy, and the driver, all of it looking as good as a photo.

By the time the girl came out, the Buddha woman was slumped into a sleep with her head bouncing a little on the wadded-up

sweater she'd jammed against the window. All the old gal did was jiggle and sweat. The girl sat in a different seat than she had before so
she could draw the woman as she dozed. Charles felt like he was in
on a secret. When the young girl finished, he got up to stretch again
and took a look.

"You done a nice job," he said softly, looking at how she'd drawn
the three soft chins and the nose wide as a lightbulb and the gold
badge on her shirt collar. The girl smiled the kind of smile that
showed she was ashamed of being proud.

They passed an auto wrecking yard. Crunched bodies were piled
on top of each other. Their engines were long gone. Waiting for
what? Doomsday. A sad little town strung itself out between the
highway and the railroad tracks. At the far end, the bus stopped at a
diner made out of a Pullman dining car. It satisfied him somehow
that the rusted green car was being used. While everybody else went
in, the girl leaned against the bus in the shade. Through the window
he watched her draw, and when they got back in the bus, he sat behind her. With a shy look on her face, she showed him. It was all right
there—the train car diner with the hand-painted sign, *Lucky Spade
Cantina,* and the cottonwoods and the arroyo coming down out of
the mountains and the trash cans and the sleeping dogs.

"You're making a nice book there."

She put a stick of gum in her mouth and wrote quickly on the
gum wrapper: "For my boyfriend. To show him what I saw."

"That's real fine of you. You know you could make money doing
that. At a carnival or something. Drawing people."

She flashed anger in her eyes and he didn't understand what he'd
said wrong. Unless it was *at a carnival.* He realized that up to now
she hadn't said a word. That struck him in the pit of his stomach. He
didn't mean she was a freak.

"You're good, I mean. Real good."

She shrugged and turned from him a little. Her braids must've taken somebody half a day to put in, he thought. She had on a clean white blouse, ironed once but wrinkled now in back where it stuck to her skin. A hurt bird was what she reminded him of.

And riding on this bus.

It's one thing, he thought, after thirty years of marriage, seeing three kids through their birthings and whooping coughs and squabbles over the bicycle until they go off and leave their own little'uns with long faces and dark scared eyes and dirty fingernails for another woman to mother all over again and a man's left rattle-brained wondering how the woman he spent all those years with could do a thing wrong enough to be locked up, it's one thing to end up here visiting a wife this way, but it's something else entirely to start off a love at this girl's age with a trip to the pen. And on top of that, if she can't talk, whoa!

Well, if she couldn't talk, then she wouldn't say anything would make another person crazy mad. But that wouldn't stop other folks saying things to her to make her mad.

He watched her draw the bare brown mountains outside the window.

She'd have kids, he thought, and someday when she's dog-tired from slinging hash and her feet ache from being on them all day and the rent's due and the kids are whining for something as impossible to give them as the moon, but she would if she could, and some jackass says something scrapes her nerves raw, then one kid'll smart-mouth her one time too many and she'll backhand that kid so hard she'd send him flying across the kitchen, and if she's prayed up and lucky, he won't crack open his head against the stove and he won't die from it, and all she'll have to feel sorry for is a welt.

She flipped a page and started in on the Mexican kid. Charles was the only one left.

He waited until she was through.

"I'd pay you if you'd do one a me," he said softly, just a suggestion, in case she was mad at him. "If you could make it look like me so's somebody'd recognize me, but make me look, you know, good 'n all." He pulled three dollar bills from his wallet.

She motioned to the seat across from her. He didn't know how to sit—looking straight forward or sideways facing her. She pointed to the rail on the seat in front of her like he was supposed to look at that. He cleared his throat and sat up straight, smoothed the hairs of his mustache, and cupped his hands together in his lap, his hands that he was trying to keep clean by not touching anything.

A fly came buzzing and bothering all around his eye but he didn't budge. He thought of old George Washington on those one-dollar bills. George had to sit still too and stare at something when somebody drew him.

Mame could tape it to the wall by her bed, if she wanted to. They'd let her do that, give her an inch of tape to do that. He had something for her. He felt better now. He wasn't coming empty-handed. If he didn't love her, if he hadn't loved her steadily for thirty years, through the drought and the Depression, through her female problems and the grandkids trying her patience, then the picture and whether she'd want to put it on the wall wouldn't be so life-and-death important to him.

What would he say to her? That was the thing, what to talk about. He'd tell her how he was managing with the other grandkids. She'd want to know that. It'd make her sad if he told her the tree in the dirt yard had blown down in a storm. She always loved to sit in its shade of a hot afternoon. Maybe he could plant another one and it'd grow big enough by the time she got out. He wouldn't tell her until he actually did it, though. What he wanted most was to say something so she wouldn't feel so bad and low about herself.

When the girl tore the page out of the notebook, each ripped hole made a little pop in his lungs. She handed it to him. Yeah, it was him, all right. Anybody could see that. "It's a better me than me," he said. Charles nodded his satisfaction and held out the three dollars. She took only the middle one. As he pulled off the ragged bits of paper on the left side of the drawing, he had an idea.

"Could you sort of draw a frame around it?"

She reached out her hand for it and began to draw.

He felt better and better as he watched. It was one of them fancy old-fashioned frames with leaves and curlicues, like for really important pictures.

"That's just fine," he said.

He folded it once and put it in his shirt pocket. He didn't want Mame to see it first thing.

Barren fields blurred past and heat wiggled up off the empty highway. The bus slowed and turned up a narrow road, and he saw the place just as he'd imagined it. Concrete buildings like solid blocks. Not a single window. Three chain-link fences. A curl of new barbed wire on the inner one. The barbs sparkling like tiny blades in the glare. Probably electrical lines too. He suddenly felt shrunken by the hardness of the place.

When they stopped at the gatehouse and the driver said, "Women's compound," he stood up and felt the stiffness of the picture there in his pocket, like a bandage over his heart. There was nothing but unowed kindness to guarantee that she'd want it.

Their Lady Tristeza

Eduardo drew on the board. That was the start of it. He came in early for my English class and drew the outline of Matisse's *Blue Nude* on the whiteboard with my blue felt tip marker, without even using the image as a reference. It was unmistakable—just like the artist's paper cutout, the figure sitting on the floor, bending over her raised knee. Only he added one thing. He drew a Band-Aid over her right breast.

It was Eduardo, all right. Eduardo, who peered rather than looked at the world from under heavy eyebrows, who seemed to have learned, somewhere in school, the less he said, the less he would be wrong. I saw the blue marker in his hand just before he set it on the railing. Big hands, adobe brickworker's hands already, thick hands that were a mistake attached to this short, narrow-shouldered boy.

I left his drawing up. It was the first time he'd done anything other than slump in his seat, draw low-riders on his vocabulary papers, and clank the bicycle chain hanging from his belt. I felt a small thrill flutter up my throat. This was what Professor Dichfield promised last year in her droning educational methods class—that where you least expect it, here, for example, behind those dark, slightly suspicious eyes, there was something wonderful inside wiggling free. How did Eddie even know about Matisse?

Admittedly, that was my New England prejudice, the conviction that culture born beyond the high desert had not penetrated this sagebrush bottom of the nation, this underfunded, forgotten border town I'd been forced to come to by need of a job.

The next period Eddie's girlfriend Anita came in. She stared at the drawing, transfixed, until she said softly, maybe to her friend Rosy, maybe to no one, "I didn't know he knew." Around the figure Rosy drew a baroque frame, and wrote "SAVE" just outside it so that Rudy, the dour-faced janitor, wouldn't erase it that night. When I came in the next day, the woman had been named *"Tristeza,"* the word inscribed inside the frame in a handwriting I didn't recognize. Rosy told me the name meant "Sadness."

Tristeza. Good name for this town, I thought. No art gallery. No library. No orchestra. Only a dusty movie hall showing third-rate horror films. I could hardly believe it was part of the same country as Boston was. One year. One year of my life was all I'd give this place. Then, back to concerts on the Esplanade, museums, the ballet, and my friends, even if I had to wait tables at the Oyster House.

All that day, kids streamed in to see the blue figure named Tristeza huddled there, her knee raised up and her head sunken down upon it. They stood there murmuring, sometimes in Spanish, with looks in their eyes that made you want to hold them. But that had been crisply forbidden by Professor Dichfield. "There are really only two rules of teaching," she'd said the last day of the semester. "Always wear hosiery so they know you're a lady, and never, never touch them." I'd broken the first one before my second week— the hot southwestern air in September so still and dry it choked you. But their dark eyes looking at Tristeza choked me too.

After school, I rubbed out the word "SAVE" so Rudy would erase the drawing along with the homework assignments when he cleaned the boards for the new week. But the figure was still there on Monday morning. Strange. Mr. Regularity himself. According to Rudy's reputation, he never forgets a thing. Then I noticed—the frame was gone. Why would he erase just that?

I had to use the space for new vocabulary words so I erased the drawing, but the next morning when I flipped on the lights, there she was. A coolness coursed through me in spite of the oppressive heat. The word list was gone, and she had come back, ghostly and blue, bleeding into the whiteboard a little, her outline edged in painful angles and contorted curves. And the Band-Aid too.

"Eduardo, did you draw this again?" I demanded when he came in, knowing as soon as I heard myself that it was a ridiculous question: I had unlocked the door myself.

A great seriousness descended as his hooded eyes roamed over the bent figure, taking in not the lines so much as the fact of its being there, her presence.

"Eddie?"

He stood up straighter than I've ever seen him do.

"Why did you draw it in the first place?"

He looked past me, at his drawing. "Just did."

In my Spanish-English dictionary on my desk, I looked up *tristeza*. Not only sadness, but pain and grief too.

After Eddie left I erased the figure, but the blue lines came back the next morning again. Rudy. It must be Rudy playing a trick on me, I thought. But when did old men with long faces and deep-set eyes ever play jokes?

I picked up the eraser just as Gabriel, the sleepy kid with the two-pound crucifix, enough heavy metal to crack some *cholo's* skull, said, "Miss Talmadge, you'd better not try erasing that again."

"Why not?"

"You just better not. *Por el bien de su alma.*"

"Tell me in English."

"I can't. It's better in Spanish."

I studied the drawing closely, standing just a few inches from the blue lines, to see if they had been laid on externally or if, somehow, they had seeped through the board. I couldn't tell.

The parade of the curious continued. Some just stared and walked away. Others speculated on the Band-Aid. Every time I escaped to look for Rudy, the janitor's room was locked. I stopped when a girl teased me for stalking him. At the doorway to my room I found Señora Sanchez in her painting smock hurrying out. "*Dios mio,* give that boy an A! He knows his Matisse."

Later, Eddie's girlfriend, Anita, said, "Her heart is broken."

"*Cállate!*" Rosy elbowed her in the ribs to quiet her.

"All she wanted was to love."

"No. *Ella es santa,*" Rosy whispered.

I saw one boy cross himself quickly, a deft, fluttery movement as if brushing away a fly. Later a boy and girl came in holding hands and stood before the blue lady as if before an altar, stood there looking at her without saying anything until the boy finally turned to the girl and she nodded and they went out.

"What was that all about?" I asked Rosy, my informant on the social pulse of the school, the first from whom I had begun to learn the facts of life here. The people were as clear and open as the desert sky at dawn, I'd thought at first, but there's more to a desert than what you see, she'd told me.

"It's Our Lady. A visitation of the Virgin."

"You can't be serious. She's nude. Naked."

Rosy gave me the kind of look you'd give to someone who had kicked a dog. "I am serious."

She told me about the time before I came to Sangre de Cristo High when the face of the Virgin appeared on a basketball and so the priest blessed it and the coach stopped drinking before games and the team won the New Mexico state championship.

"So what happened to the basketball?" I asked. "Did they use that ball in every game, her face pawed by sweaty hands?" I imagined the orange nubby face of the Virgin smacking against the gym floor.

Rosy turned her shoulder to me and I felt suddenly exposed, as if she had read my mind.

I tried one more time to erase the drawing, without success, so I stopped trying and just avoided looking at it. Two days later, when I had my back to the board and was dragging my second period through *The Scarlet Letter,* reading aloud the bittersweet part when Hester Prynne and Arthur Dimmesdale finally kiss in the forest, the whole class gasped and pointed. I turned, and Tristeza had a tear, one blue tear on her cheek just under her right eye. Had I not noticed someone drawing it between classes? Some students looked knowingly at their friends. Others began talking in Spanish, their words tumbling over each other so fast that I could make out only one. *Milagro.*

"What's *milagro?*" I asked Rosy.

"A miracle."

Between every class for the rest of the day, my room was filled with students. Some murmured, "Hector," and the girls lowered their eyes. I had to shoo them out to start each class, afraid Mrs. Hardgrove, the principal, would come clomping down the hallway in her resolute shoes and correct maroon dress twenty years out of date and discover the commotion—the principal who reminded me rather too much of Professor Dichfield, who used to say, "The authority of logic leads all thinking persons to believe . . ." and then she'd finish the sentence with her own opinion on matters of comma placement or achievement scores. What would the authority of her logical mind think of the nude Virgin visiting a class studying the Puritan *Scarlet Letter?*

At lunch the math teacher next door came in to have a look. Tugging at his gray mustache, he declared, "It's because you're new, you know, and young. One year they soaped a new teacher's wind-shield every day for a month until he packed up his books and his fancy desk set and walked out of here. Never saw him since. They locked his replacement in a closet. Don't let it get to you. They're just kids."

The crinkles around his eyes, which had seemed Santa-ish be-fore, now took on a prophetic meanness, a self-importance that an-nounced he thought he knew all the answers, and I was just a rookie.

A tiny drop of resentment at his dismissal of the Lady bubbled up and surprised me. "What makes you so sure it's a student pulling a trick?" I said, feeling that I was betraying Professor Dichfield, who would surely hold that the authority of all logic leads all thinking persons to believe that marks on boards are made by human hands. I was going to ask him if he knew a guy named Hector, but instead I just wanted him and his grim sympathy to go right back out the same way he came in.

I held Rosy after school.

"You haven't talked to me all day," I said. "What's wrong? Be-cause I said that about the basketball?"

The corner of her burgundy-painted lips lifted in an unwilling smile.

"The last time you were this quiet was after you had an argument with Anita. Did you have a fight again?"

"My mom and dad did."

"With Anita?"

"With each other."

"I'm sorry. Is everything back to normal now?"

"Yeah, after she shot him."

"*Shot* him?"

"Just in the shoulder. She told him he couldn't come home until he had a job, so he went to Mexico and came home drunk. We found him climbing through the bedroom window to get in so she got out my brother's pellet gun and shot him. He just fell back out the window."

"Did you see if he was all right?"

"No. I was reloading for her." She shrugged and laughed at my shock.

Her stories always made me feel the newness of my arrival, as if I were the bumpkin ignorant of the way things were. "That tear. What do you make of it?" I asked.

"You ever see some guys have a tear tattooed on their cheek? One tear each time they're sent up."

"Sent where?"

"To juvie, or the pen."

I looked back at Lady Tristeza. One blue tear, not what I'd imagine to be the color of blue tattoo ink under brown skin.

"Who's Hector?"

"Nobody. Just a guy used to go here."

Rosy shouldered her backpack. Her lips, dark as Communion wine, closed up. A whole world lay just beyond me, a network of interlaced lives bearing secret, weighty cargo. I felt a prick of desperation that Rosy, this sixteen-year-old to whom everything was clear and simple, would leave without telling me more.

"So why our school?" I asked. "Of all the schools in the country, why choose this one? Why not at least a parochial school? Why not one in Spain or Chile or Mexico? Or Boston?"

"She came because she knew we needed her."

I thought of the Virgin of the Basketball and how the coach stopped drinking. "It's just a drawing. Eddie drew it."

"Nobody drew the tear," she said.

The whole school became quieter. The weekly counseling office report indicated fewer discipline referrals than anytime since November

1963. There were no fights in the hallways, and even Bert, the science teacher who had told me to use the janitor's cleaning fluid on the board and forget about the drawing "for good and all," found nothing to complain about in the faculty lunchroom.

During my afternoon prep period one day, Mrs. Hardgrove marched into my room with a priest.

"This is Father Corcoran. He heard about this . . . phenomenon"—she glanced at the board—"and came to see."

The Holy Father examined the drawing from various angles in the room, holding one hand in the other over his belly in a monkish pose. If he corroborated Rosy's claim, what would that do to my classroom? Make it a pilgrimage site?

"Don't you think it's a bit unusual for the Virgin not to be clothed?" I asked. Preposterous was the word that came to mind, but I had to be cautious.

He squinted his eyes in contemplation. "The lines could represent a robe."

"But her position. Have you ever seen a Mary all hunched over on the ground? Maybe she's only Mary Magdalene. The penitent Magdalene. Sorrowful. That fits her pose, don't you think?"

If he agreed, that might save room 204 from being beset by the barefoot faithful entering on their knees, and the church wouldn't put my blue marker in a reliquary.

"You haven't touched her, have you?" he asked, a rattle in his voice.

"No."

"If you don't mind, Miss Talmadge, tell me the events of this appearance as they happened," he said.

"Certainly." I gave an account, day by day.

"Is there anyone in your classroom whom you think has done a wicked deed?"

"No."

"Anyone suffering guilt?"

"That I can't say."

"Is there anything else you might have left out in your account? A person you don't know coming or going?"

"Not that I can recall."

"Can you be sure the room has been locked anytime you haven't been here?" Mrs. Hardgrove asked. "In accordance with the school rules."

What was this? The Inquisition?

"Yes, I suppose I'm sure, except for Rudy being here at night."

"The janitor," Mrs. Hardgrove explained.

Father Corcoran stood before the drawing for a long time, hands behind his back, his fingers twitching, itchy for the coffers of his down-at-the-heels parish to be filled, no doubt.

"Sometimes it's easier for the young to believe. They haven't been hardened by skepticism." He looked sideways at me.

"But why in my room? It could have been anywhere."

"But it wasn't. You'll have to answer that for yourself."

This was getting ridiculous. I had compositions to grade.

"Can't we say it's just a drawing that means something to some people, and leave it at that?"

"But her presence persists," he said.

"So what do we do?" Mrs. Hardgrove asked, the first time I'd ever seen her acquiesce her authority to another person.

"We wait and see," he said.

"See what?" I asked.

"See what she does."

"Don't let her disrupt your lessons," Mrs. Hardgrove said on their way out.

Not even if she gets up and dances a jig? Disrupting lessons—no, I wouldn't think of it, as if I had any control over that, but disrupting my prep period, that, apparently, was just fine. Now I had to stay late correcting the papers I would have finished if they hadn't come.

When Rudy came in with the sweeping compound and push broom I asked him if he had anything to do with that blue nude.

"*La Virgen de la Lágrima?* No, ma'am."

Him too!

"Did you ever erase it?"

"Three times. And the frame too." He wouldn't look at me, but just kept his nose down sweeping the floor. "She came back each time, so now I sweep just like I always do, and empty the trash, but I don't touch her no more."

"Nobody comes into the room in the morning before I get here?"

"No."

"And you've never noticed anything unusual?"

He squinted his sunken eyes at me a moment, sizing me up, then looked sideways at her as if asking forgiveness for something he was about to say. "Last night, I haven't told this to no one, last night right under her eye, right there . . ." His arm jerked out to trace an invisible line downward.

"Well?"

He drew his arm into his chest. "Just keep a careful watch."

"What do you mean?"

"I hope saying this isn't out of place, but it seems to me she's a sign to you."

"To *me*?"

"Miss Talmadge, these kids need something stable in their lives, that's all. It's a poor town, a poor school. Teachers don't stay."

Was my intention to bail after one year that transparent?

He swung his arm toward her bowed face and said with more emotion in his voice that I'd thought possible for him, "This Virgin has a tear, you can't deny that."

"You mean to say this Virgin came to—"

"I mean to say they like you, but they're afraid. They see you cross off the days on your wall calendar and write ninety-one. Ninety. Eighty-nine."

"That doesn't mean anything."

"To them it does."

This conversation was going too far.

"I'm sorry, Rudy. I've got to go."

I crossed off one more day and gathered up my papers to finish grading them at home, feeling I'd been riding a seesaw all week.

For a grown man to believe a kid's drawing was the Virgin . . .

I wouldn't buy one stick of furniture for my dumpy studio apartment. Nor a single towel or saucepan. Nothing that wouldn't fit in my car if I wanted to evacuate. "One contractual year. Nine months," I said, less firmly, through the windshield to the town. The town that had no science museum celebrating rational thought, no literary society, no dress boutiques, no fine restaurants. Not a single person I could imagine becoming a friend, or something more.

Two things happened the following week. Rosy finally had enough money to pay off her lost textbook debt. "My dad got a job," she said, counting out the money into my hand without a hint of embarrassment in her voice. And I finally had the opportunity to speak to Anita alone. I sat down at a student desk and folded my hands on the desktop.

"I hope you know you can trust me." She blinked and nodded. Not exactly agreement, but I took it as a sign I could go on. "The first day Eddie drew that, you said to Rosy something curious that I haven't forgotten. You said, 'I didn't know he knew.' What did you mean by that?"

"I didn't know he knew I gave her up."

"Who up?"

"My baby."

"Your *baby*." I tried not to let my voice show surprise or shock or judgment. "I didn't know you had a baby."

"Last summer. His too. Only I didn't tell him."

"That you had his child?" She nodded, and her eyes slicked over like the mirages on hot pavement here. "You mean to say his drawing told you he knew?"

"Well, what else? The Band-Aid's right there on her heart."

"Your heart?"

"He's a sweet guy, but I didn't want him to have to marry me just for that, you know. It was stupid, my dream of an apartment with me and him and the baby."

"No, Anita. Not stupid. Everyone dreams of love. Not everyone recognizes it when it's right in front of her, though."

"You're the first adult who's ever said anything like that to me."

I had to wait another two days until I caught Eddie coming in late so I could make him do afternoon detention. When he shuffled in after school, the laces on his high tops dragging, he looked at Tristeza right off, as everyone did coming into the room these days. No more "Hi, Miss Talmadge." I was sharing occupancy of room 204, and I was obviously of lesser importance.

"Your drawing has caused a lot of commotion around here."

"I didn't mean it to."

"Can you tell me now why you drew it?"

Pain shaded his cheek even browner. "My mom has—"

I waited a moment, then ducked my head low so he'd see my face. "Has what? That piece of art? A copy of it, I mean."

"Cancer." He pinched his lips together. "Breast cancer."

I did hold him then, despite Professor Dichfield's rule, and he let me, his head dropping onto my shoulder and his chest quivering in a way that ran right through me.

"They're going to cut her." I held him tighter. The words shot out with a hint of disgust, as though it shamed *him* somehow. In the weight of his head on my shoulder, his pain seemed not entirely for her, but for himself too. The weight traveled down my shoulder to settle in my heart and I wanted more than anything to say something that might help.

"*Milagros,* Eddie. *Milagros* come to those who are open to them, who love enough. And you drew her out of love." His body became still in my arms.

Across his shoulder I could see Tristeza. How could he, they— Matisse and Eddie—get that pain in such simple lines? The attitude of the head dropping forward and the hand cupping the back of the skull could move a stone to tears.

"Does Anita know why you drew it?" I whispered.

He rolled his head against my shoulder in a "no." I looked down at those brickworker's hands and knew there was no boy attached to them.

"Maybe it's best if you don't tell her, if you let her think— whatever."

I was absent from work Thursday and Friday with some strange malaise, overwhelmitis. I needed a retreat from this slippery world where a drawing could mean so many different things and belief was simple and easy. What if Professor Dichfield's sentence stopped without a dependent clause? The authority of logic leads all thinking persons to believe. Period. I lay in bed, my head and my heart pulled in opposite directions. Every so often I glanced at the clock. First period. Eddie. Second period. Anita and Rosy. Third. Fourth. Lunch. Prep. By sixth, the bed was littered with lists of school districts in big cities where rational people live, and with scratched-out drafts of letters to them. I kept thinking of Rudy, his deep-set eyes darting away from me, his concern for the students, the sincerity of his preposterous theory. Would he . . . had he done something after all?

On Saturday morning, Eduardo knocked on my door.

"How did you know where I live?"

"Everybody knows. Small town. We know you only pay month to month too."

He thrust forward a covered earthenware pot. "It's *caldo de res.* Beef soup. My mom. She wants that you eat this so you'll get better."

"*Me?* So that *I'll* get better?"

My conviction that this was the last place on earth where I'd ever want to fit in was being eroded by the purity of her gift.

I had nothing commensurate to offer her. "Tell her . . . tell her you got a B-plus on vocabulary last week."

When I came back to school Monday, I knew the drawing would still be there, even if the substitute had erased it. *La Doña de la Lágrima,* I would call her. The Lady of the Tear, but I was never going to call her *Nuestra Señora* or *La Virgen de la Lágrima.* Though I tried to pass by her casually, my eyes moved against my will. The blue was that kind of silky deep aquamarine blue you'd hope for if you'd never seen the sea but only dreamed of it. Living here midway between the Pacific and the Gulf of Mexico, Eddie and Anita and Rosy had probably never seen an ocean, never heard the crash of surf, never tasted its salt. It would be nice to take them, to be there when they grasped its unfathomable presence.

Right beneath *La Doña's* eye there was a glistening on the metal chalk tray. I looked up at the ceiling, but there was no dark spot, no moisture up there. I watched my finger slowly reach toward the tiny puddle, slowly dip into the wetness, slowly come toward my mouth, and on my tongue I tasted salt.

Tableaux Vivants

My son's vintage VW put-putting into the driveway with his speakers blaring Louie Armstrong splits me with joy and a surprising little pang. Joy, because it's my week with him. As for the pang, Louie Armstrong's responsible. Jeff's father is the jazz aficionado. Me, I'm only an elevator-music lady trying to catch up. Catch up, grow up, and have a life of my own before my son does.

Jeff comes into the kitchen, taller and broader than I remember him from this morning. I point at his feet and he tiptoes backward to rinse off sand at the outdoor faucet. I revel in this childlike obedience.

"Occupational hazard," he says, proud of his new status as beach lifeguard.

"A Mrs. Larsen called from the Pageant," I tell him.

"Cool. A callback. She's the artistic director this year." He sets down his before-dinner snack: burger, fries, and a shake. "I think I've either got the part of a flagbearer on the Iwo Jima Memorial or a triton in the Fontana di Trevi."

"A triton?"

"A Roman god. Son of Neptune."

Seeing my only child transformed at eighteen into a World War II soldier in fatigues would probably make me cry, even though the Pageant is just a theatrical romp of role-playing for the sake of art. I'd prefer a Roman god. It's probably the way every girl on the beach sees him when he climbs down from his lifeguard tower to knock off an elaborate aerial gymnastic routine on the rings, ending with an iron cross, the most difficult maneuver, holding it, suspended in that muscle-burning T position.

"What would you wear? If you're a triton?"

"Grease."

"Naked! My boy naked in front of all of Southern California!"

He raises one eyebrow and deepens his voice to sound professorial. "I believe the art term is nude."

"Intellectually I grasp the difference."

"With body paint, I'll look just like a statue."

"Right. You're going to be presented as an object, to be enjoyed by strangers—what women have been subjected to since antiquity. I approve of turning the tables, but I have one question. How, pray tell, did you audition for this role?"

He holds up a french fry, twirls it slowly as if examining it for the part. "Use your imagination."

The Pageant of the Masters, a summer tradition in arty Laguna Beach, is a high-tech production of tableaux vivants. One at a time, two dozen famous paintings and sculptures are reproduced life-size with real people posing as figures against painted backdrops in an amphitheater—a bizarre illusion of life imitating art which originally imitated life.

Being a part of the Pageant comes naturally for Jeff. This is a boy who cherishes Halloween infinitely more than Christmas, who gave up baseball in order to be Ariel in the community theater production of *The Tempest.* He's a card-carrying member of the Society for Creative Anachronism, an organization that acts out historical events in character. In order to "be" Sir Stephen Pettigrew, a Yorkshire knight proven in battle, he fashioned articulated armor out of papier-mâché. Though it looked real enough, he was dissatisfied because it didn't clank. His girlfriend that year "was" Lady Margaret Westmoreland, but they broke up and so he "became" a monk and listened to Gregorian chants and posted a sign in calligraphy on his bedroom door: *Cell of Geoffrey of Monmouth. Enter only when summoned.*

"Only last year I watched you play the sweet, good boy in straw hat and bow tie holding the oars and waiting for a bonneted Renoir girl to step daintily into your red skiff. I loved it. The innocence of youth in summer. And now you're either a marine or a naked fountain. I'm not ready for this."

He takes a long pull at the double straws of his shake. "Why don't you do the Pageant too? Auditions are still open."

"Oh, sure. *Whistler's Mother* knitting in a rocker. Or one of those ugly peasants in van Gogh's *Potato Eaters.* I'll get to wear burlap and they'll smudge my face with cow shit."

"Greta wouldn't do that. Trust me."

"Greta? Greta?"

"Mrs. Larsen. The artistic director."

"Since when do you call adult women by their first names?"

"Since I was twelve, Ei-*leen,* only you haven't noticed."

I wonder if he asked Richard to do the Pageant. It would be just like Jeff to try to get us together again that way. How cozy, a happy three-some in disguise. The last thing I want is to do it *with* Richard. It's doing things by myself, for myself that I need. I can't seem to shake that man and lead an independent life. By the time we cut the cake together at twenty-four, we'd already known each other half our lives, which puts our first date sometime in sixth grade. He's always so *there* that I don't know who I am, separate from him. So I left to find out.

Richard and I have cordial enough relations, sharing Jeff one-week-on and one-week-off ever since he was in tenth grade. If Richard were auditioning for the Pageant, I'd stop thinking about it on the spot. Using the issue of Jeff's dorm accommodation at the university in the fall as an excuse, I call Richard to see if he mentions it. We discuss what we need to, and then there's silence. He doesn't say anything about the Pageant.

"What did you really want to talk about?" Richard asks. "Whether I've fed the roses and the goldfish? Or how much you miss me?"

"I miss Gertrude."

"I'll be sure to tell her."

"Don't do that sucking fish imitation when you feed her. She doesn't like it."

"Did you audition?" Jeff asks when he comes in from work.

"No. I have no desire to melt and droop myself over a table wearing a clock around my face for the sake of Salvadore Dali. 'Local Woman Running Out of Time Dies Trying.' " I dish out Chinese food from paper boxes and think of Gertrude and the day Richard and I brought her home in a box just like these.

"You still can," Jeff says.

"Every night for seven weeks just to stand still while two thousand people say how wonderfully flat I look? Give me three good reasons." We sit down to eat.

"Brandon's doing it."

"Huge attraction, to be with my son's friend whose idea of a good time is to make electronic gadgets that give you a shock when you shake hands with him."

"Maybe you'll meet someone."

"It'll happen when it's—"

"Ready to happen, I know. They're doing *Washington Crossing the Delaware*. That means soldiers. And Rembrandt's *Nightwatch*. Rich merchants. Maybe you'd prefer a disciple from *The Last Supper*?"

"Too old." I try to dismiss this hovering concern he gets from his dad.

"How about an intellectual? Vermeer's *Geographer*. Or a good dancer from *Le Moulin de la Galette*?"

My son's spirit of fantasy is not only unrelenting, it's infectious. "Mmm, now, that's a possibility. You know I like to dance. And reason number three?"

"Cool. It's just a cool thing to do. By the way, I'm in the Trevi Fountain." A Cheshire cat grin spreads across his face.

At work the next morning I go online to look up Fontana di Trevi. It's gorgeous, and exuberantly sensual. Backed by a columned façade, the central figure of Neptune is riding his seashell chariot over a wave. There are two tritons. The Youthful Triton is in the rushing pool, his muscular arms flexed in struggle to control a rearing horse galloping through waves to pull the chariot. Yes, that could be my son. A sort of merman with scales and tail. Naked enough.

I drive to the pageant amphitheater to find out just how naked. If he were to do this nude posing, he would pass through some rite of passage and become a sensual being, a transformation that I myself have missed in my own life. I just want to be close enough to see the glow, or catch the pieces. I ask for Mrs. Larsen and am told to wait in the patio. "If you fill out this form, you'll hear your name." Age, height, weight, allergies to makeup. An audition form.

Well, I was here. I could tell Jeff I came, and get credit for trying. I don't have to agree to anything. If I got a part, it would mean I was doing something on my own, with only myself to blame or congratulate. I fill out the form using my maiden name. I don't want to get in just because I'm Jeff's mother. "Do you consent to pose nude?" it asks.

I blacken in the "no" box so vigorously it leaves a hole in the paper. Oops, maybe they'd take that to mean I changed my mind. I write "Not on your life" in block letters next to it.

A group is called in through the stage door, and the door monitor snaps up the audition form out of my hand. I see Jeff's former girlfriend, Lady Margaret, whose real name I've forgotten. "Patty," she reminds me. "Cool that you're doing it too."

"We'll see. I just want to find out what it's like."

The staff is introduced. Greta Larsen is a dragonfly of gauzy turquoise, purple and black. When she skims across the stage, it's as if the wind is rising. When she speaks, a hint of dusky accent leaps out, Slavic or Scandinavian. With auburn hair too long for a woman of her age, my age probably, held by a comb she keeps repositioning, long supercilious nose, carefully made-up eyes, jade green shadow, perfect teeth, and forty-five-dollar magenta nails, she is what I, at twenty, dreamed of being, a beauty who makes all other women in the room combative and desperate.

"Arlene—" This woman who has the power to make my son into a god flings the name at me like a hiccup.

"Eileen," I say to correct her.

It's not much of an audition. I stand in front of a board with feet and inches marked and get my picture taken, front, back, and side, and then have every square inch of my body measured.

Jeff would die on the spot if I made a big deal about his nudity in front of his former girlfriend, so I leave without asking this Larsen lady anything.

"How far does this fish thing come up?" I ask Jeff when he's back with me after his father's week.

"Up? Fish thing?" His legs are swung over the back of the sofa and his head is in a reference book, *Timetables of History*, with dates and columns labeled Literature, Religion, Art and Music, Science and Technology, Daily Life. "It's a shame that Joan of Arc, who died at the stake in 1431, was not able to enjoy the efficiency of the friction match, not devised until the early 1800s," he says.

"The triton tail. You have a triton tail with scales like a fish. How far up?"

"Hips."

Intentional ambiguity. A tease, just like his father.

"How do you walk with a fish tail instead of legs?

"The tail's part of the set. I fit into it. Naked. You'll see." He lets the book fall to his chest. "Don't worry, Mom. It's easier in our society to be naked physically than emotionally."

My extraordinary philosopher child, old beyond his years. It makes me proud. It makes me ache too. I'm forever running along behind.

Jeff spends more and more evenings working on set construction. He's Greta's assistant now, he says. With his coming home so late, I feel I hardly have him at all on my weeks. I am suspicious and wonder if he comes home late on Richard's weeks too, but I refuse to call. Richard would convince himself he heard loneliness in my voice— he'd be right, of course—and he'd invite me over for a fun-filled evening of watching Gertrude in her tank.

One day Jeff comes in the door thrusting at me a fistful of daylilies from our yard. "I'm stoked."

"Why?"

"You're in the Pageant."

"You don't know that."

"Look at your mail." He thumbs through the stack and tosses me an envelope. It's a letter thanking me in advance for volunteering, with a call sheet and costuming schedule.

"But it doesn't say what I am."

"Ask me."

"How do you know?"

"Greta showed me the cast list. You're the major female in Georges Seurat's *A Sunday Afternoon on the Island of La Grande Jatte*. It's a terrific part."

"You're kidding."

He brandishes a photocopy of the painting full of dabby little strokes. I am giddy with the aura of acceptance. The woman is in profile carrying a parasol and strolling with a man in a top hat. "Me? This dot woman is me?" People are lounging on the grass, fishing, enjoying a summer day. "That outrageous bustle. Looks like the rump of a horse." I chortle. "I have to hold this monkey on a leash? Don't tell me that's real too. I don't even like dogs." I nearly spit the word "dogs" I'm so excited.

"You'll be fantastic."

On the night I am scheduled to go for my fitting, Jeff says, "Don't wear that, Eileen. Put it in the back of your closet and forget it's there. Wear jeans and a silk blouse."

"Since when have you become such a keen observer of women's fashion?"

He smiles in an abashed way, and I indulge his wishes. I wonder what kind of drapery Greta will be wearing tonight. I am surprised. Skin-tight white jeans, untucked black silk shirt with a toucan amid leaves brightly hand-painted on the back, a monstrous green crystal dangling from a thick gold rope of a necklace. Her working uniform? Yes, for Laguna Beach. She's the epitome of sexiness. I expect Jeff to be watching her every move, but no. He goes about his work moving sets, handing her chalk, recording on a clipboard the things she murmurs. A small shock shoots through me. They are moving with the ease and intimacy of husband and wife making a Sunday morning breakfast. This son who leaps over years in a single bound is now a partner to Rana, Queen of the Jungle.

The costumer straps on me a padded rump the size of a beach ball, winches me into a corset and a muslin dress stiff with paint, with a black bodice and a full blue skirt that drapes over my hump in a most fetching manner. There is even a left flesh-colored glove painted with dots. I look around for the man whose arm I'm supposed to take. I find him painted on the scenery with a hole through which I'm supposed to put my right arm to grip a handle behind the flat to steady me. It's a bit disappointing. I had hoped for some real arm-gripping, and witty conversations with a dashing, top-hatted Frenchman, or perhaps some words of affection whispered in the wings.

There are holes in the scenery for other figures who are farther back in the painting. To give the illusion of depth and distance, they are played by children made up as adults. All around me these wee folk are dressed up for Sunday in the park—and here I am, elephantine, with a hump for a rump.

Everything is dots. Dots on trees. Dots on the grass. Dots on the water. We learn our poses and practice positioning ourselves in the foot pads quickly. Artists paint in final corrections on the set and our costumes while we're wearing them, in dots of course, and someone takes pictures. After the flash, I'm dizzy with dots.

"I think you need a hook and eye on the back of your costume, Eileen. It gapes." Jeff's voice comes out of the swirl of spots.

Hook and eye? How does he know hooks and eyes?

Don't get excited, I tell myself. He'd naturally learn about them with all this theater costuming.

I remember coming into the kitchen one morning tugging at my dress zipper. He stood up from his bowl of cornflakes, zipped me in one smooth motion, and said, "A shame the wildly amorous Lord Byron didn't know the swift joy of the zipper, not in common use until the early twentieth century." He was telling me something then. Of course he knows about hooks and eyes, and the bras they're found on, and the breasts they cover. Of course. And of course he is sexually active. The mere thought wilts me.

"Jeffrey, I forgot a color swatch of the right lime green for the grass," Greta says. "This grass is too yellow. It's washed out under the lights. I think it's on my dining room table. Would you?" Greta dangles her keys.

A lump the size of a green lime solidifies in my throat. She didn't give him any directions. It could mean only one thing. He's been there before. To her slinky house. Those late nights. After the vise-like vice of those stretch white jeans, she slips into something loose, woven of blue midnight, turns her back to him, lifts her long auburn hair, definitely too long for a woman her age, and says over her shoulder in a breathy voice, "Be a good boy and fasten me."

And does he? Or does he leave her unfastened? Has he had more clandestine trysts, more erotic adventures than I've had?

I'm in a panic driving home, convinced that my son is falling prey to The Intoxication of the Older Woman. Girls claiming they're protected, girls claiming they're pregnant, girls claiming they love him, the effects of alcohol, of marijuana, of sunburn—all of that I'd warned him about, but the trap of the older woman, I hadn't. He's innocent and vulnerable, and it's my fault.

I put the key in the front door lock and it doesn't turn. I step back, disoriented. Oh. Our old house, Richard's now. I was the one who moved. The door opens.

"Eileen! You came for a nightcap?" Gesturing gallantly for me to enter, he acts only the least bit surprised.

"No. I . . . I came because I didn't know where I was going. I mean, I was going home but I ended up here. A mistake, Richard. That's all. It doesn't mean anything."

"You do need a nightcap." He closes the door behind me and I'm grateful he doesn't make me feel like an idiot. I spill out all my suspicions. Smiling, he's more amused than concerned.

"Well, not old. My age," I say.

He laughs.

"Our age, Richard. I'm serious, and I'm worried sick." In a tumble of words I tell him about the hooks and eyes, about Greta dangling her keys. I tell him she didn't give him directions.

"That doesn't prove anything."

"I think you underestimate him. Can't you see it? A tableau vivant. *The Seductress.* Some posh ocean-view house lit by candlelight, Greta in tangerine silk caftan offering him Turkish coffee."

"Better that than opium."

"Apologizing in a lungy voice, 'because you are too young for scotch,' then sinking down sideways on a white leather sofa, and saying, 'Now, Jeffrey, my pet, tell me about yourself.' "

"As she languidly strokes her Persian cat with her naked toe," Richard adds. "Don't forget the cat. It adds a certain *je ne sais quoi.*"

"And Jeff, our Jeff, takes a sip and says, 'Did you know that coffee didn't reach Europe until 1517, the year Martin Luther posted his Ninety-Five Theses on that church in Wittenburg? Imagine! The whole Protestant Reformation caused by caffeine overdoses.' "

"We raised him to be charming and to interact well with adults. This is what we get," Richard says.

It makes me feel like my son is passing me by in the exotic life department, but I can't say that.

"I think he can handle himself. It's you that—"

"There hasn't been a woman with auburn hair slinking around your place?"

"Ei-*leen.*" Looking over his reading glasses. "We promised we'd never ask about each other's visitors."

"I'm not asking about *yours.*" My voice pinches to a squeak.

"Blondes, brunettes, dozens of them, even one purple-haired surfer with a ring in her nostril, but no redheads."

"Well, just be on the lookout."

"I'll keep my sentries posted and e-mail you directly with all the particulars. Or would you prefer a fax?"

I ignore that. Any wonder I moved out? We're stuck with sixth-grade social skills in which love and teasing are synonymous, so he never takes me seriously. I watch Gertrude swim into the underwater castle and come out the other side with a swish of filmy orange tail. I really do miss her.

"Have you gotten an aquarium yet?" he asks.

"No. It wouldn't be the same." I lift my hand to say no to the drink, straighten Matisse's *Blue Nude* on the wall and turn to go. "I hate it when you don't keep the pictures straight."

He grins. "See you opening night."

"That rat. He told you?"

Richard's laugh was both hearty and tender. "No. You did. Just now. Why else were you at the rehearsal?"

I slap my forehead.

"That rat did tell me, though. He wanted me to do the Pageant too."

"You're not, are you?"

"No. I thought you'd want to do it yourself." He smiles a genuine smile, maybe even a sad one, but definitely not a teasing one. "Maybe next year."

Two casts perform on alternating weeks. The walk-through with both takes a whole Saturday. We're told to find our body double and to exchange phone numbers. It's like looking for a long-lost twin. I shudder to think what mine will look like. When I find her, I'm delirious with happiness. She's a decade younger, has only a four-year-old son. For once I feel superior.

Each cast has a separate dress rehearsal the following Saturday. I'm in the blue cast, Jeff's in the red. We get to watch the opposite cast do the show. I sit in the third row with the steep fan of seats behind me rising to the wooded hill on one side which will be used for Manet's picnic scene, *Déjeuner sur l'herbe*.

A soprano sings an aria from *La Traviata* just prior to the unveiling of the Fontana di Trevi. The music swells and the curtain lifts, and I am struck breathless. The massive figure of Neptune stands in his sea chariot astride a foaming wave. A trick of lighting makes the moving, pale green plastic look for all the world like water rushing over rocks and falling from pool to pool. And my son, a Roman god, is taming a wild steed in the churning waters. The bulge of his gymnast's shoulders I recognize. His torso is twisted just enough to leave his manliness a mystery. Turned toward me, the bottom I powdered religiously when he was a baby—prone to diaper rash—round as country loaves, greased luminescent white, like wet Carrara marble. He is magnificent. I am awash with awe, and wish Richard were beside me. My mind buckles and in an instant of joyful agony I see a younger Richard as that triton, and then the illusion vanishes and I see only my son, a work of art.

On opening night with my dinner of Oreos and coffee, I head for makeup where I get my face, one ear, and my neck spotted in Seurat's pointillist style. Then off to headgear and costuming, and finally to the cast courtyard to wait for my cue. The first thing I see is George Washington talking on a cell phone. Judas in black robes is playing poker with a sad-sack Picasso harlequin and two bronzed-faced marines whose real eyes moving in their heads practically glow by contrast. One of them says hi. "It's me, Brandon."

"Oh! You look—old." I'm glad to see he has bronze paint on his hands, which makes a handshake out of the question.

"It happens. We grow up, I mean."

Everyone but me, it seems.

"Have you seen Jeff?" I ask, half afraid I'll find him standing white and naked in the patio, substituting for his double who chickened out.

"He's up top helping stage crew tonight."

Tutankhamen is listening to a Dodgers game on a small radio, volume low. Judas asks, "Who's up?"

"Dodgers. Bottom of the seventh. Giants leading 3–2. Two outs." When a Dodgers player hits one into the stands, Tut gets excited. It's definitely unnerving to see that gold face crack into a smile. In fact, the whole scene is something out of Poe's "Masque of the Red Death."

I want to sit down but can't fit in a chair. I look for a bench so my rump can hang out the back. There's only one, and Jesus is sitting in the middle of it smoking a cigarette and talking to his disciples. Jesus kindly moves over on the bench and gestures so I can sit down. He smiles a know-it-all English gentleman sappy smile, and I flash on an entirely different view of the Savior. "I don't mean to interrupt any parable," I say.

"You're not. We were just griping about what we'll get for supper. Always Italian. Spaghetti for thirteen."

I can't get it into my head that there's a real man behind that scraggly hair and sorry excuse for a goatee, but that only makes it intriguing. I offer him an Oreo. "I don't have chicken pox or anything. Just spots."

He breaks the cookie in two like it's the Holy Eucharist, and slides half of it toward me on the wrapper. Then he gives me an exaggerated holier-than-thou look.

I want to make him notice me. But which me—a painted French beauty or just me? "I read the book about you," I say. "Liked it a lot." Before he has a chance to answer, I get my call. He says, "Good luck." Something is fundamentally wrong with Jesus Christ saying "good luck."

The children in *Grande Jatte* are nervous and twittering, which makes me wired. Our set is lowered, and we get into position quickly as our set slides downstage. The posing director corrects the spread of my skirt, the angle of the smallest girl's head, the lounging man's pipe. She hooks the leash sewn onto my glove to the monkey painted on the set. The curtain is raised, the lights go up and I hear the audience suck in their breaths. A charge passes between us like an electric current, and I know they are stunned, admiring, and I feel beautiful. I feel like art. I feel like a masterpiece. This is real. This is wonderful. I am transformed. I am not myself anymore. I am greater than myself. I understand immediately why Jeff loves this. And I love him for wanting me to experience it.

A twinge crawls up my back. The more I try to ignore it, the more intense it gets. My upstage hand holding the grip behind the flat begins to cramp. I'm afraid to let go. One one-thousand, two one-thousand, three one-thousand. No, that's a dumb thing to think about. Think about art, I tell myself. Think about beauty, about Seurat persisting with his dots against all criticism, going his own way. About the courage, the nobility in that. Appreciation of what he's created washes over me and I'm lost in a Sunday afternoon in a Parisian riverside park. All too soon the lights begin to dim and I feel a different kind of twinge—disappointment that it's over. The applause thunders, and my eyes get damp with joy.

A few weeks into the season Jeff doesn't come home at all one night. The next day when I ask, he fixes me with a steely look and says he went to his dad's instead, daring me to call Richard and ask. I shrink from knowing.

"Did you know, Seurat's mistress was the model for your character?"

"Mistress. What do you know about mistresses?"

"Greta told me. She thinks her name was Dot. Get it?"

"All I *get* is a sleepless night of worry. Call when you're going to do that."

"I didn't want to wake you."

"Call."

The delicious feeling I get from being admired as art lingers between performances. I find myself speaking pleasantries to men in cafés. When my apartment neighbor is out sunning himself by the pool, I do the same. I clear out from my closet everything that makes me look frumpy, and I get a new style of haircut. Jeff whistles at me and I blush.

Jesus and I make awkward moves to become friends. Oddly, we don't share names. That and our costumes lend us a kind of freedom. Others might say that if you put a man in a robe and sandals, let his hair get raggedy, and starve him half to death, it erases any possible sexual appeal. And when you know what's going to happen to him, why bother?

I bring my mind back to the here and now. What would it take to bed down the Christ, or rather the man within the getup? I can't even imagine that with any man other than Richard, but I am curious. You have to give a possible relationship a chance. How does a person begin? Just plunge in?

While waiting for our cues on the cast patio, I ask him out for a drink after the show. "Maybe you can show me your water-into-wine trick."

"I'd like to, but I've got to relieve the babysitter by eleven."

"Single parent?"

"Yes. My boy is seven. You?"

My nerve shrivels. What am I? Not a single parent *officially*. I hadn't anticipated having to categorize myself.

"My boy is seventeen. He's the Youthful Triton in the Fontana di Trevi. Red cast." I can't control myself and I beam with pride.

"I never would have guessed. I mean, that you could have a son that old."

"Well, maybe we can meet on the beach some weekend. You can bring your son. Mine'll already be there. He's a lifeguard."

"That would be nice. I'm always trying to think of things I can do with him."

"We can take a swim, pretend it's the Sea of Galilee."

"Or roast some fish over a fire pit."

"Great." Then I could see what he really looks like, and I might be able to forget who he is in the Pageant and just talk normally. Right now, I can't seem to get beyond thinking that he's only thirty. No. He's in *The Last Supper,* so he must be thirty-three. He must realize I'm not his age.

That reminds me of Jeff and Greta and the night before last when he didn't come home, and I'm upset all over again. I excuse myself and ask George Washington if I can use his cell phone, and I call Richard. I can't go to his house because now this is Jeff's week there. He might barge in on us before we have a plan.

"Can you meet me after the show at Barnaby's?" I ask. On such short notice, I can only think of the restaurant where we've had our anniversaries.

"This show business is turning you into a raging night owl. I'm a working man."

I bite my thumbnail, waiting for him to realize I'm serious.

"You think I'm a theater groupie?" he asks. "Okay. Barnaby's. I'll be the man waiting under the potted palm."

As I hang up, a collective gasp goes through the patio and Tut points to the stage video monitor. A pigeon has landed on Venus de Milo's shoulder and slithers down the slick makeup to her breast.

She doesn't move. Not a twitch. Her skin leaks a thin line of red over the white. Wild applause drowns out the orchestra. We give her a cheer.

"That's what it's all about," Jesus says. "Illusion. Mistaking the unreal for the real."

"Or the real for the unreal," Tut says.

Richard has two brandies waiting at our old corner table at Barnaby's. "I see the theater life agrees with you," he says. "You look terrific."

I smile, pleased at his reaction. There is candlelight, and a rose in a crystal vase. I tell him about the pigeon on Venus, thinking there's something in both interpretations relevant to me.

"You brought me out this late to tell me this?"

"Did Jeff stay with you the night before last?"

"No."

"He didn't come home."

I wait for the reality of my suspicion to register.

"That doesn't mean he was with some middle-aged, art-struck vamp."

"There's a relationship implied between nude subject and artist, however unstated, and in this case, she's the artist," I say. He considers this. "Do we confront him?" I ask.

"We? Together?"

"I mean, do we tell him to stop?"

"We shouldn't jump to conclusions."

"Fine for you to say. You weren't the one awake all night listening for his VW. Awake alone."

He gives me a rueful look. I feel my toes curl.

"Until now, he's had no evasive instinct," I say. "He assumes everyone's morals match his, so he tells us everything."

Richard's chest expands with a big, weary breath. "We might have to admit that for once our perfect son might be blowing it."

I'm relieved Richard is taking me seriously, but that makes the possibilities all the more real.

"He may have told us everything before now, but he's going to tell us less and less," he says.

That threatens to sink me, and my eyes moisten. We are lost in our separate imaginings until Richard reaches up with utter natural-ness and rubs at my chin. I can see him realize, the same instant I do, that he has not touched my face in three years. "Just a smudge," he explains. "A dot of makeup."

We both turn to look at the fake waterfall.

"We'll be able to tell when it's over, won't we?" I say. "Over for him, I mean."

His mouth slides into a wry smile. "It'll probably end at the close of the season."

"Just when he goes off to college."

"And we'll scramble to get any shred of news," he says.

"We'll be lucky if we see him at Christmas."

"Might even have to spend Christmas together just to have a whole day with him." I pretend I didn't hear the invitation. "Even though he may tell us someday, we'll never know the truth," he says.

"You think he'd lie?"

"No. We'd just hear his truth."

"No one knows, really, about someone else's life," I say.

"Or love." He looks right in my eyes. A warmth passes through me. "You were exquisite, Eilie."

"You've seen the show?"

"Three times." He looks abashed. "Well, you're only on for a minute and a half."

"Have you seen Jeff?"

"Once.

"He's magnificent, isn't he?"

Richard nods. "Two masterpieces of untouchable art."

"Who made him magnificent? We, or she?"

He places his hand next to mine, an inch of mauve tablecloth between. "We did."

A few days after the end of the season, there is a big party at Greta's beachfront house. When I come home from work I find laid out on my bed a long coral silk tunic with white storks among jade green leaves, and with it, jade silk pants. "Jeffrey," I say, liking the sound of his full name, the way Greta says it. "Do you know anything about this?"

"Looks like clothes to me." He squints his eyes, touches the fabric. "Yes. Definitely, it's clothes."

I purse my lips, hands on hips. "Where did this come from?" I have visions of Greta's closet.

"Store. I'm sure of it." He shrugs. "My choice. Dad's money. He knew your size."

The thought of their collaboration chokes me with tenderness. I slip on the cool silk, something rich and strange and beautiful, and feel vastly loved—by both of the men of my life.

The party seems to be mostly strangers until we figure out who was whom in the Pageant. It becomes a boisterous guessing game with people bursting out with, "You've got to be kidding." In plain clothes, people have lost the luster of the footlights, except for Greta. She is wearing a dress of flowing water, iridescence itself. Her hair is wound in a sweeping chignon. Everything about her reveals a life of the senses. I swallow down a sliver of envy. Her house shouts wildness and confidence. In Living Room One, red and purple accents against black and white. Brazilian pillows. Fierce ethnic masks glower at each other from opposite walls. I try to find something to criticize but I can't. The effect is stunning.

Greta looks at Jeff with a gaze which implores and commands

at once, a look men leap to answer. "You were beautiful, Jeffrey. My Youthful Triton. And next year, we'll do something even more spectacular."

Her? *Her* youthful triton?

"Superb bone structure, that son of yours." She gives me an oily smile.

Nothing about his intellect? His appreciation for historical ironies? The breadth of his reading? Did she just get down to business those late nights without talking first?

"He's going to Stanford, you know. In just a week."

"I know, I know." Condescension drips from her words, and a rage threatens to erupt in me. Across those high, artificially shaped cheekbones there passes something wistful as she looks at me. "You must be very proud."

I practically choke.

She claps her jewel-weighted hands and announces, "Prizes on the lanai. Come."

She raises her arm in the air and wiggles her fingers in command. People follow. One award goes to Venus de Milo "for grace under pressure." Jeff gets one for "hardest working." Music plays in the hot September night, and everyone dances, everyone shines.

Bob Jones, whom I knew last week only as Jesus, is ridiculously young without his beard and scanty wig. He picks out a gardenia floating in a bowl and fastens it in my hair. His hand pressing the small of my back as we dance feels nice, but it's just an ordinary hand, not a two-thousand-year-old hand. He is no savior. The appeal is gone. I was fascinated by the illusion, not the reality.

In the moonlight shining on the sea I notice silhouettes of two people entering the surf, hand in hand. Naked. A tableau vivant. By his two peasant loaves I recognize the Youthful Triton. But the woman? I look around and don't see Greta. I splash down my drink and rampage through the party—Living Room One, Living Room

Two, dining room, elbowing people out of the way, pushing past a waiter, through the sunken garden, back outside, and am overjoyed to find Greta lit sideways by the lanai fireplace.

"Looking for Jeffrey?" she asks. "Sweet, aren't they, he and Patty? They've become inseparable."

Patty? His former girlfriend? Inseparable? It burns me that she knows something about my son I don't.

"She was in Winslow Homer's *Croquet Scene*. The one in teal blue. Lovely. They just took a walk." Greta's fingernails flutter toward the beach.

I sink into a wicker chair, into the relief of having discovered my mistake. Into the strange comfort that he may be having sex tonight, but it will be with someone age-appropriate. I listen to the waves awhile, and then prepare a plate of hors d'oeuvres to take to Richard on the way home. I have to tell him about Jeff's return to Patty. And more.

Author's Afterword

In these stories the characters who are not identified as members of the painters' families, their artistic circles, or their models can be assumed to be fictional, with the exception of "Crayon, 1955," which was written to honor the two very real people who widened my world. Nevertheless, these stories, spanning twelve years of my writing life, are firmly based in research.

Although many books speculate on the intimacy of Claude Monet and Alice Hoschedé before their marriage in 1892, my source for identifying Claude Monet as the likely father of Alice Hoschedé's baby, Jean-Pierre, is Daniel Wildenstein's *Claude Monet: Biographie et Catalog Raisonné* (La Bibliothèque des Arts, 1974–1985), vol. I, p. 83. That Monet burned thirty canvases one morning at Giverny is recollected by Lilla Cabot Perry in her article "Reminiscences of Claude Monet from 1889 to 1909," *American Magazine of Art*, XVIII, no. 3, March 1927. Monet's remarks, "I'm no better than a pig," "It's a damned obsession," and "It's beyond an old man's powers," are all recorded in Charles Stuckey's *Monet Water Lilies* (Park Lane, 1988).

That Berthe Morisot was given to moodiness and melancholy and that her love for Édouard Manet was the emotional vortex of her life are presented in Margaret Shennan's *Berthe Morisot: First Lady of Impressionism* (Sutton, 1996).

The manner and cause of Édouard Manet's death is reported in, among other places, Pierre Schneider's *World of Manet, 1832–1883* (Time-Life Books, 1968).

Of Paul Cézanne, Rainer Maria Rilke wrote in his *Letters on Cézanne* (Fromm International, 1985): "I know a few things from his last years when he was old and shabby and children followed him every day on his way to his studio, throwing stones at him as if at a stray dog." Cézanne's comments that Mont Sainte-Victoire is "The spectacle that God the Father spreads before our eyes" and that "The artist should consider the world as his catechism" come from John Canaday's *The Lives of the Painters*, vol. III (Norton, 1969).

Given what is generally known about van Gogh, the statements he makes in the three volumes of *The Complete Letters of Vincent van Gogh* (Bullfinch, 1958) are sometimes startlingly positive, as when he wrote, "No evil exists in this best of worlds. . . . Everything is for the best."

I am grateful to Jeanne Modigliani for her forthrightness in *Modigliani: Man and Myth* (Orion Press, 1958), as I am to all of these sources, and those listed on my Web site, www.svreeland.com.

As always, I'm grateful to the members of the Asilomar Writers' Consortium and its founder, C. Jerry Hannah, for their insightful criticism; my extraordinary copy editor, Dave Cole; my agent, Barbara Braun, for her constancy and guidance; and my editor, Jane von Mehren, for her clarity of vision enticing and challenging me ever onward.